"ON THE BRINK, ALL THE WAY . . .

A supersonic air adventure . . . every horror is penned with graphic detail and reveals the real human beings within the wire-tense pilots."
— *Kirkus Reviews*

"This is the most strongly realistic novel . . . I've ever read about carrier pilots. Imagine a fogbound carrier deck rising to cream you in an uncertain wind as you descend at 350 miles an hour with errors of reckoning and electronic failures bursting like popcorn in your cockpit. Outta gas and you can't even land by the seat of your pants. Horror and disaster, superbly realized."
— *Gallery*

"THE BRINK could be the classic novel of the Era of Undeclared Wars."
— *San Francisco Examiner*

"Rammed inside the cockpit of a jetfighter from page one . . . you eject yourself from your armchair at the end with your own everyday problems forgotten. . . . A unique reading experience."
— Colin Forbes

"A continually exciting book. Not a good read, a great read. . . . It'll probably make an excellent movie."
— Herb Caen, *San Francisco Chronicle*

THE BRINK

Rick Setlowe

PYRAMID BOOKS NEW YORK

THE BRINK

A PYRAMID BOOK

Published by arrangement with Arthur Fields Books, a division of E. P. Dutton & Company, Inc.
Copyright © 1976 by Rick Setlowe

Pyramid edition published July 1977

Library of Congress Catalog Card Number: 74-23660

Printed in the United States of America

Pyramid Books are published by Pyramid Publications (Harcourt Brace Jovanovich, Inc.). Its trademarks, consisting of the word "Pyramid" and the portrayal of a pyramid, are registered in the United States Patent Office.

Pyramid Publications
(Harcourt Brace Jovanovich, Inc.)
757 Third Avenue, New York, N.Y. 10017

To Ernest and Marion Setlowe
and
To Beverly

The ability to get to the verge [of war] without getting into the war is the necessary art. If you are scared to go to the brink, you are lost.

—John Foster Dulles

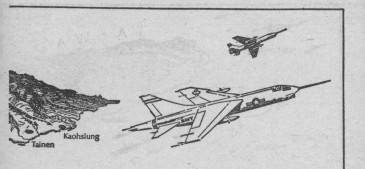

Prologue

Loud male voices at the end of the hall filtered through the paper walls and woke me. The dark morning cold splashed my face, and I squirmed down into the cocoon of the tatami roll, trying to seal out the chilly dawn air.

My memories of the previous night were the disjointed, surreal erotic images of a dream. A girl's bared breasts framed by her dark flowered kimono. A plump brown body sprawled, legs apart, on the hard glaring white tiles of the bath house.

The voices in the hallway now seemed to be approaching, as if someone were moving from room to room, but the sounds were too subdued to make out.

I wondered what time it was. The room was illuminated in a faint gray light, and I could just make out the dark outline of the low black lacquer table that was the room's only furnishing.

Bam! Bam! Bam!

Bam! Bam! Bam!

"What? Huh?" I rose up on one elbow, stupid and bleary, rubbing my eyes with my fists.

Bam! Bam! Bam! The fragile paper walls of the room shuddered under the ham-fisted blows.

"What? What is it, for Chrissakes?"

"Sorry to disturb you, sir," a hoarse, masculine voice right outside the door called out loudly. "Are you military personnel, sir?"

"Am I *what?*"

"Sorry to disturb you, sir," the voice outside repeated. "This is the Shore Patrol. Are you Naval or military personnel, sir?"

I rolled over, alarmed, and started to get up. The abrupt movement stripped the slippery silk quilt off the

11

girl. She howled at the cold and clutched at the blanket, recovering her nakedness with a yank.

"Are you Naval or military personnel, sir?" the matter-of-fact but insistent voice asked again.

"Fucking A, I am. Wait one, huh." I heaved to my feet and stumbled about in a circle, still punchy. The dark air, chilled as well water, was a shock to my naked body.

A black heap on the floor turned out to be the girl's kimono. I thrust my arms into the wide, draping sleeves and wrapped the kimono about my chest, bursting the seam in the back.

The man standing outside in the dim light of the hall was a thick-gutted, middle-aged chief petty officer wearing a Shore Patrol brassard. "Very sorry to disturb you, sir," he said again in a heavy, weary voice. "Are you Naval or other military personnel, sir?"

"Yeah, sure."

"May I see your ID please, sir?"

"What's this all about?"

"May I see your ID first, please, sir?" the chief repeated in the same tired, policeman voice.

I frowned, looked back over my shoulder and then shuffled across the room to a sliding door. I thrashed about in the closet for a moment and emerged with my wallet.

The chief was leaning into the room, staring at the girl who was now wide awake and cowering down into the bed roll, peering back at him with confused, frightened eyes.

"Where are you stationed, Mr. Rohr?" the chief asked, examining the ID card.

I named the aircraft carrier and my squadron. "Why?"

The chief handed me back the wallet. "You're to report back to your unit immediately, sir. A general order to all personnel has just been issued."

"What's up?"

"I don't really know. Our job is just to shake the walls and get everybody the hell back to their ships on the double," he said. "Your carrier is pulling out right away, if it hasn't already!"

I dressed in a groggy panic and scouted up Hooks Lewis. He was already up, hopping about in his shorts and T-shirt with one sock on, searching for the other,

12

cursing the Shore Patrol, the Communists, Chiang Kai-shek, CincPac, Eisenhower, and John Foster Dulles, all in the same unremitting tone. I yelled in that I would wait for him outside.

The air and sky outside were cold, gray, slimy, and dripping wet, looming heavily overhead like the shell of some great cosmic oyster hinged at the horizon, swallowing the port of Yokosuka. I looked up, somehow already knowing that there would be great rolling smoke clouds surging south in angry swells.

Behind me a door slammed, and two guys in their twenties, dressed almost identically in tweed sports coats and flannel slacks, their rep ties and button-down collars undone, scampered out and took off down the street at a trot.

There I was, Charly Rohr, the All-American boy, hauled wham-bam out of an officer's whorehouse in Japan to launch World War III.

1

On August 28, 1958, shortly after high noon, we scrambled from Atsugi Air Base in Japan and now, paraded across the sky in diamond formations of glittering silver aircraft, we streaked south.

I flew at the butt end of the parade, buffeted by the churning slip-streams of the jets blasting through the air ahead of me. My head throbbed and a soaking sweat poured off me into a sopping pool in my seat, but I did not dare take my eyes off the jet, an F-8 Crusader fighter-bomber, hovering just a few feet away, off my left wing.

My eyes were riveted on the Black Knight, the squadron heraldic coat of arms emblazoned in Day-Glo colors on the fuselage of the other plane. The knight in black armor, brandishing a long, slender missile like a jousting lance, charged through a circle of flames on a white-winged horse. Just above the squadron insignia Red Lucas peered out of the cockpit. The pilot was himself armored in a Day-Glo gold and black crash helmet, plastic face visor, and rubber oxygen mask. Red's eyes, in turn, were fixed on the painted knight charging to his painted battle on the fuselage of a third jet just ahead of his own right wing. There Chub Harris flew at the point of the formation, directly ahead of my aircraft. And tucked behind Harris' right wing flew a fourth Crusader, completing the four-point diamond.

Our four jets were the rear of a larger formation of warplanes, made up of four such diamond-shaped elements. The smaller gems coalesced into one large diamond, a squadron of sixteen silver jets in all. The formation blasted across the sky, outracing the continuous thunderclap that exploded in our wake and angrily pursued us.

15

Below, the Japanese landscape flowed beneath us, blanketed under an overcast of scud. Off to the left, Mount Fuji thrust through the cottony layers, its white nipple glistening moistly in the sunlight. Through other tears in the clouds, there were glimpses of an intricate patchwork of geometrically shaped farms and terraced gardens, and then the rents took on a blue tinge through which we could see the deeper blue-gray of sea below.

But I was only vaguely aware of that skyscape. My entire perception was focused on that cartoon knight and, looming just above it in the cockpit, Lucas' gold helmet. Flying at eight hundred miles an hour, tucked behind the wing of another jet, I measured my margins in inches and struggled desperately to stay within them.

Whatever terrible beauty there may have been in that parade of shining warplanes, it could be appreciated only by MacCafferty, the squadron commander, flying at the forward point of that spearhead. Looking over his shoulder, MacCafferty could see his entire squadron in a tight disciplined cluster behind him. Then he scanned ahead, and his eyes eagerly swept the sky and horizon as if searching for the smoke of a new battle, one to replace the memories of Korea and the Philippine Sea that had given his life ever afterward the stale taste of anticlimax. I am not creating fantasies about how MacCafferty looked that day, for that was the man. And that was how he had looked a half hour before, at the airfield at Atsugi, when he had climbed up into the cockpit and poised a moment, one hand gripping the canopy, his eyes seeking, a little wistfully, for something in the clouds overhead.

Now airborne, MacCafferty looked over at his wingman, hovering a wing-width away, and nodded his head emphatically to the right, twice, the Day-Glo gold paint of his helmet flashing. The signal was transmitted cockpit to cockpit, an electric nod from each element leader to his wingmen. Then MacCafferty banked to the south, and almost simultaneously, as if all the fragile wings were connected, the squadron turned with him.

There was a lot about MacCafferty summed up in that maneuver. No other squadron commander of whom I was aware made his pilots fly a tight parade as a routine discipline. Periodically, each pilot in the squadron had to fly wing on MacCafferty, and he made you fly tighter than, according to the book, was safe. But by that very proximity, dangerous as it was, he forced you to fly as he flew. Quick, tight maneuvers executed with a fluid grace and hairline precision. If you did not fight him, he led you through whirling gavottes as a great dancer leads his partner, and you never flew more smoothly or more boldly. But there were those it unnerved, and they did not stay long with the squadron. It was in this way that MacCafferty extended invisible filaments from the controls of his aircraft to your aircraft.

I am not imagining this. All of the pilots in the squadron had similar experiences. It is necessary to understand this to understand what happened later in the Straits of Taiwan when men began to die.

2

Far below, against the slate-gray surface of the sea, the aircraft carrier and its wake looked like a toy boat pulling a long curving white streamer. Our echelon of four planes swooped down, down, down, but against the flatness of the sea nothing changed in perspective except the toy ship, which grew larger and more awesome, no longer resembling a ship at all but an enormous iron mesa abruptly rising from the blue-black desert of the sea.

The four jets swept down the starboard length of the ship, almost at masthead level, in a tight formation with each plane slightly stepped down from the one on its left. A few hundred yards ahead of the ship, the aircraft on the far left snapped into an almost vertical bank, followed at an interval by the second, then third plane. When the last plane had rolled to a position behind my wings, I banked after him, the sudden centrifugal force of the high speed turn sucking at my flesh as if trying to pull it off my bones.

I maneuvered into the carrier's landing pattern, all the while rushing to set the plane up for the landing. But I was still too high and too fast when I banked over the ship's wake into the final approach. "You're high, bring it down," the voice of the landing signal officer stationed on the ship's fantail suddenly crackled over the radio headphones.

I corrected my altitude and speed, but then overcorrected, shoving the jet's nose too far forward and chopping off too much power.

The plane dropped alarmingly. The crushing armored stern of the carrier suddenly thrust toward me, the red lights flashed on and off. "Wave off! Wave off!" the urgent voice in my ears demanded.

Shit!

I rammed on power and aborted the landing, blasting over the flight deck. I flashed by the green-glass bubble of primary flight control from which the air boss frowned down at me, up past the bridge from which the captain scowled, and climbed back into the landing pattern and began the approach all over again.

This time I settled down. I centered the "meatball," the red orb of the landing signal lights, and held it all the way down the final glide slope to the deck. But at the last minute, the fantail of the carrier suddenly pitched, dropping out from beneath me. Instinctively, panicked that I was going to miss the landing again, I pushed the nose over and dove for the deck.

The jet slammed down on the carrier's fantail. It was violent and wrenching and the shock and the pain stunned me for a split second. Then I hit the throttle, and the plane leaped forward to be airborne again. But the aircraft's tail hook snared one of the half-dozen thick steel cables stretched across the afterdeck like trip wires. The jet abruptly jerked to a stop, straining and shrieking at its tether like some giant falcon brought to wrist.

"KEEErist!!!" I bellowed at the top of my lungs down at the deck crew scurrying ten feet below me, but my voice traveled only inches. It was drowned out by the hysterical, tympanum-piercing shriek from the twin turbojets of a Douglas A-3 Skywarrior bomber that rolled ponderously into the parking space immediately forward of my own aircraft.

I gingerly taxied forward, straining to follow the hand signals of the airman who maneuvered me into a tight parking spot directly behind the bomber. Then I just sat there, waiting for the plane captain to find me. Hot, hung over, and choking on the A-3's exhaust fumes, I sat boiling in an encasement of nylon, foam rubber, and steel—getting madder by the second. Finally, I couldn't wait it out any longer. I furiously unstrapped and unplugged everything in sight and scraped and squeezed my bulk out from among the computers, circuit breakers, consoles, radios, radar gun sights, precision bombing systems, and electronic avionic whiz-bangs.

When I ripped off my helmet, the roar from the flight deck exploded in my ears, deafening and painful as if I had been punched in the eardrum. I shrieked back at the turbojet in front of me, but once again the sound of my own voice never even made it to my ears. I screamed again at the other plane, then I flung my crash helmet down to the deck. It bounced high and almost bowled over the plane captain, Giles, who was now trotting up to assist me out of my straps.

I didn't wait for him. Using the strength of my arms like a gymnast, I swung out of the cockpit, got one toe-hold on the fuselage, and vaulted the ten feet to the deck. I almost landed on Giles. The long drop onto the armored steel plates of the deck jolted the hell out of me, and startled him. "Mr. Rohr, what the hell's happening?" He handed me back my helmet.

"I don't know. It's World War III," I shouted. "We're going to burn Red China. Now you know as much as I do."

Giles stood there a moment, blinking, trying to figure if I was serious.

I wiped my face and massaged the back of my neck with my flight scarf. The scarf was originally a flashy gold silk, but now it was sweat-stained and hung around my neck like last week's locker room towel.

"Look, you better double-check the landing gear and hydraulic lines," I shouted at Giles. "I really slammed aboard."

I ducked under the fuselage into the wheel recess to give the gear a quick check, then emerged and worked my way through the chaotic jumble of silver aircraft and yellow towing machinery.

The flight deck was a plateau of steel approximately as large as three football fields. It extended from the aircraft catapults on the bow to landing area aft. On the starboard side, the aircraft carrier's only superstructure, known as the island, towered up from the deck like a lighthouse from the sea. On the afterpart of the island, directly above the open signal bridge, lines of red, white, blue, and yellow signal pennants were hoisted, flapping in the bright sunlight like festival flags.

Directly beneath the bunting, MacCafferty's Crusader was parked, its thin wings broken and folded overhead to take up less room on the jammed flight deck. Its plane captain hung from the aircraft's side by a toehold, busily helping the squadron commander unstrap and remove his helmet. MacCafferty sat slumped, a knight being attended by his squire. Then he pulled himself from the plane with a painful slowness, twisting around to lean on his strong leg, pulling the game leg after.

Once down on the flight deck, he stood a moment with legs apart, braced against the gale that whipped down the length of the deck. He absently combed his thinning, short, dark hair with his fingers as he checked out the other planes in the landing pattern.

KKKKKKRRRRRRRRRRRRRRREEEEEEEEEEEE-EE Another Crusader slammed down into the landing area and now stood shrieking and trembling, trapped in the landing wires. The tail hood was released, and the plane surged forward and taxied to a parking spot alongside MacCafferty's plane. In the open cockpit, the pilot, his face hidden by his visor and oxygen mask, gave Mac-Cafferty a "thumbs up" by way of greeting.

MacCafferty nodded, then he whirled and strode toward the island where I stood, his big frame rocking and pitching with that pronounced hobble. He jangled with the movement. His parachute, life belt, the .38 caliber revolver in a shoulder holster and the heavy bandoleer of bullets draped across his chest like a chain-metal sash, Mexican-bandit style, all clinked and clanged together. Behind him, his gold silk flight scarf caught the wind and fluttered out from his thick neck like a battle pennant.

MacCafferty had a beak of a nose, but his hard, shining eyes dominated his face like a hawk's. He was a big man, beefy, with an older man's foreshadows of jowls and paunch. If anything, it made him look tougher, like scruffy old saddle leather. He pulled up in front of me. He started to say something, but his voice was suddenly silenced by the thunderclap of four Crusader jets booming down the starboard side of the carrier. Once forward of the ship, the lead aircraft snapped into a violent perpendicular bank into the landing pattern.

MacCafferty frowned at the maneuver, and his frown was like a fist clenching. Then he turned back to me, and stood a moment studying me, measuring. There was something about him that always reminded me of my old high school football coach, a big, broken-down, ex-pro tackle. It was MacCafferty's bulk, partly, but mainly it

21

was his eyes, remorseless and faintly hostile, that stated he demanded sixty minutes of crashing, head-banging, balls-to-the-wall football from you and he was not going to accept any excuses.

"When we get out there on the line, you're not always going to get that second shot at a landing," he said, his voice flat and low but nonetheless threatening for its lack of expression.

I met his eyes directly and nodded, "Yes, sir." We stood toe to toe. MacCafferty was several inches taller, but I was just about as broad as he was and, at twenty-four years old, a lot younger and leaner.

He studied me a moment longer, then his eyes grew friendlier, or rather, half-amused, and he cuffed me on the shoulder. "Hang in there, Charly. We're going to make a goddamn ace fighter pilot out of you yet."

He glanced down to check the chunky, stainless-steel watch on his wrist. "We're briefing at fourteen hundred. Pass the word to the others." With that, he lurched through the hatch and disappeared into the gloom of the interior of the ship.

I turned back to check the operations on the flight deck. Back aft, the landing signal officer's platform jutted precariously out over the water at the end of the flight deck. On it, I could just make out Hooks Lewis, the LSO, bobbing up and down behind the small canvas screen that inadequately shielded him from the direct blast of the wind. An F-8 Crusader jet fighter, its abbreviated silver wings flashing sunlight, banked into its final landing approach. Hooks' body was contorted as if he were trying with body English to place the fast-settling jet *just so* onto the small landing area, which was storming over the waves away from the descending aircraft.

Just above where I stood on the flight deck, the red diamond pennant that signaled "fixed wing aircraft operations now underway" flapped noisily on its halyard, held steady a moment, and then luffed again like a jib sail turned too close into the wind. It was an erratic, dangerous wind.

The fierce but intermittent gusts were playing hell with the landings. I had stood duty alongside the landing signal officer enough times to fill in the dialogue for that mime act I could see going on on the fantail.

"Oh, what's that boy trying to do, kill us all?" Hooks Lewis whined, and then in another tone—a quiet, confident voice—he commanded into his radio hand mike, "Goose it two-zero-six. You're a scosh low."

The F-8 fighter screamed down at more than one hundred sixty miles an hour, and the ship barreled directly into the wind so that, in theory, the gale sweeping down the deck and the high speed of the ship neutralized the aircraft's flying speed, reducing it to within safe limits. A jet carrier landing is not a landing at all, but a precision-controlled crash. The fourteen-ton jet now in its final approach had to slam down and be abruptly stopped within that small, quaking area on the ship's fantail.

Without taking his eyes off the plane, Hooks yelled at the enlisted man with a headphone set who stood shivering in the cold wind next to him. "Can't those jokers give us any more wind than this here?"

"The bridge says *that's it*. They're tearing the ship apart to get this here speed up now." As if to confirm the report, the deck beneath them shook with the strain of the engines.

"Sheeit!" Hooks loudly cursed the captain, the pilots, but especially the inconstant wind.

The plane swooped down, its engines in a high-pitched scream, its landing gear extended like a hawk's talons as if, instead of landing, it intended to snatch up Hooks Lewis and carry him off. Lewis shouted at the plane, yelling into the wind, then wiped his wind-lashed running eyes and nose with the back of his sleeve. His eyes made a quick sweep of the landing area to make sure the flight deck crew were all clear, crouched down below the level of the deck in the relative safety of the catwalk that ran around the perimeter of the ship. Across the deck, crewmen in green, red, blue, yellow, brown, and purple jerseys scattered and disappeared over the edge and into protecting nooks and crannies.

The plane fell toward the fantail, the thin stubby wings trembling just above stalled flight, as if it were sliding down a guy wire. At that moment, as if the action were timed to the landing, the carrier's stern suddenly pitched up over a sea swell and the jet brutally crunched down on the deck. The left landing gear, striking an instant before the other, took the full force of the blow. It snapped clean

23

off and slingshot across the deck. A green shirt leaped, eager beaver, from the shelter of the catwalk a moment too soon and caught the gear full in his groin. He was lifted up bodily and hurled back, sprawling finally with his limbs and torso crumpled at odd contorted angles. His eyes, frozen open, stared in astonishment at the gear which had dropped next to him, the wheel still spinning furiously.

The crippled plane bounced once, then skidded crazily on its belly and one gear across the landing area without catching an arresting wire. The full power of the engine suddenly burst on with a clap of thunder, and the jet vaulted off the edge of the deck and dropped from sight. A moment later, it reappeared, skimming over the water like a flat pebble that had hit and glanced off. It flew low to the surface, its jet blasting a trough behind it, and then pulled up into a steep, frantic arch.

I stared after the F-8, at first horrified, holding my breath for the crash, and then stood awed at the plane's—the pilot's—desperate insistence on flying, watching until it was lost in the bright haze and sky glare.

On the fantail, the green-shirted body was now surrounded by flight deck crew. Two medical corpsmen wearing white pullovers emblazoned with foot-high red crosses knelt over him. From a distance, the two corpsmen on their knees looked like Crusaders praying over a fallen comrade. There was nothing I could do there. I turned and charged through a hatch.

Primary flight control was a bubble of green-tinted glass that popped out from the side of the carrier's superstructure, overseeing the flight deck like a control tower at an airfield. It was deadly quiet when I burst into the room. The air boss and his assistants were all staring dumbly at a wall speaker, which at the moment was emitting only the low static crackle of radio silence. Presently, a strong unhurried voice came over: "Homeland, this is Charger six . . . Leveling off at ten thousand . . . Plane vibrating a bit but otherwise the controls seem to be responding normally . . . so far. I'm going to check them out now, real easy like. Over."

The air boss grabbed a hand mike. "Charger six, this is Homeland. You left your left gear on the deck. Look,

24

Alexander, if your controls start stiffening up, get the hell out of there. Over."

"Roger. I'll call you back in a minute with the word."

The air boss, a stocky, bald-headed commander with a perpetual scowl, turned and nodded curtly to me, his eyes demanding information.

"The hydraulic reservoirs are in the gear struts," I said. "The primary system for the controls is in the right one. So if it's not damaged he might be okay." I snapped out the information like a schoolboy reciting a well-drilled lesson. "He'll know soon enough. The utility hydraulic system works out of the busted strut. That probably wipes out his tail hook flaps, and brakes."

"Great!" the air boss snarled bitterly, then resumed monitoring the speaker.

Another voice, languid and casual, suddenly came out of the speaker. "Homeland, this is Mixmaster two at the one-eighty. Three showing down and locked. Over." It was another pilot, now turning into his final landing approach and reporting that his landing gear was down and locked.

"Oh, Jesus!" The air boss dove for his hand mike and barked into it, "Mixmaster two, we have an emergency and fouled deck. Abort your landing and continue circling in the pattern."

The voice, higher pitched and quicker, came back, "Mixmaster two. Roger. Out!"

The air boss bent pungnaciously over the intercom box and flicked the switch to the Combat Information Center, the carrier's electronic nerve center which controlled the incoming aircraft on radar and radio until they swooped down into the landing pattern. "Combat, this is Pri-Fly. We have an emergency on the deck up here. Keep all the jets holding over the ship *at altitude*. Keep them under your control. We have our hands full here. Over."

There was a quick "Roger" from the box, then it clicked off. Jet engines were just the opposite of propeller plane internal combustion engines in that they consumed less fuel at higher altitudes than at sea level. The air boss had to hold all the aircraft overhead while the damage to the landing area was evaluated. He might be forced to send all the planes back to Atsugi Air Base before they burned too low on fuel.

The intercom box crackled for attention. "This is the LSO. The deck is clear. Wires are okay. None were cut up. We can start landing aircraft again."

"Good! That's something at least. How's the green shirt?"

"Wait one," the box requested, and there was a long stillness. Then it clicked on again. "They just took him down to sick bay, but someone said the doc thought he was dead already."

"Roger," said the air boss, then as an afterthought added softly, "I'm sorry. Thank you." The room was suddenly quiet, an embarrassed stillness in which those alive and present groped to acknowledge the significance of another man's death, although no one there knew the green shirt.

Then, just behind us, there was the clang of a heavy metal door closing. MacCafferty lurched into the room.

The air boss and I briefed him in low, tense voices. MacCafferty asked several quick questions, then all three of us turned to stare in silent concern at the crackling wall speaker. Another pilot who had been dispatched to look over Alexander's plane now reported in on the radio that the one remaining gear looked firm, but Alexander's underbelly and a wing tip were smashed up. Then Alexander himself called in again, his voice surprisingly cheerful under the circumstances. "The controls seem all right. Hydraulic pressure is holding up, so far. It yaws a bit though, and there's a whole lot of shaking going on. But I'm pretty sure I can handle it without too much sweat. I'm game to bring her in. Over."

The air boss looked at MacCafferty and shook his head, then keyed his mike: "Charger Six, this is Homeland. Fuel state? Over."

Alexander reported back the amount of fuel he still had. MacCafferty suddenly stepped forward and gripped the air boss by the arm. "I don't want that plane sent back to the beach," he said fiercely. "I want him on board." There was no question of compromise in his voice.

The air boss turned and stared at MacCafferty, somewhat startled. Both officers were equal in rank, full commanders, but the air boss was technically in charge. "Landing the plane is out of the question," he reasoned.

"It's too hairy. It's a fifty-fifty shot at best in his condition. They can handle him at Atsugi without any sweat."

"Let the pilot make that decision," MacCafferty snapped back. "He knows how he can fly the plane."

The air boss shot an angry glance at me, then glared back at MacCafferty. "That goddamn flying circus of yours knows *exactly* what you want them to do. And they either risk busting their ass doing it or find themselves transferred to a ferry squadron."

MacCafferty neither acknowledged nor denied it. "Alexander's my operations officer. He's one of my best pilots. When we get out there on the line, I'm going to need him. If he's stuck on the beach, he's as lost to us as if he were shot down."

The air boss shook his head. "Even if he makes it aboard, he'll foul the deck so bad I won't be able to land another plane."

But MacCafferty would not back down an inch. "He'll hold in the air until the rest of the air group is landed."

"It's too hairy. I can't take that responsibility."

"I'll take the responsibility," MacCafferty answered without hesitation.

"You can't take the responsibility," the air boss snapped back, his voice quavering and hushed with suppressed anger. "The air group commander can't take the responsibility." He gestured belligerently to the expanse of the ship just outside the green window. "That's *my* deck down there. *I'm* in charge there."

He and MacCafferty stood staring hard at one another for a long moment, then MacCafferty let out a breath and said quietly, "Call the captain."

The air boos stared at MacCafferty, then said, "You always push it too hard, Tom." He ducked his head, bent over the intercom, and flicked the switch to the bridge.

The captain was immediately on the line. "I've been monitoring the emergency on the radio," he said without preamble. "What's your recommendation?"

"I recommend that we immediately bingo the plane to the beach," the air boss stated emphatically. "A landing in the plane's damaged condition is hazardous, and we risk damage to the deck. They can foam down the runway at Atsugi and Alexander can belly it in without any problems." The air boss looked up at MacCafferty, then added

27

in a flat expressionless voice, "However, the squadron commander, Tom MacCafferty, does not agree with that recommendation."

"Let me speak to Tom," the captain said.

MacCafferty was already bent over a second intercom box. "Yes, sir," he said by way of announcing himself. "I think it would be unnecessarily losing a plane and one of my best pilots, my operations officer. If he splats it down at Atsugi, they'll either scratch the aircraft or take months to repair it. Once we're out at sea, Alexander will have no way of getting back to the ship. If Alexander says he can bring it aboard, then he can do it, sir. He brought them aboard with flack in them in Korea."

The captain's acknowledging grunt sounded over the speaker like a bullfrog's croak. "The plane will probably be busted up in the landing," the captain said.

"I can replace a wing or fuselage panels overnight, sir," MacCafferty responded. "But I can't replace that pilot or that missile system, once we're out there on the line. They're each one of a kind. If they push the button, we are going to need them."

There was a long silence. "Okay," the captain said heavily, almost with a sigh. "Put the air boss back on."

"Yes, sir," the air boss immediately answered.

"I think, under the circumstances, that we'll go along with the squadron commander and the pilot's recommendation. I don't anticipate any irreparable damage to the flight deck."

"Yes, sir," the air boss said to the speaker box. He turned and nodded brusquely to MacCafferty and immediately plunged into the task of bringing aboard the other planes now bunched up in the landing pattern.

MacCafferty grabbed a second hand mike from the control console. "Alexander, this is Commander MacCafferty. The captain has given his permission to bring you aboard if that's what you elect to do. It's tricky. The plane is damaged so it will be difficult to control in the approach. You're probably going to have to hold extra speed in the approach or you'll stall out. Your tail hook may be fouled up, and it may or may not grab."

MacCafferty glanced inquiringly at the air boss, who emphatically nodded back at him. "We'll rig the barricade," the air boss said.

"Okay. The barricade will be up," MacCafferty said into the mike. "But if you hit it too fast, you'll rip right through it. You're going to have to play your speed by ear all the way, depending on how the plane is flying. Remember, you get only *one shot* at it. Just one. It's very marginal. The air boss recommends that you take it to Atsugi. They'll foam down the runway and you can take all the room you need and crunch down there without any sweat. I suggest you strongly consider it. But it's your decision. You know how the plane's handling and what you can do with it."

Alexander's answer was immediate and very cool. "Yes, sir, I already have thought a lot about it, Skipper. It won't be the prettiest landing I ever made, but it will be a sincerely heartfelt one. We'll drive her aboard okay."

MacCafferty gave a tight little smile. "Okay, Luke, hang in there for a while."

Alexander circled overhead while the rest of the planes landed, and all the aircraft on the aftersection of the flight deck were hurriedly shoved forward out of danger. A pair of steel stanchions that had been lying flush with the deck now swung upright like fence posts, and a net of thick nylon webbing was strung between them and anchored to one of the landing wires.

In flight control, MacCafferty leaned back against one of the radio consoles, smoking a cigar, seemingly relaxed. Only his eyes, bright and intense, betrayed any excitement. I studied him. I was taking all my cues from Mac-Cafferty now. I unzipped one of the pockets of my flight suit, took out a soggy pack of cigarettes and lit one. Squinting through the smoke, I leaned back against the bulkhead, thumbs hitched in my pockets, but almost immediately I straightened up again and stepped forward anxiously to peer out.

Alexander flew the damaged aircraft once over the ship and then circled back, making a very wide approach. The wings wobbled as if the plane were searching for direction. Then it descended rapidly, heading toward us.

"He's too damned low!" the air boss cried out.

Even aboard the carrier, I could feel Alexander fighting the plane, and something in my chest caught and skipped.

The F-8 yawed badly because of the damage, and Alexander tried to correct it with a heavy rudder, skid-

29

ding the plane to its landing lineup. In the unbalanced flight, his altitude and speed fell off sharply, and he desperately dropped the plane's nose to keep from stalling and spinning out of control. Simultaneously, he shoved on power to hold his altitude above the ship's armored stern that now thrust up before him, massive and crushing as mountain rock. The plane stalled out just before it reached the carrier and dropped heavily.

Its forward momentum carried the jet just over the edge of the fantail, clearing the stern by inches, and it crashed to the deck, lurching on the gearless wing. It slid sideways across the wires with a terrible tearing sound and struck the nylon barricade broadside. In one agonizing shock, the net gave way, strands burst, the striking wing collapsed into pleats like an aluminum accordian. A few feet from the port edge of the deck, shuddering, the plane finally stopped.

The fire crew immediately surrounded the wreck and began smothering it with foam. Two men encased in silvery asbestos suits, their movements slow and encumbered as robots, struggled toward the cockpit. Before they reached it, the canopy popped open, and Alexander vaulted to the ground and frantically scrambled away from the plane on his hands and feet.

Once at a safe distance, he stood up and turned back to study the broken aircraft. His eyes carefully measured the short distance from the plane to the drop-off into the sea. Then he took off his crash helmet, and, cradling it in his arm, removed his gloves, finger by finger, like a boulevard dandy. With a theatrical flourish, he flipped the gloves into the hard hat, all the while beaming up at the bridge and primary flight control with an absurd grin.

Alexander did not learn about the dead boy under a sheet in sick bay until late that evening, long after that dire briefing in the ready room, and by then, the death of one boy in a freak accident had little meaning.

3

At fourteen hundred, the squadron pilots were all assembled in the ready room. MacCafferty stood at the front off to one side, gripping a thick wooden pointer across his thighs with both hands, his feet in a wide stance against the quaking deck underfoot. The compartment rattled like the interior of a subway as sixty-five thousand tons of steel crashed through the sea, propelled by turbines shaking themselves apart. At the rear of the ready room, the crockery in the coffee mess on one side and the steel lockers on the other hand set up a loud clatter. I sat in the midst of this commotion, worrying an unlit cigar to shreds.

Steinberg, the intelligence officer who was briefing the group, stood before an enormous chart of Taiwan, the Straits of Taiwan, and the coast of Red China that practically covered the front wall. He was a tall, thin young man with horn-rimmed glasses and the pedantic, low-key manner of a teaching assistant in political science. He had to shout to be heard over the noise. "We feel that they are definitely planning and waiting on this weather front moving down now from the northeast. The Red armies that they've massed around the ports of Amoy and Foochow, according to our intelligence, are under General Chiu Chien-hung. He made his mark in Korea by managing to operate his army and move supplies under our air superiority. He's a past master at sneaking them at night, but especially in lousy weather when we're blind and grounded."

A sharp splintering crack startled Steinberg. MacCafferty had snapped the pointer he was holding in both hands. "Just how soon will this low front hit and how far does it extend back?" he interrogated Steinberg. MacCafferty's voice was an intimidation in itself. It was a harsh, scraping, gravelly noise that came from a larynx long abused by cigarettes and whiskey and broken sleep. A voice that rumbled awake one morning in middle age and could no longer retune from that first raucous, croaking note.

Momentarily shaken, the intelligence officer stuttered. "The front ... I ... we ... we don't really know. The front's moving down from the northwest. We really don't have any reliable weather reports from inside China or Siberia. Just indications."

Luke Alexander, the squadron operations officer, raised his hand like a schoolboy vying for attention. "I thought you've been telling us all along that *they've* got the immediate air superiority," Alexander said, almost shouting. "Something like sixteen hundred jet fighters and four hundred or so tactical bombers spaced out on bases along the whole coast."

Steinberg regained his professional composure and gave Alexander a small smile. "That's right," he nodded. "But so far, they've been holding back their air force. At first, they made a careful aerial reconnaissance of Quemoy Island. Then a little over a week ago, August 18 to be exact, the Communist batteries around Amoy fired a hundred rounds at the island. Some MIG-17's overflew Quemoy, but they didn't drop any bombs. Then several days ago, on August 23, the Communist big guns really opened up. They threw approximately fifty thousand rounds into the island, and they've kept up that intensive barrage daily. But they've continued to hold back their air power. We think they are deliberately trying to avoid any direct confrontation in the air, because it might draw the United States into the action. If they attempt a massive amphibious assault on Quemoy under this muck, they could conceivably secure their positions before the weather lifts and our air support could hit them." Steinberg again gave a small conspiratorial smile. "If, of course, we were ordered to."

He jabbed at the wall chart with his forefinger. "Quemoy Island sits right at the mouth of Amoy harbor. It is only a mile and a half from Red-held islands and only three miles from mainland China itself here at its closest point. And Matsu Island *here,* off Foochow, is not one hell of a lot further away. When the Communists con-

32

quered the mainland of China in 1949, Chiang Kai-shek managed to hang on to these islands for outposts, but by his fingernails. The offshore islands have been a thorn in Red China's side ever since."

Steinberg rubbed the bridge of his nose, where his glasses had made two little indentations in the flesh, then checked his notes briefly. "Three times in the past nine years, the Chinese Communists have made amphibious raids on Quemoy, but never in the force they are now massing. How much longer the Nationalists can hold on to the islands without *direct* American Navy and air support is the question."

Steinberg paused and looked around, but there was no reaction. "It's *not* as simple as it sounds," he insisted with emphasis. "It's *not* just another skirmish for two barren hunks of rock and sand. Mao Tse-tung and Khrushchev recently met in Peking. We don't, of course, know what they agreed on but, shortly afterward, Radio Peking officially proclaimed that Quemoy and Matsu islands would be conquered as the prelude to an attack on Taiwan. Just to what extent the Russians will back the Red Chinese play we have no way of knowing at this point."

Steinberg cocked an eyebrow for emphasis, then added, "It is, of course, the United States' declared military policy to defend Taiwan and pursue any attack against it into the mainland of Red China itself."

There was a heavy silence, then one of the pilots, Red Lucas, broke in. "In short, what you're saying is that we don't really know *eggsactly* what in hell they're going to do. Nor do we know *eggsactly* what in hell *we're* going to do."

Steinberg's eyebrows arched. "Of course, that's a political decision," he answered in a supercilious tone.

Lucas gave a contemptuous snort.

MacCafferty interrupted. "That's all I think we'll need by way of background briefing for the time being, Mr. Steinberg. Thank you." He turned and faced the group, holding both pieces of the broken pointer in his right hand, swatting them against his thigh like a swagger stick. "The situation may be as yet unclarified, but our orders are quite explicit," he said in his sharp, harsh voice. "We've received a Special Weapons alert. All pilots will be rebriefed on their targets."

Special Weapons. In the lexicon of the Navy, Special Weapons meant *nuclear* or *atomic* warheads. It was as if we had a special vocabulary to hide from others, and perhaps from ourselves, just what we did. Nuclear bombs are not dropped, they are *lofted.* The practice bombs—dummies that are aerodynamically designed to have the same drop characteristics as the actual nuclear bombs—were referred to as *shapes.*

Special. Loft. Shapes. Graceful gentle words. In the bleak, remote stretches of the Nevada desert, we practiced our *lofts* with *shapes.* Insulated by jargon from the reality of the *special* mission for which we trained. Not really believing . . . most of us . . . that that day would come to pass.

But now we'd scrambled. This time out, it was no training exercise. It had been heating up for months in the Taiwan Straits, like a pile of greasy rags kindling itself. The carrier was booming south, knocking down the waves in its path. And MacCafferty was standing before us, indomitable as a war lord, passing the word.

He nodded to Steinberg, who again took the stage.

"For most of you, it will simply be a review and update of your present assignments," the intelligence officer spoke up. "There have been some changes however, and you'll be told them when you come in for your individual briefings."

MacCafferty took over again. "The loading officers will immediately start pulling static checks on each plane's delivery system. Each pilot will man an assigned plane during the checks. Each of you is personally responsible to see it is checked out. You're the only one who knows what sort of drop you're making and what the fusing is. We'll be holding loading drills right through the night, until we're sure we've got it down pat. If they ring the bell, we have to be loaded and off within minutes. Frank is getting together with Special Weapons as soon as we break," he said, indicating the squadron executive officer, Frank Pastori, a thin, dark man who was sitting right behind me. "He'll have your loading schedule ready right afterward."

Glancing back at MacCafferty's reference, I was struck by Pastori's expression. The executive officer was seated apart from the rest of the pilots in one of the last seats, as

34

if he were not really a member of the group but merely on the edge of it. He leaned forward in his seat, staring intently, but not at MacCafferty. His dark, melancholy eyes were focused somewhere far beyond the front wall of the ready room—and what he saw there seemed to grip him with profound horror. MacCafferty's next words swung me around again.

"If the engine room can keep up this pace, we should arrive at Station Zulu *here* tomorrow night, just after midnight." MacCafferty pointed to a spot off the north end of Taiwan. "From that time on, this ship will launch and continually maintain an armed combat patrol in the Straits."

"Skipper," called out Walt Stovall, "from what you've all just been telling us, there aren't going to be any sort of flying conditions in that area for very long."

MacCafferty turned toward Stovall, and his expression was very odd—expectant, vaguely amused but somehow menacing. He nodded slowly. "That's why, as conditions become less marginal, *this* squadron will be responsible for maintaining that patrol."

For a prolonged moment, the only sound was the clatter of the ship bulling its way to a distant rendezvous. Then a discordant, quickly rising chorus of protest swelled up from the pilots. MacCafferty slammed his broken pointer down on the desk with a loud crack and angrily ordered us to knock it off. He proceeded immediately with the briefing, and all the while those squinty falcon eyes—cold, hard, and glaring—swept the room, individually challenging each man there but recognizing no dissent. At the end of the briefing, MacCafferty strode out of the ready room in long pitching steps, passing through the rows of silent, and temporarily quelled, pilots.

One by one, we were summoned to the Mission Plans Center to be secretly briefed. I waited, slumped in my chair, brooding. The mangy cigar stub that I had been gnawing suddenly disintegrated completely, covering me with tobacco shreds. I cursed and brushed myself off, then got up and grubbed a cigarette from Red Lucas.

"What the fuck's happening here, Charly?" Lucas asked, holding out a match to light my cigarette. "Are we going to take on World War III just to save that old gook

35

Chiang Kai-shek's two-bitty island?" He spit out the generalissimo's name with contempt.

I shrugged. "That's what we're paid for."

Lucas gave me a look, then shook his head. *"Sheeit."*

About a half-dozen cigarettes later, I was called, in my turn, to the Mission Plans Center and assigned a new target. An auxiliary airfield at Cheng-Hai.

"There are several fields along here—Cheng-Hai and here, at Liencheng," Steinberg explained, indicating the positions on the map covering the table. "They *were* unoccupied. Then about three weeks ago, Chinese Nationalist reconnaissance pilots spotted MIGs moving on to them. The fields conveniently face Taiwan and the offshore islands." The air intelligence officer spread a series of aerial photographs on top of the map.

"How'd we get these?" I asked.

"F-84 photo planes. Our planes, ChiNat pilots."

I nodded and hunched over the photos.

"Here, look at this chart to get a general picture of the area layout," the AI suggested. "As you can see, they have tight radar and flack concentrated along the coast there."

"Those Sammy sites?" I asked, pointing to the indicated surface-to-air missile locations.

"Yes. But we don't know how effective they are. They're the earliest Russian types, and we're pretty sure you can be over them and gone before they can fix on you . . . if you hug the ground."

"If it's all the same to you, I'd just as soon go around them," I said uneasily.

Steinberg nodded. "Here are your weapon specs and radius of action," he said, laying down a file card on the table.

I studied it a moment. "Ground burst, huh?"

"That'll give you a good-sized crater so they won't be able to utilize the terrain as an airfield, and it'll also level everything for a mile around. You have a choice of attacks. You can either stand off and lob an air-to-ground missile or come right in on it with your low altitude delivery system. The radar overlays for this one are fairly sharp, if you want to stand off."

I shook my head. "I don't like those Sammies. I'd just

as soon stay low until I'm right on top of it and drop over the shoulder."

"Probably be safer," Steinberg agreed. He stood examining the display of aerial photographs proudly, as if he had taken them himself.

I plunked down into a chair and meticulously arranged the pencils, scrap paper, a slide rule, and several technical tables and graphs about me like a schoolboy stalling before tackling a math problem. I picked up a pencil, absently nibbled the end for a moment, and then began to write out a series of numbers, frequently cross-checking the tables.

I had to figure out a profile of my attack—the jinking courses and times on course, speed and altitude changes, the trajectory of the drop, and then the fast, direct retreat. It was basic algebra. Essentially, the problem was no more complicated than the navigation and gunnery exercises I had been working out since my Naval ROTC courses at Southern Cal. It was simply a matter of going from A to B to C. The one absolute, inflexible value from which I worked—the one from which all the other figures were derived—was the amount of fuel I had to fly from the ship to Cheng-Hai and then back to the carrier's new recovery area, wherever the Christ that was. The problem fascinated me. It had a beautiful clean straight-line slide-rule logic to it. The mathematics precisely defined my alternatives.

Once over my release point, Cheng-Hai, the immediate problem was getting back to the carrier. What happened at Cheng-Hai, whatever Vesuvian hell erupted in my wake, was simply not part of the problem. And I found it very convenient at the moment not to prod my imagination.

After a while, I leaned back and lit up a cigar. "I figure my best penetration to avoid those Sammy sites and most of the radar and flak would be here," I pointed out on the map with the cigar. "Then head straight in, hugging the deck all the way. Anything more oblique would cut me too short on fuel." I hunched back over the calculations, rechecking the arithmetic, the tables, and the slide rule.

"You'll be given the ship's plan of intended movement just before launching," Steinberg commented offhand, checking over my strike profile. "Good, good," he nodded, evidently satisfied with it. "When you're clear of the mainland, remember to check in with Dogmeat on Taiwan if the carrier is still in operation."

"What if I can't raise Dogmeat?" I asked, squinting through thick cigar smoke.

Steinberg shrugged and gave a sardonic little smile. "Then it's your decision. Either take a chance, and come out and look for us anyways or head directly for one of your alternate fields."

"Chances are, if Dogmeat's been hit, neither of my alternates are going to be very available."

"That's one of the things to worry about when the time comes."

We went over the mission until I had it committed to memory. Then I left, passing through the heavy green curtains and the Mission Plans Center's double bank of security doors.

4

I scrambled down a ladder to the hangar bays just below the flight deck. The upper hull of the aircraft carrier was made up of four enormous plane hangars running the width of the ship and closed off from one another, forward and aft, by great armored-steel sliding doors. Each door was two or three stories high. They were now shut tight. There were man-sized hatches at the sides, and at each access stood an armed Marine guard, grim-faced kids dressed in green fatigues. The fatigues were so heavily starched and pressed they looked like they were cut from sheets of cardboard. I was stopped and my Special Weapons Clearance card checked a half-dozen times before I finally made it to Hangar Bay Three where the squadron planes were loading. Pastori, the executive officer, was in the middle of the hangar, flanked by rows of F-8's and dart-shaped A-4 Skyhawk jets. He stood gripping a clipboard, looking about with dark, troubled eyes at the activity around him. He seemed startled when I asked him to which plane I was assigned.

"What? Oh yes," he mumbled absently, and then ran his finger down a list attached to the clipboard. "You have two-zero-nine," he said finally, with an indefinite gesture toward the port side. "It's over there."

I located the plane and an ensign from the ship's Special Weapons Division. The ensign was a towhead with the smooth pink face of a seminarian. He did not look old enough to be an officer, but he had his job down pat and zipped me through the static checks in nothing flat.

I secured the systems just as Red Lucas sauntered up with his loading crew and spoke briefly to the ensign. Up in the cockpit, I could not hear what they were saying over the rumble of the ship, thundering and echoing in

39

the steel sea cave of the hangar like a storm. Lucas walked over under the nose and shouted up, "Hey, Charly, since you're all checked out, how 'bout staying up there for a little while longer? I want to use your plane for a loading drill, okay?"

"Yes, sure."

I lolled back in the ejection seat, while several crewmen shoved the plane forward into the roped-off area alongside an opened elevator shaft in the deck. From my perch, the pit appeared black and bottomless, plunging straight down into unknown depths below.

"Okay, gang, let's move," Lucas boomed, holding up his wristwatch. He had a voice like a kettledrum. "I want to knock off at least a minute from our last time, and immediately hit the next one. Go, go, go."

Several crewmen scooted under the wings to rig the special weapons pylons. Once more I hit the checkoffs to secure the arming and fusing system. Beneath me, heard but not seen, the hydraulic lift whined under the dead weight of the bomb, hauling it up from the deep, dark secret hold of the ship. There was a great deal of jockeying with the bomb and the lift under the wing, and then Lucas hollered up at me to confirm the contacts. They shoved the plane, now loaded, off to one side and immediately pushed another F-8 over the shaft.

I scampered out of the plane and stood forward of the wing, hands on hips, to look at the bomb. The Crusader was normally outfitted with Goshawk air-to-air missiles, which were as slender and graceful as needles. In contrast, the bomb looked thick and bloated, hanging from the underside of the aircraft like a cancerous growth.

"Is that *it*, sir?" a hushed voice alongside me asked.

One of the Marine guards, a private no more than eighteen, stood next to me, intently staring at the bomb with an awed, respectful expression. A conscientious high school student on tour in Washington, D.C., who had just spotted the President would have had that same expression. The Marine shook his head. "Wow! That's *it*, huh? I've never seen one close up like this before. That's really something. I'll have to write my girl about this."

I had to laugh. Actually, it came out more of a bark, but then something caught my eye. On the bomb somebody had scrawled in red grease pencil. "Fuck the Reds,"

40

and the smudged scarlet letters glistened in the flat light of the hangar bay, looking strangely as if they had been written in lipstick.

The Marine backed off, and Pastori was at my elbow.

"Forgot. We have to check all the weapons in the locker tonight. Get together with the Special Weapons boys as soon as the loading drills wrap up," Pastori said.

I grunted an acknowledgment. Like the squadron's other junior officers, I had "collateral duties" besides flying. My job was to be the squadron's assistant ordnance officer.

Just behind us, there was a sudden chorus of mutterings and curses. The loading crew had spotted the next plane badly over the Special Weapons lift, and now they couldn't jockey the bomb under the wing pylon. They had to lower the lift and shove the plane around to respot it. Red Lucas impatiently checked and rechecked his wristwatch, his broad florid face, mottled thickly with freckles like bright pennies, screwed up in an angry frown.

"Okay. Okay. For Chrissakes, let's get the goddamn nuke set right this time."

I nodded toward the loaded plane and gave Pastori a vague embarrassed grin. "That *thing,* it scares the shit out of me, Frank."

Pastori did not appear to have heard me. He gazed distractedly across the hangar, as if focused on the pools of shadow there. When he finally spoke, his voice was bitter and the bitterness welled up into his eyes, dark, sad, and fluid in their anxiety. "You know, Charly, if they do push the button, we'll be making the first strikes."

I shook my head. "Never happen."

"You sure about that?"

I nodded. "Peace is our profession," I said.

Pastori didn't say anything. His eyes were fixed upon my face, as if reading something that was indelibly written in my football-battered features.

I turned back toward the aircraft. Just beyond the Black Knight in armor squadron insignia on the fuselage, there was an open outside hatch, and through it there was a brief view of the darkening sky—clouds and stars rushing by. The backdrop gave the cartoon knight charging to battle on his white-winged horse an urgent sense of motion.

I knew what was troubling Pastori. There had been a sick hollowness in the pit of my guts from the moment we had scrambled from Atsugi Air Base, and it was getting worse by the minute. But I'll be goddamned if I knew what Charly Rohr, the All-American boy, could do about it. Except watch the way the game broke and make the plays that the situation called for. I checked out with the Special Weapons detail and then headed for the wardroom.

"Charly, for Chrissakes, look where the hell you're going."

I stopped in my tracks.

"You all but stumbled right into that goddamn hole," Red Lucas warned in his deep rumbling voice, coming up alongside.

I stared down into the dark, deepening pit formed by the lowered weapons elevator.

"Damned thing is flush with the deck. You got to watch out for it. Where the hell is the lookout man I had posted? Before someone falls in." Lucas looked around accusingly.

In the wardroom lounge, I sat huddled with a mug of steaming coffee, clasping it tightly with both hands, trying to draw warmth from it. Cups and saucers, stacked on the cupboard behind me, rattled hysterically with the vibrations set up by the ship's screws, driving at full power directly beneath.

I got up and glanced into the main dining room next door. There was a full house for the evening movie, which was being shown right on schedule come hell or high water.

5

In the open cockpit of his fighter plane, John Wayne of "The Flying Tigers," his white scarf fluttering in the prop wash, gave a thumbs up and shoved down his goggles. Six engines roared as one, and like a swarm of angry hornets the stinger-nosed Curtiss-Wright P-40 Tomahawks soared into the air. The painted shark eyes and ranks of man-eater teeth on the engine nacelle gleamed hungrily.

A flight of twin-engine Misubishi bombers suddenly appeared overhead. The Jap bombardier, his simian face contorted with sadistic pleasure, bent over his bomb sight.

A string of bombs hurtled to earth.

The truck stacked with rice parked in front of the China Relief Mission disintegrated into flames and splinters. Amid the smoke and rubble, a ragged Chinese baby bawled its heart out.

The monkey face smiled and pressed off another load.

John Wayne frowned angrily and dove head on at the bomber, directly into the fiery hail of bullets spitting from the Jap's nose gun . . .

"Mr. Rohr."

"What . . . ho."

A Marine corporal of the guard leaned over and whispered in my ear. "The Special Weapons check," he said nervously, uncomfortable about being in the wardroom. "The others are waiting in Hangar Bay One."

"Oh, right. Jesus, almost forgot. Thanks."

I took one last look at the silver screen on which John Wayne zoomed, looped, and Immelmanned as he single-handedly blasted the Japanese Imperial Air Force from the China sky. Then I got up and followed the Marine out of the wardroom.

"Whoops. Excuse me, sir. Sorry. Excuse me." I picked my way in the dark through the congested obstacle course of dining chairs. The flickering light from the screen faintly illuminated the officers about me. Their faces were expressionless, staring straight ahead, fading in and out in the phantom glow—more like ectoplasm than flesh—as if they themselves were the ghosts of battles past.

Outside the wardroom, the corridors were jammed with shoppers. The second deck—the level just below the hangar bays—was the one on which the ship's stores, mess halls, kitchens, bakery, tailor and cobbler shops were located. This first night at sea, there were long lines of shoving, bellyaching enlisted men in front of each ship's store. They were stocking up on cigarettes, soap, toothpaste, razor blades—all the items that were considerably cheaper aboard ship than ashore. Young, razor-scraped, pimply faces jammed about the *gedunk,* the ship's soda fountain, clamoring for "two Hershey bars here." "Hey, a strawberry sundae, huh. How about it?" "Six Eskimo Pies."

A sailor in dungarees squirted out of the press of bodies and collided with me, damn near dumping a chocolate malt all over us both. "Oops, sorry, sir. You all right?" He bolted for the mess hall in order not to miss a moment more of the enlisted men's evening movie.

The Marine corporal and I worked our way forward through the darkened mess hall and up a ladder to Hangar Bay One. The Special Weapons Officer, a short, pudgy lieutenant commander with the middle-aged, flaccid face of a high school science teacher hanging on until retirement, was waiting there. With him was the eager-beaver ensign who had zipped me through the static checks. They stood lounging against the port side, watching the nightly exercising of the prisoners in the brig.

The prisoners, with gleaming shaven skulls and expressions as dispirited as their baggy, stained old dungarees, looked like DP's. A Marine guard, not older than nineteen, stood before them, braced in parade rest in that grotesque stance Marines are taught, hips thrust lewdly forward, gripping a billy club with both hands tightly across his thighs. He wore a tight, tailor-made, sharply pressed uniform, and his cap was jammed down almost over his eyes. In order to peer out, he had to tilt his head way back, making a taut bow of his body. He scowled at the men in his charge with contempt. He whacked his club

44

loudly, and probably painfully, against his thigh. His act was faultless, his model the drill instructor who had terrorized and humiliated him in boot camp in San Diego.

The guard bawled out an order, and the prisoners immediately flopped to the steel deck. He barked cadence, and they began pressing out push-ups. Painfully, their faces red and bloated with strain, the prisoners were ordered to continue beyond their strength and endurance, bodies quivering and contorted, to where the form of the calisthenic was no longer recognizable.

"What are most of them in for anyways?" the lieutenant commander asked.

The corporal of the guard started to answer but I cut him off. "Nothing much. A.W.O.L., insubordination to petty officers."

"We are reeducating them, sir, instilling them with a sense of discipline they missed during their original training," the Marine corporal put in, his voice mechanical as that of a cop reciting a statute he has memorized. But underlying it, there was a heavy note of contempt. He looked me squarely in the eye, the line of his mouth grim and tough. A Marine corporal is better than a goddamn officer in any other branch, he had been told when he won that second stripe, and his expression left no doubt that he believed it in the pit of his guts.

I turned my back on the Marine and said to the Special Weapons Officer, "Ready?"

With the corporal leading, we went back below to the mess hall. A hatch in the bulkhead opened up into a dimly lit, narrow, vertical shaft that dropped away beneath my feet like a well. In a line like a string of cave explorers, the two Special Weapons officers, the Marine, and I struggled down a series of vertical ladders. The metallic ringing of our steps and our labored breathing echoed hollowly off the walls.

At the bottom of the well, another Marine guard in gleaming combat boots and severely starched and pressed fatigues stood braced at parade rest like a men's store mannequin. I jumped the last three or four steps and as my foot hit the steel deck, the Marine guard snapped to attention and saluted as if my foot had struck the button that galvanized him.

"Your ID card, please, sir."

I produced the white Special Weapons Clearance card. Behind me, the lieutenant commander, sweating and breathing heavily, fumbled about. Directly in front of us was a locked hatch, and after clearing with the guard, the other officer and I each inserted separate keys into the lock. The hatch swung open heavily with a harsh, metallic groan.

The compartment had the thick, musty chill of a mausoleum. The overhead light threw strong, distorting shadows, and the nuclear missiles, sleek shark shapes with stubby side fins, were laid out in racks like the corpses of savage sea creatures.

The two Special Weapons officers bent to work with quick efficiency. They made their checks swiftly, the ensign occasionally singing out to me, and I made the notations on my checkoff list. While they worked, I prowled the weapons locker, restlessly padding back and forth like a caged cat.

The lieutenant commander inspected the last detonator, bolted its covering plate back in place, and straightened up. As he did, he gave the nose of the missile a resounding farewell slap. I jumped.

"Relax," the Special Weapons Officer assured me, smiling oddly. "We could explode a conventional bomb in here, and it wouldn't set off these devices. Not at the moment."

"Let's hope that nothing ever does happen to disturb them," I said. "If you're all finished, sir, shall we secure?"

The lieutenant commander lingered a moment. With the same weird smile, he patted the nose of the missile almost affectionately. "Innocent-looking enough, isn't it?" he asked.

"May we secure here?" I insisted. "The air conditioning is giving me one hell of a chill."

Jesus, that place made me jumpy. I felt as if the steel walls were pressing in on me, relentlessly sliding in on silent rollers to crush us all. I had only been in the nuclear armory once before, in Pearl Harbor, when the Special Weapons had been loaded aboard. I had had that same feeling then, It went very deep, a horror that seemed to penetrate to my very genes, back to the beginnings and ends of life. Once in college, at Southern Cal, when I was working at one of the part-time campus jobs

46

they gave to jock straps to make us earn our living expenses, I had to deliver a package to one of the medical school labs. A glass cabinet at the rear of the lab was filled with precisely labeled, sealed glass cups, and with the same spooky, Boris Karloff smile as the SW Officer, the researcher had casually mentioned that they were plague cultures with which he was working. Those missiles made my skin crawl the same way. I recoiled from them physically as if they were canisters of plague culture that would spread wildly, littering the world with smoking heaps of corpses if they were ever broken open.

I could not get out of that armory fast enough. I scrambled up the ladder and suddenly I was on the mess decks again right in the middle of the evening movie. On my left, ten feet tall and surrounded by flames and bleeding bodies, John Wayne was waving a smoking forty-five over his head and bellowing a war cry. And on my right, a pimply faced, teen-age sailor sat slurping a milk shake in one hand and gripping a Baby Ruth bar for dear life in the other.

6

Pastori was waiting, alone, in the ready room for the report. He took the key and the report from me, studied the latter for a long moment, and then locked both in the squadron safe. When he stood up he had a strange expression on his face, half horrified and half amused, as if he could not quite take what he had been reading seriously.

"Sweet Jesus, Charly," he said, shaking his head, "you know we've got enough nuclear weapons aboard this ship to incinerate half the world."

"It won't go that far, Frank."

"Oh, won't it?" He sat down behind the duty desk, tilting back in the chair. The squadron exec was a slender man, almost gaunt, with the deceptive thinness that disguises tough, wiry strength. His dark, deep eyes and vaguely melancholy half-smile invited confidences. His expression said that he understood, and accepted, all his own frailties and mine and all the lousy tricks that fate or women or friends might play on us both. But on top of that, tonight, there was something else. A look of embarrassment, as if he had been unexpectedly caught in a place he was not supposed to be.

"This is my third trip out here, Charly," he said suddenly. "Count them. World War II, Korea, and now this—whatever the hell it is."

He paused and stared at me, as if expecting a comment. I had none.

"You know, Charly, each time I've come, it seems the reasons are a little more obscure, more abstract, but the potential is greater."

Pastori's voice was low, puzzled, as if he were not really talking to me at all, but trying to figure it out for himself out loud. "When I flew in Korea, we weren't quite ready to fight a nuclear war. But even then, MacArthur was pushing it. Pushing to strike over the border into Red China. Even use nuclear weapons against the Red Army and the Chinese industrial cities, *if need be*. And half the nation and the Congress thought MacArthur was the hero and Truman a gutless *politician* for firing him." He shook his head in awe. "Well, this time out, we *are* ready for a nuclear war."

The squadron exec had just been promoted to the rank of full commander, although he had not yet gotten around to changing his rank insignia. Normally, he probably would not have discussed politics with a lieutenant junior grade only two and a half years out of college and a year out of flight school, but at that late hour at sea, men often react in strange ways. On quiet watches or in the wardroom lounge where men unready to sleep may drift in, the older officers tell you stories of World War II and Korea, of native girls on Palau Island, or another man's wife in San Diego. Their adventures, philosophies, secret lusts, and fears tumble out in the weak lonely hours of night when they look into some younger man's unlined face and suddenly recognize that their own youth has somehow evaporated. They then feel the weight of middle age in the heaviness of their shoulders and the dim ache in their eyes. And they recollect where they have been, and sometimes they are frightened by where they are going. There was a hint of that fear in Pastori's eyes that night.

"I don't think it'll ever get to that point," I insisted.

"It *is* at that point," Pastori said, his voice hushed with menace. "Look around you on this carrier and a dozen ships like it."

He stared at me, then gave a short mocking laugh and shook his head. "Jesus, you don't even see it. It's all you've ever known. One of the twenty-three-, twenty-four-year-old kids who are specialists in nuclear warfare. *Look at it*, Charly," he quietly exhorted me. "All this fantastic equipment didn't exist five years ago. A fortune in research went into it. Years of our lives spent training with it. And now it's all developed a will and momentum of its own, like a runaway horse. This time out there's not a ward-heeling Kansas City politician in the White House to put the generals on a leash. This time out there is a general in the White House. And this carrier is charging across the Pacific, fired up and primed to launch World War III. It's America's new Manifest Destiny. In a couple of days, Charly, you're going to be catapulting off this deck with a nuke weapon under your belly and heading for the Chinese mainland."

A third time I shook my head. "No one is insane enough to push the button."

Pastori's voice was quiet, like that of a patient teacher, but it had a hard bitter undertone to it. "Why do you believe that, Charly? Do you think that all this equipment, the billions of dollars, the research and development, the years of training are all just for a gigantic bluff? Or is it because you think it's a horror too great to imagine? It isn't. We've already done it. Twice. The use of nuclear weapons is already a matter of established military and political procedure for this country. And believe me, when it become strategically practical to use them against a ChiCom invasion fleet or troop concentration, Eisenhower—the ex-Supreme Allied Commander of the invasion of Europe—will make that decision with a great deal less soul-searching than the ex-haberdasher from Missouri did."

Pastori stared at me, his eyes probing. "And when that order comes, Charly, are you going to obey it?"

I didn't say anything. With my thumbs hitched in my belt, I rocked back and forth slightly on the back legs of the chair and gave Pastori my poker-playing look, alert but expressionless, waiting for the other man to declare himself.

He looked at me intently, then nodded to himself, as if the answer to his question was unmistakably written in the trim of my crew-cut hair and the gnarl on my broken nose.

"I guess, Charly, you have as great a need-to-know as any man," Pastori said, his voice almost inaudible. "The word is that Eisenhower has already approved hitting the Chinese mainland with nuclear weapons. The only question remaining is when."

The exec glanced down at his desk as if embarrassed, absently picked up some papers, then looked back at me. "That information goes no further," he said.

I nodded.

"You better get some sleep. We've got long days and nights ahead of us." He looked back down at the papers. I was dismissed.

The ready room was directly below the flight deck, and I climbed out onto the open catwalk that ran around the perimeter of the carrier. The ship's blocky island with its towering radar masts was a black silhouette against the pale backdrop of moon-illuminated clouds. On the deck the planes were already spotted for the launch, wedged together as tightly as the pieces of a jigsaw puzzle. A few hundred yards from the ship I could make out ghostly phosphorescent wakes and bobbing lights haunting our track. They were the guard destroyers in an antisubmarine screen around the aircraft carrier.

> *Well, fools fall in love in a hur-ray.*
> *Fools give their hearts much too soo-oon.*

It was absolutely insane. An aircraft carrier with four thousand men aboard is smashing crash-bang across the Pacific loaded with nuclear weapons, heading for a launch point off South China, and suddenly music strikes up and it's . . . *The Drifters.*

> *Just bathe in two balls of stardust.*
> *Just hang up one silly moo-oon.*

I started to laugh. There I was, grim-jawed and scared, staring off into the pitch black night with the deck quaking underneath me, feeling like one of Columbus's men. I mean I felt like we were all going to plunge over the edge of the world at any second. Then that music came up out of nowhere. I leaned back against the steel bulkhead and roared, and the cold sea whipped in my face and dried the tears running down my cheeks.

> *Uh-oh, they've got the love torches burn-ing.*
> *When they should be playing it coo-ool.*

The sound was very strong and pure, broadcasting from a high-fidelity setup that one of the electronic technicians had rigged in one of the shops just off the deck.

But the sound of the music and voices was eerie. It hung in the air just above the clatter and roar of the boiler room, as if it were emanating not from the ship but from another world, or another time in my life.

7

The drive from the University of Southern California to the Naval Air Training Command at Pensacola, Florida, was a three-day barrel-ass to El Paso to Houston to Mobile, rolling due east like the prevailing winds. The final sprint from Mobile Bay along Route 90 cuts through weedy grasslands and pine clumps, then mounts a sterile steel-and-concrete bridge across a narrow river which a metal road sign identifies as the River Styx. Feeble portents of the gods.

A Navy public relations man once tagged Pensacola "The Annapolis of the Air," and they had a Navy blue and gold billboard heralding that slogan right outside the main gate. But by the time I signed aboard freshly minted as an ensign, U.S.N.R., by the Southern Cal Naval Reserve Officer Training Corps, that description was inaccurate on a couple of counts. The Navy's strict air cadet program was now a small part of the picture, and most of the student pilots were young Navy and Marine Corps officers right out of college with commissions from the N.R.O.T.C. or the officer candidate schools at Newport and Quantico. The general atmosphere was considerably more relaxed than the shit-and-Shinola of the Naval Academy, and the bachelor officers' quarters was more like the Sigma Chi house than a midshipmen's dorm.

In preflight and primary flight training, the first heavy cuts were made, and the Navy then pretty well knew who was varsity material. Those of us in the "jet pipeline" were transferred to Whiting Field about thirty miles outside of Pensacola, but several nights a week I boomed back into town with my BOQ roommate, a Dartmouth man named Bob Ferrara. We each had brand new cars. I had a sky-blue Chevy convertible and Bob a red MG,

53

both of which were bought with the Instant E-Z Credit of newly commissioned Navy officers on flight pay.

Our first watering stop was the main officers' club, a sprawling white, colonnaded building that against the swamp oaks and Spanish moss looked like a commandeered Southern mansion. After a few drinks there, we invariably moved on to Trader Jon's, a downtown honky-tonk decorated in World War II South Pacific. An enormous fish net covered the ceiling, and from it hung festoons of dried starfish, ammunition belts, blowfish, a bullet-pocked Marine helmet, a Samurai sword, exotic sea shells, cork floats, a shattered wooden propeller, a shark's jawbone, and models of World War II fighter planes. There was a black rhythm-and-blues band at Trader Jon's, but the main attraction was the barmaids, who wore skin-tight shorts and halters and jiggled right along with the beat.

Un-oh, they've got the love torches burn-ing.
When they should be playing it coo-ol.
I used to lay-aff but
Now I un-der-stand,
Shake the hand of
A brand new foo-ol.

Ferrara was going with one of the girls, Nancy, who had just graduated from the University of North Carolina. A sorority girl, a Theta, she had decided two weeks before graduation that she really did not want to marry the guy whose fraternity pin she had worn for the past two semesters.

Now she was in Pensacola for the summer, visiting with friends from college. During the day, she lay on the white beach and water skied in the Gulf of Mexico. At night, she played at working as a barmaid in a spot that catered to eligible young Navy and Marine officers.

Ferrara had jumped the moment he saw her. She had soft, flowing, copperish hair that framed a delicately boned face, and a slender figure that spectacularly set off full, round breasts. My jealousy of Ferrara was totally out in the open, the source of constant banter, lewd suggestions, and innuendoes. But after eight months of a Southern military town, of beer-glutted, sweaty nights

54

spent trying to pluck the pants off third-rate secretaries, Navy exchange clerks, and loom workers, there was a hard muscle of truth beneath the banter. Nancy was under my skin.

She had provocative ways, perhaps innocent, perhaps deliberate, of standing or sitting too near so that her hand or her breast or thigh touched, and the electricity of that touch inevitably rattled me. Her voice, a murmurous Southern accent an octave lower than most women's, made hushed exciting promises out of innocuous information.

"It's not too busy tonight, so I can get off early," Nancy crooned sliding into a seat next to Ferrara, cuddling up under his arm and giving him an affectionate nuzzle. He and I were drinking beer in one of the bare wooden booths at Trader Jon's, and Nancy joined us for a moment on her break.

Ferrara nodded and silently lit two cigarettes at once, passing one to Nancy. "How about it, Charly," he asked. "Why don't you put the old boyish charm in gear and hustle one of the girls here? We'll all go for a ride in the boat and a moonlight dip. Our flight tomorrow isn't scheduled until the afternoon wing anyway." He and I each owned a part interest, along with two other flight students, in a battered old runabout that we used for beer parties and weekend water skiing.

"Fine," I nodded. "Anything to forget the lieutenant for a while."

"I don't see why you two can't get along with your new instructor," Nancy scolded us.

"Because his whole purpose in life," said Ferrara, "is to make *ours* miserable. We've drawn a very definite line. He hates us, and we hate him."

"Now that's silly. The idea—grown men."

"No, it isn't," I insisted. "It's totally ideological. First of all, he's a Marine aviator, which only means he's a Navy pilot in a dung-colored uniform, and if he doesn't make a lot of noise, everyone will forget he's a Marine. Two, he's a Texan, a Southerner, and we're . . ."

"Well, now, I don't . . ."

"No, listen," I interrupted, "there's a hell of a lot more to it. He's just a little shit, a midget Marine among the jolly green giants, and we're both big, or at least bigger

55

guys than he is, and that bugs him too. And then we're college graduates and he didn't finish college, probably flunked out or something, and he had to go through flight training as a cadet getting ninety bucks a month and all the shit he could eat, while we're going through flight training as officers with the same rank and pay and privileges he now gets, even though he's our instructor, and that *really* bugs him. So you see that our reasons for mutual contempt are totally rational and reasonable."

"And I drew that asshole because I took two weeks leave *just* so you and I could go through formation flying together," complained Ferrara. "Would you do that for me, roomie?"

"Not if I live through this."

Nancy rose to go back to work, and Ferrara and I both silently studied her departure. Her lush figure was hourglassed in an oversized man's shirt and in shorts that pinched her hips and thighs tighter than skin.

Ferrara turned back and grinned at me. "In the last couple of weeks, she's confiscated all my button-downs."

"They look very much *hers*."

"She has a way of tucking them in."

"She certainly does, and if we can patent it and get it on the market, we'll make millions."

Ferrara laughed easily. He was a tall, exceptionally good-looking guy with dark, curly hair—the romantic type you always see gazing dreamily over the girl's shoulder at the fadeout of mouthwash commercials on TV.

Trader Jon's had a good crowd of stags, the post-college used-Porsche set. Almost to a man they were wearing the same uniform—tartan sport shirts or button-down dress shirts with the sleeves rolled halfway up the forearm, wash khaki slacks, and white tennis shoes. They leaned on the long horseshoe bar drinking and playing Liar's Dice to see who paid for the drinks, talking loudly but not really looking at one another. Their eyes drifted, restless and bored, about the room, tailing a bouncing barmaid, envying a couple on the dance floor, sizing up a dog pack of girls that had just strayed into the club. And if, for a moment, we forgot how lonely or horny we were, there was the music to remind us. Five black men with drums, electric guitars, and slushy saxophones wailing away, throbbing like a weeping heart.

Dev-vil, or ang-gel,
Dear, whichever you are.
I-need-you.
I-need-you.
I-need-you.

A team of barroom athletes climbed up into the fish net hanging from the ceiling, shouting hoarsely and rolling over one another in the convulsing net. They tried to bounce on it like a trampoline and execute the flips and somersaults they had just mastered in preflight physical training, but they kept tripping in the wide mesh or over their own feet or each other. Finally they just sprawled flat in the net gasping and laughing.

If I didn't get my mind off Nancy, I was going to end up climbing the nets myself. Right across from me was the table of girls who had just come in. They were only about two blocks from Tobacco Road, but what the hell. I sort of grinned speculatively at the best-looking gal and she sort of smiled back, but she was wary as a hound bitch that's been kicked as often as she's been petted.

As soon as I took her hand to lead her to the dance floor, I knew she worked at the Chemstrand mill. She had the tough-hided hands of a shortstop from working the spools.

"You dance pretty good," she said after a couple of turns.

"I've got natural rhythm."

She leaned her head back and looked me over. She was chewing gum, and her jaw was keeping time with the music, not missing a beat.

"Yeah, well, you look it. You an athlete or something?"

"I scout for a girl's softball team. You play ball?"

She actually laughed and moved in tighter. We didn't exactly dance, just stood there rubbing our bellies together in time to the music, dirty boogie style. What more can I tell you about her? She could chew gum and drink beer simultaneously.

You look like an ang-gel,
Your smile is dee-vine-ne.

But you keep me guessing
Will you ev-ver be mi-ine-ne.

But suddenly I looked up and spotted Nancy watching me romance Daisy Mae. Nancy smiled at me, you know the way women do when you're with another girl who doesn't quite cut it—sort of indulgently. And, well, sheeit, that did it. I was not about to spend half the night trying to get the pants off some hard-handed muchacha from the Chemstrand mills, at least not while Ferrara was romping with Nancy.

"Look," I told him, "you and Nancy go ahead. I think I'll just have a beer with the boys and turn in early. I'm going to try and get in eighteen holes before the afternoon hop. My game's getting pretty rusty."

"Where do you play?" Nancy asked.

"There's a golf course right on base. They've made the flat land all around the runways into fairways. It's a dull course, but you can't beat it for convenience."

"Pretty rough life you guys have," Nancy said, half mocking but also a little envious.

"Not rough," I said, winking at her, "but intense."

There was a bull session going at the bar. A strapping jock, a 230-pound ex-guard from the University of Michigan, was telling the others about a student pilot review board he had gone before that day because he had flunked his instrument flight check. The captain on the board had just taken one look at him, quietly inquired at what college he had played football, and commented that he hoped old strap was coming out for the Training Command's team in the fall. Then the officer recommended a few extra training hops to correct his deficiency. A student who came before the board right after him was washed out for the same deficiency. "The Navy's no different than any place else," the reprieved man concluded. He winked at me. "Right, Charly? The ball players make out."

Riiight. The majority of my flight schoolmates were simply unmyopic, reasonably bright, and physically fit young men whose interest in flying was as vague and romantic as my own. Very few had done any flying before, although there was one Marine, short and stocky as a fire

58

plug, who had worked his way through Alabama Aggie as a crop duster.

Just down the bar from me a squad of Yalemen stood drinking together. They had come down to Pensacola in a group, just as they might have gone to Bermuda for the yacht races—led by an Eastern prep-school patrician whose name was synonymous with big steel and sprawling shipyards. They were polite and friendly enough, but they always moved about in a tight little phalanx that shielded them from outsiders.

Among us, however, were others who seemed to have an almost mystic calling. A dark, moody rodeo champion from the University of Texas, and a handsome Irishman from Queens with an infectious grin. He had quit a Catholic seminary for Navy flight school and now drank hard and tried to lay every woman between fifteen and fifty. There were Annapolis men, sons of admirals, and others from Iowa State and Kansas whose fathers had flown in the South Pacific in World War II and had sent their sons to Pensacola drunk on legends.

There was a future astronaut and Apollo commander, already self-contained, competent and tough at twenty-two years old. But he was married, a brown-bagger who spent his evenings at home doing his homework and was at the head of the class.

And then there were the officers of the foreign legion—our allies in the Cold War. Canadians, South Americans, Japanese and Germans. The Japanese and Germans were older than the rest, almost middle-aged. They had all been pilots in World War II, but after the war their countries had been forbidden to have air forces. Now the United States government was completely retraining them to fly the latest jets. In the flip-flops of international politics, they were on our side now. The Japanese, I'd heard, had been kamikazes, but the war had ended before their final banzais had come up. I felt very strange whenever I passed them in the BOQ, the superpolite Japanese officers always smiling and bobbing their heads up and down automatically like wind-up toys. They and the Germans were from an age when I was reading "War Comics" and acting out my Flying Tiger fantasies with balsa wood P-40 fighters. "Pow! Pow! Take that, you Jap-a-Nazi rats!"

I now looked around the bar for the Germans. The Japanese kept quietly to themselves, but the Germans liked a good time after working hours. I immediately spotted one of them, a beaming moon-faced officer who looked like a prosperous Bavarian innkeeper. Scuttlebutt had it he was a Luftwaffe multi-ace who had shot down forty Allied airplanes in World War II. I didn't really believe the story at first, but one day the Germans received a large shipment of wine, beer, sausages, cheese and assorted imported delicacies from their embassy in Washington and threw a helluva party. I took advantage of the general gemütlichkeit to inquire, sort of jokingly, about the forty planes.

"Not *sooo* many," the innkeeper laughed, rolling his eyes. "Anyways, they were all Russians," he added, giving me a tremendous wink.

"All Russians?" I laughed with him, because it was crazy anyway you looked at it.
man confided, pounding me on the back jovially and refilling my glass.

"Well, maybe a few English and Greek, eh," the Ger-

> *Dev-vil, or ang-gel,*
> *Dear, whichever you are,*
> *I-love-you.*
> *I-love-you.*
> *I-love-you.*

Wherever I was in the South that year the black rhythm-and-blues wove about me from Saturday night barroom bands, juke boxes, and car radios. It was primitive and compelling, throbbing in the air and in my blood like a series of interweaving harmonics on the basic beats of life itself, stirring pains and joys I couldn't quite put my finger on, things I had either forgotten or not experienced yet.

I sat in my new Chevy with the top down, feeling the music. I had stopped at a drive-in for a cup of coffee and a hamburger on my way from Trader Jon's back to Whiting Field and was lounging with a cup and a cigarette, the blues wailing about me. *Crash bang caroooooooommm.* A couple of tank-town commandos cruising in a chopped Ford pulled up into the slot next to mine, their dual exhausts in afterburner. Out of the Ford's tin speaker, a Nashville ex-pig farmer was screaming about gunning down a man in Laredo, and I was stirred to murder. My beautiful bluesy mood was shattered, its glass crashing about me as if a rock had come through the window.

"Turn down that goddamn hillbilly."

I think they were even more startled than I at the anger in my voice—a challenge suddenly hurled at them. Three cracker youngbloods in their go-to-town crotch-cutting jeans. They weren't very bright, but they could count to three. And there were three of them and one of me.

They sat there a moment counting, sucking on their cigarettes, eyes squinty like the hired guns in a western. Then one of them said in a badman drawl, "Y'all planning on making us?"

Growing up in Southern California gives you an instinct for certain things—one of them is how to play "High Noon" in the drive-in. In a moment, they were going to be charging out of that car and all over me. So I slowly climbed out the door opposite them and ambled around to the trunk, opened it up, and took out the jack handle. I paused a moment, just so they could get an idea of my size—I figure even a pack of wolves will hesitate to attack a bear—and then I got back into the car, jack handle in hand.

"I just thought it might be more neighborly if I could hear my music and you could hear yours," I said, leaning across the door toward them. I couldn't see their faces, only the red glow of their cigarettes stoking up. Then I noticed the carhop standing right in front of my Chevy, her eyes flicking nervously from one car to the other. She was ready to bolt. "No trouble," I grinned at her. "I'm a lover, not a fighter."

That set the wolves in the other car howling and baying, and after a minute of talking loud and leaving the radio up, they turned it down.

The carhop sashayed over and idly wiped at my tray as if she was looking for something to do and asked if I'd like a warm-up on my coffee. She wasn't bad looking, kind of jaunty in her little red carhop cap and red shorts. And busty. She was stacked like an ice cream cone with the scoops pressed side by side rather than on top of one another.

"Y'all work around here?" she asked, friendly like. She had looked me and the car over and hadn't missed the Navy Air Training Command sticker on the windshield, but she was making conversation.

I gave her my best grin. "No, I don't work. I'm one of the flight students."

"Cadet?" She knew perfectly well cadets weren't allowed to wear civvies. I shook my head. "An officer and a gentleman."

We got this big nonverbal thing going now, all eyes and smiles. I offered her a cigarette, and she shook her head, not so much refusing as asking, "What else are you offering?" She leaned lightly on the door, listening to the music, nodding her head slightly to the beat. "I like your taste in music."

"Want to go hear some *live?* There's a place down the highway, toward Mobile."

Bull's eye! Her smile was right there. "Why sure."

"How soon are you off?"

My arm was draped on the door top, and she leaned over it, those cool mounds of vanilla ice cream squeezing against my arm like it was the banana in a banana split, and without a word she took my hand to look at my Omega Seamaster wristwatch. Then, with her face inches away from mine, she licked her lips and asked, "Do y'all think you could sit tight for fifteen minutes more?"

Her hair and the moist warmth of her neck emanated the sugary fragrance of S & W root beer syrup. It enveloped me, permeated the air in sweet, sticky perfume. S & W root beer and vanilla ice cream. I had me a walking, balling root beer float.

8

Ferrara and I each made it back to Whiting Field the next day just in time for our hop.

"Well, are you two college boys ready to fly today?" piped up Lieutenant Olson. He was a skinny little guy, almost adolescent-looking, with a squeaky voice and a round head of severely cropped tow hair that gave him the fuzzy appearance of a newly hatched bird. He wore his cap jammed so far down he had to lean his head way back in order to squint up at Ferrara and me. "Well, let's keep a few points in mind today, shall we, gentlemen? First, Mr. Rohr, this is formation flying we're working on. You are supposed to stay within fifteen feet of the other plane. I got the feeling yesterday you were on your own instrument flight plan. Now don't be afraid of him. The worst thing that can happen is that you two might collide with each other." Olson grinned evilly for punctuation. "And when you make that rendezvous, it's *Check. Check. Check.* Like so," he explained, passing one hand closely under the other in three distinct movements. "Got it? It's not *whoosh* and off we go. And Ferrari . . ."

"Ferrara," he was corrected.

"Okay, Ferrarah. You make another landing like that one yesterday, and your name will be mud. I'll down you. I'd have downed you yesterday, except then I'd have had to ride in the back seat with you."

Ferrara nodded. "I wasn't used to landing from a break like that. I was a little rushed."

"Well, today, you'll be used to it. These aren't those Maytag Messerschmitts that you learned to fly when you were little boys in primary and they forgave you everything. These are planes for the big boys, and they have a lot of power and torque, and if you try to wrap up a landing like you did yesterday, it's going to spin you right on

63

your curly head." He paused for effect. "Any questions?" Another pause. "Okay, men, let's move out."

Ferrara and I exchanged looks of silent disgust, and then followed behind Olson. Chest out, head up and straining for height, the instructor strode out to the flight line of blunt, muscular T-28 trainers as if he fancied himself at the head of a parade platoon of Marines.

We took off in three separate planes in quick succession. As soon as we were clear of the field, Ferrara, the first off, banked into a rendezvous circle, and I joined on his wing a few feet away. For the next two hours we maneuvered between towering cotton pillars of afternoon cumulo-nimbus, repeatedly practicing turns, climbs, and letdowns in tight formation, changing the lead, breaking off in sharp vertical banks, and rendezvousing again. All the while, Olson's shrill, fretful voice constantly rasped in the earphones and scraped across the raw edges of my nerves like a file. "Okay, Ferrari, pull it tighter . . . Rohr, heads up. Stay with him . . . Jesus Christ, don't swing in that fast. What are you trying to do, kill us all? . . . Will someone please shoot down these two jokers."

At the end of the flight, Ferrara led back to the field. As we crossed over the runway, he turned toward my plane, blew a kiss, and broke off, banking steeply into the landing pattern over the field.

I followed him at a distance, making a wider turn to give myself more space in which to make a more gradual landing approach. I lost sight of Ferrara's plane as I turned into the final letdown. I concentrated fiercely on holding my airspeed right on the button, aiming the plane to fly right onto the small square that was outlined in yellow paint at the end of the runway. The square represented the size of the landing area aboard an aircraft carrier.

I caught a glimpse of Ferrara's T-28 ahead of me in an exceptionally steep bank, cutting for the end of the runway. The wings appeared to wobble. Then the plane, as if in slow motion, rolled in the direction of the bank, almost over onto its back, and dropped. It crashed, upside down, into the grass field to the left of the runway.

I do not remember landing my own plane. The next thing I recall was rolling down the runway, fighting to brake the plane, the wail of the crash alarm in my ears. I careened onto the taxiway and jammed on the brakes.

The plane pitched to a stop. I stood on the rudder pedals and thrust up out of the cockpit to peer down the field.

Just off the end of the runway, Ferrara's plane lay on its back, a wing and the canopy crushed beneath the fuselage. Red snake tongues of flames flicked from its ruptured engine nacelle, darting out and then disappearing, but growing bolder and bigger with each appearance.

"NO!" I bellowed. It was a cry of outrage and protest, a command meant to carry the length of the field. I yanked off my harness and scrambled out of the cockpit. Halfway out, my head was almost jerked off my shoulders by the radio cords still attached to my helmet.

I was panting and staggering from the long sprint when I finally reached Ferrara's plane. The plane was on its back, its gears up like the claws of a mortally wounded bird, and the crushed canopy made it impossible to get at the pilot. The crash crew had already smothered the fire with foam, and a crane hoist had to be rigged to lift the plane. Through the work, I hung back, staring at the cockpit, terrified by what horror might emerge from the wreck. The fuselage shifted, exposing a pool of unfoamed gasoline, which immediately flared up and enveloped the cockpit in flames and black smoke until it too was smothered.

"You left your plane on the runway. You better move it right away, mister."

"What?" I whirled about. Olson, anxious and sweating, stood behind me.

"You left your goddamn plane on the runway. Move it off," he ordered.

I stared at Olson, trembling with rage, and in the next instant, I was going to step forward and smash that little shit. But just then, the crane raised the wreck further. A black scarecrow figure, fire-charred and ragged, flopped halfway out of the cockpit, still pinioned by the seat belt.

I was paralyzed. The acrid smell of burnt flesh doubled me over like a kick to the stomach. I dropped to my knees, as all my juices exploded out of me.

When I finally staggered to my feet, I was half blind with tears and my shirt front was wringing wet. Olson handed me a handkerchief. "We better go," he suggested gently. "There's nothing we can do here."

The crash crew had freed Ferrara's remains from the

wreck, and the crushed, burnt husk of his life was now lying on the ground, covered with a parachute cloth.

I followed Olson across the field, walking very slowly. I stumbled and, focusing for the first time, discovered I was on a golf green. Ferrara had crashed in the middle of the third fairway of the Whiting Field golf course. On the edge of the green, a foursome of cadets, who had been playing in their cotton khaki uniforms, stood rooted in one spot. Their adolescent faces, pale and bloodless, stared at the parachute cloth that covered the tortured, charred corpse.

I turned to Olson. "The plane," I muttered.

"Screw it!" Olson said savagely. "Let the tower worry about the goddamn plane." And then in another voice, plaintive and almost whining, he said, "Oh shit, I told him he was going to stall if he tried to bank like that in the approach. He wrapped it up too tight again. I told him," and then he shut up.

When we arrived at the squadron area, there were several commanders and a captain waiting for us. Olson conferred with them a long while, and then they asked me several questions. I answered as best I could, but I was in a daze, and my most vivid sensations, like those of a drunk, were confusion and nausea.

"I think we both need a drink," Olson said, taking me by the arm after the interrogation.

"The last thing in the world I want is a drink," I said weakly.

"I think a good drink is just what you need," Olson insisted. "In fact, I order you to have one." Despite his authoritative tone, he looked like a very worried man.

I was too stunned to resist further, and Olson led me to his BOQ room where he broke out an almost full bottle of Old Crow.

The first straight drink made me gag, then took hold. I smiled weakly at Olson and staggered to the sink for a glass of cold water. Then I came back and held out the glass for the Marine to refill with whiskey. It wasn't very long before I had a good heat on.

"I think I should go to church or something," I suddenly announced.

"What for? What kind of church?"

"Any kind of church."

"Why? The base chapel's probably closed now, anyways."

"Not the base chapel. A real church."

Olson looked at me closely. "What's *Rohr?* Are you a Catholic too?"

"No, it's a proper old Anglo-Saxon name. Don't worry. My presence won't desecrate the goddamned place."

"Oh. Well, there's a Baptist church outside Milton," Olson suggested, still puzzled but solicitous.

He drove with me slumped next to him, regularly pulling at the bottle. It was late by the time we got to the church Olson had in mind, a white, wood-framed, and steepled building with an adjoining graveyard. Mounted against the deep blue cloth of dusk, it stood out like a model for Currier and Ives. The door was locked.

"What the hell do they lock the door for?" I complained loudly.

"Shhh!" cautioned Olson. "It's probably just to keep the niggers out. Tramps'll sneak in at night to sleep and get warm."

"God forbid." I wandered over to the graveyard and stared gloomily at the ranks of weathered headstones that glowed gently in the moonlight. "There are sure a hell of a lot of dead people in the world," I muttered.

I took another healthy swig from the bottle, but there wasn't a drink left. I studied the empty, and then suddenly hurled it into the graveyard where it exploded against a headstone.

"Come on, wake up, Rohr! We've got a hop at eight."

I couldn't focus on the figure hovering over me in the painful morning sunlight, etched in black and white glare like a solarized photo. At first, the apparition materialized as Ferrara, but it gradually resolved itself into Lieutenant Olson. "What . . . what are you doing?" I croaked and covered my eyes.

Olson nudged me again. "Come on. We've got a hop in less than an hour."

Automatically, every move feeling drugged and lead-weighted, I checked my watch and then Ferrara's bunk. It was still made up from several days before. "Who? . . . what the hell are you talking about?"

"You're gonna take a check hop this morning," Olson insisted. "CO's orders. Come on."

With Olson prodding me, I lumbered out of bed and over to the small sink in the corner of the room. The instructor remained adamant but vague. And I was too groggy and hung-over to organize questions or objections.

We stopped briefly at the officers' mess for breakfast. A plate of sunnyside-up eggs stared up at me like a Halloween fright mask with two runny, baleful yellow eyes and black slices of bacon for lips. My stomach surged, and I shoved it away and just managed to down a cup of coffee and nibble a roll.

Olson hustled me onto the runway and into an airplane for the same two-plane formation practice as the day before, this time with another instructor acting as the wingman. My flying was extremely shaky at first, and Olson was merciless in his sniping. Too dopey to get angry, I simply focused on flying to Olson's instructions as the only way to survive the flight, and by its end I had settled down.

Afterward, instead of lying in wait to give his usual debriefing harassment, Olson was mysteriously absent from the ready room. Puzzled but feeling weak and very hollow in the stomach, I wandered to the canteen, where I wolfed down a beef sandwich and several cups of coffee.

"Come on," Olson summoned, suddenly popping down next to me. "You're being transferred to another squadron. They need you. Some plumber just washed out, and they've been waiting a week for someone to round out a four-plane formation."

"I'm not finished with two-plane yet."

"You are now. We checked you out this morning. That was it."

"Now wait a minute!" I protested. "I'm not ready. I'm not even sure I want to stay in this fucking program anymore."

"Come on," Olson insisted, ignoring what I said. "There are half a dozen people waiting on you over there."

"Now look! I don't want to."

Olson turned on me. "Whataya doing? Chickening out on me?" he spat. "Come on! There are three guys waiting on you over there so *they* can finish up the program. Forget about yourself." He turned on his heel and strode off.

I stood smoldering a moment and then charged after Olson into the next squadron cubicle, where I was immediately embraced by another instructor and three students who lost no time in getting airborne again.

When we landed, I was again intercepted by Olson who pulled me into the operations office. A Wave handed me Ferrara's accident report. It was a step-by-step, bloodless account of the previous day's flight. The crash was attributed to a stall and spin on landing, caused by the student's excessively tight approach. The report stated that the day before the accident the instructor had pointed out to Ferrara this error in his landing technique.

I read over the report silently, and then signed it. "There's really nothing more to it, is there?" I said to Olson and left the office.

Right outside the door, I remembered.

"Oh, my God." I bolted for a telephone booth.

"Oh, Charly," Nancy cried in a pitiful voice. "I've been praying you'd call. I've been trying to get you all last night and today. Why didn't you call?"

"I've been in a state of shock," I said. The other end of the line was silent. "I'm sorry, Nancy. I didn't mean that the way it sounded. I've just been in a complete daze. I don't know whether I'm coming or going. I'm sorry. I haven't had a chance to think, not about anything. It was thoughtless and stupid of me not to call. I'm sorry."

On the phone, the thrilling familiar voice now sounded heavy, grief-stricken. "Oh, Charly, it's so awful," Nancy began again in a low, tragic voice. "I can't cry, and I didn't know what to do. Some jerk last night . . . I don't know what his name is. I think it was one of the Yalies. Dick something-or-other. I don't know. He came in early last night and said he was sorry about Bob, and I didn't know what the hell he was talking about. I just couldn't believe it. I didn't know what to do. I just kept wandering around serving drinks and wiping off tables and then all of a sudden I just ran out . . . without telling anyone. *Why* didn't you call me?"

"I'm sorry," I said again.

"I've just been sitting here ever since. I haven't been to

69

bed or washed my face or anything. Just sitting here. It's awful. I'm hysterical and I can't cry."

"Look, I'll drive over there, if you want me to," I offered.

"Oh, please," she pleaded. "I need someone I can talk to."

By the time I stepped into Nancy's apartment, she had evidently washed her face and combed her long auburn hair. Through the opened door of the bedroom, I could see the still unmade bed where, just the morning before, Ferrara had laughed with her, drunk orange juice, and made love. Nancy greeted me with a very shaky smile. She was holding onto herself very tightly, as if each muscle of her being were a clenched finger. If she had ever seen what was left of Ferrara, she would wake up screaming every night of her life.

"I have to go to work in a little while," she informed me immediately after I arrived.

"For Christ's sakes, take a few days off at least."

"I can't. I don't know what to do. I'm so broke now I don't know how I'm going to pay my rent or anything. I've been skipping out I don't know how many nights to see Bob, and last night, I just cut out without telling anyone. I'll be lucky to have a job at all." Her voice had a numb quality, her preoccupation was that of someone still half asleep.

"How much money do you need to tide you over?" I asked.

"Charly, you're sweet, but I couldn't."

"It's okay," I assured her.

I wanted to get the hell out of the apartment. We drove to the boat and held a wake in the runabout, drifting in the bay a hundred yards offshore. We drank from a six pack of beer and talked quietly in the somber velvet night. But mostly we just sat listening to the water softly slapping the side of the boat. I told Nancy a little about Olson and about flying that day.

From some dark corner of the bay a loon screamed out its chilling night call that sounds like a woman on the rack. Nancy hugged herself tightly and shivered dreadfully, although the air was warm as dishwater.

I crushed another drained can of beer and hurled it

overboard, where it became the last in a line of cans that bobbed listlessly along a yellow path of moonlight.

"The wake of a wake," I said.

"What?" she asked, punchy, as if rousing from sleep.

"The wake of a wake," I repeated, indicating the trail of cans. "Mourners."

She attempted a smile, but suddenly she broke up and her tears surged all at once, driven by a moan that sprang from the roots of her heart. I was completely at a loss. I hugged her and said hoarsely over and over, "It's all right. There, there. It's all right. There, there." My own eyes were spilling freely, and my tears ran together with hers, as I awkwardly tried to kiss her tears away.

Her stormy sobbing gradually quieted, but still she clung to me, her breasts burning into my chest. I kissed her wet cheeks, her throat and mouth, then hesitated.

Like two desperate drowning swimmers, we clutched one another.

"Oh, Charly," she cried out, grasping me to stay afloat. "Stay alive. Please don't get killed, Charly."

There was a moment in the boat, alone there with Nancy before she let it all out, that I tried to think about Ferrara. I sat there quietly, waiting for grief to come—as if grief, like sleep, could be coaxed if I sat still in the dark long enough. But life had already moved on to somewhere else.

I was again flying and booming along in the program. Olson, the little asshole, was sitting at the officers' club bragging to the other instructors about how he had gotten me "right back up on the horse." I hated his guts for it, but there was no doubt in my mind that if I had been allowed to mourn for Ferrara, perhaps wait a few days for a new wingman—in short, do the respectful Christian thing—I never would have flown again.

But I was still flying, and that made all the difference in the world. I moved in with Nancy. I exorcised Ferrara's haunting spirit by rationalizing that I, Charly Rohr, had been the winner in some vague undefined contest of natural selection.

Whatever rationalization Nancy clutched at, I never knew. If Ferrara's name was ever mentioned, it was simply with the affection and respect due a very dear, mutual

71

friend. Nancy seemed to accept the new relationship without question, almost compulsively. I would wake up in the middle of the night and find her clinging tightly to me, and then and there, I'd make love to her again, as if she required it before she could sleep. She clung to me—as she had that night in the boat—as if she were drowning, thrashing desperately and gasping to ease some unbearable tension in her lungs, until she finally burst through the suffocating pressure, crying aloud.

But there were nights I lay awake wondering. Wondering what it had been like between her and Ferrara. And if I thought about it too much, then it got to me. I lay there next to Nancy, holding her close, but I was limp as a bait worm. I might be that way for days.

About three months after Ferrara's death, I flew out into the Gulf of Mexico. Out beyond the beach strewn with volleyballs and the bikinied breasts and bottoms of vacationing college girls. Past the sandbar, the sailboats and water skiers, and the commercial fishing boat dredging for red snapper. Out to where the water was dark and deep and no longer the vivid offshore aquamarine mottled and shadowed by the caves and grottoes just below the surface. I was in a formation of six T-28's, and one by one we broke, very smartly, and spiraled down to a clunky old World War II carrier gently plowing its way through the Gulf. I plunked aboard perfectly on the first shot.

The carrier landing marked the official end of my basic training, and I was reassigned to a bleak base outside Corpus Christi, Texas, for advanced training in jet fighters. I said good-bye to Nancy. I didn't make any promises, and she told me to take care of myself. She stood in the doorway, dry-eyed but hugging herself tightly and again shivering with some deep unseasonal chill, as she had the night after Ferrara had died.

"Long, long, and lonely nights ..." Clyde McPhatter was wailing, and I picked up my Motorola beach portable and hurled it right out the window of the BOQ into the black, sticky, mosquito-miserable Texas night.

Nancy had gone back home to Atlanta to teach school, to become an airline stewardess, to go to graduate school.

wasn't exactly sure what, and neither, I guess, was she.

There was a blonde in Corpus Christi. She was good-looking enough, but after a couple of movie dates and nights of dancing at the O Club she brought me home to family dinner of real Southern-fried chicken, real corn bread, and real RC Cola. Her mother, sun-dried and desiccated and resembling the daughter the way a prune does a plum, urged me to join them all for church the next Sunday. After that, I cooled it.

I brooded about visiting Nancy, thought about perhaps arranging a cross-country navigational training hop to Atlanta. I even considered asking her to come to Texas, but then where would it end? I could not see a future with Nancy, as much as I ached for her, ached along with Clyde McPhatter through the long, long, and lonely nights. Faced with my indecision, my instructor laid out the cross-country himself, and we went to San Diego. Atlanta and Nancy were three thousand miles away. And then I got my wings, I was assigned to a training squadron in San Diego, as I had requested.

The wings! Having them pinned on was like earning a Red Cross life guard badge, a football letter, and a diploma, all at once. I felt like an Apache receiving the headband of manhood. There is magic in those bits of cloth, paper, and metal, and I could actually feel the electricity running through my arms and legs.

And, oh man, that little winged gold talisman did have mystic powers over women. I started wearing a lapel pin of miniature Navy wings in the boutonniere hole of my civilian jackets and then consciously worked at contradicting whatever cocky first impression my build and my looks might make. Women like strong men and little boys, and I worked at giving them both in the same package. I cultivated a boyish, self-effacing grin and often flustered unnecessarily. Alone with them, I acted out scenes of revelation, self-doubt, tenderness, and affection, speaking hesitantly in a soft voice. It was not really an act, but more a self-conscious kind of loving.

For all my mooning about it, the affair with Nancy had been pretty straightforward, the break clean. Not so with the women that followed. They flapped in soft, fragile protest like butterflies being impaled for display. There was the *zoftig* dimpled little Western Airlines stewardess

whose favorite sport, indoor or out, was cuddling. Sh
wanted to get married, settle down, and have six kids. Sh
wasn't a stickler about the order of events, and we starte
off by settling down. But then I discovered she had
similar setup at the other end of the line in San Francisc
Well, you can't expect a girl like that to put all her egg
in one bed.

And then there was the San Diego State co-ed with th
sun-and-surf bleached hair who would never make love i
bed, protesting, "It seems so . . . so premeditated," bu
dropped her pants with instant abandon in cars, o
couches, or on the beach. Or Lois, the prototype o
several divorcees I dated who all seemed to work in insu
ance or real estate offices—well-groomed but not spectac
ular girls with nervous laughs who chain-smoked, drank
lot of Daiquiris, and pretended not to mind if I didn't ca
for a month. And there was the WestPac widow. (Did th
men of the Atlantic Fleet also have an alliterative labe
for bored and horny wives whose husbands were away
sea?) She would move the baby from her bedroom to ar
other room whenever I slept with her.

But the girls that really touched me were the ones
never dated. The loners I spotted on the beach when
went to surf. Young, often lovely girls who sat quietly b
themselves reading, or hugging their knees deep i
thought. There was something about the way they smile
the way their mouths flashed but not their eyes. The
wanted to be friendly, but they held back like a child wh
has been badly hurt. They were invariably on vacatio
and had just been on a side trip to Mexico—Tijuana t
be specific. The beach at San Diego is a nice place t
recover from a Tijuana abortion.

Then suddenly, without any letters to warn me, ther
was a phone call from Nancy.

"I'm right here in Chula Vista. Chula Vista! I sta
teaching school next week. I just got the appointmen
You can't believe the competition for these teaching jo
out here in California. The pay is fantastic compared t
what I'd get back home."

The next evening I drove to Chula Vista, a suburb ju
south of San Diego, with mixed feelings about Nancy
reappearance.

She was already settled into an apartment in a ne

wo-level stucco complex sprawling about a giant kidney-haped communal swimming pool. She was sunburned, nd slimmer than I remembered, with a breakfast cereal ir of health, as if she had been playing tennis every day or the past six months. The soap and lemon cleanness of er made me feel soiled and a little older and flabbier by ontrast.

She hesitated a moment and then gave me a kiss and a ug, not that of a lover but of a long-lost friend.

Nancy had a roommate, another schoolteacher, and af-er brief introductions the roommate excused herself to isit other friends, leaving Nancy and me sitting on the ouch with cups of coffee sprinkled with cinnamon in ront of us.

"Would you like to see San Diego by night, or La olla?"

"We don't have to go anywhere, Charly. I haven't seen *ou* in a long time."

I reached forward to kiss her, but she warded me off vith a hand on my chest. "That's not what I meant, Charly."

"What did you mean?"

She studied me a moment, then said, "Let's go see San Diego by night."

Why do lovers always seek out public bars for the most bersonal conversations of their lives? We drove north along San Diego Bay to the Coronado ferry, and then churned across the neon light-speckled bay in silence to he Naval air base at North Island. The Officers' club was crowded, and there was a cluster of stags drinking at the bar, their arms rising and falling as if they were literally bumping themselves up with booze and bullshit.

With one exception, they were all dressed in civvies. The exception was MacCafferty, standing up at the bar in he midst of the others in full uniform with a chestful of confetti campaign ribbons.

I pointed out my new squadron commander to Nancy, but he had already caught her attention. His voice, loud and gravelly as a cement mixer, carried to the table. "I'm ight above the ground, zapping through the flames, trafing that truck convoy, and then—Pow! I get hit sol-dly. Pieces of the plane are flying off, and I'm knocked ass-over-tea-kettle upside down right above the ground.

I'm so close I can read the serial numbers on thos trucks. Everything is hitting me like the hammers of hell but I manage to extricate myself and roll out. I glance down and, *Jeezus,* my leg is hanging there all blood and rags. And that no sooner registers, than—Pow! I ge slammed again."

"You must have been shitting bricks," one of the othe officers said.

"Hell, I didn't have time or brains enough to b frightened. I was too damn busy coping. But, by Jesus they have definitely got my attention."

The explosion of laughter caused half the heads in th club to turn.

Just then the waitress brought our drinks, and after w had settled, Nancy took a token sip of her drink an asked, "Have you been pretty busy out here?"

"I get the feeling that's not what you're really asking."

Nancy played with her drink a moment. "What yo didn't say in your brief letters and calls from Corpu Christi, and your silence since you've been out here, ha been pretty eloquent by itself. I don't have any othe questions, Charly."

I thought, here it comes.

"Not that I blame you. There I was the night after m lover, or whatever you want to call Bob, is killed, and I'r screwing his best friend on the greasy floorboards of thei boat. We've never ever talked about that, Charly."

"It's just something that happened."

"But it left me pretty screwed up. I had to go to a psy chiatrist for a while in Atlanta to get it all straightene out. I thought I was going to become one of those cas histories where the girl sleeps with every young soldier c sailor she meets after her fiancé gets killed. It wasn't any thing that melodramatic."

"What was it?"

"Just delayed hysteria, according to the doctor, an confusion."

"What were you confused about?"

"You and Bob. I was never in love with Bob. I came Pensacola right after graduation to have a good time b fore I had to settle down to work, and having an affa with a good-looking young officer was just part of it. was already involved with Bob when I met you. And th felt very strange because I was attracted to you, and you and Bob were so close. I may have imagined it, but I thought you felt something too. Then suddenly Bob was dead. Nothing like that had ever happened to me before. He was dead. Someone said his plane had crashed, caught fire and he was burned to death. I couldn't think about it. I tried to think about him alive and all I could see was him being burned to death. So I thought about you. Because you were alive, and I could picture you that way, drinking beer and dancing, even sweating. I could picture the play of your muscles when you water skied, and there were no unbearable pictures. I just thought of you that whole day to keep from going crazy, and then you were here and I just wanted to feel you and cling to you and fill myself up with you and not thinking about anything else." She looked at me, her eyes brimming with tears, but not crying. "Do you understand that?"

I nodded. "Yes . . . It wasn't very different for me."

We sat in silence, until the silence itself became an embarrassment.

Nancy looked away. She idly examined the stags at the bar, then turned back to me. "Why is he the only one wearing a uniform?" she asked, indicating MacCafferty.

"He always wears one, even after working hours," I said, as if that were the answer. I glanced at MacCafferty, holding court at the bar. There was an arrogance in his stance—the weight on one foot—that suddenly answered Nancy's question.

"His leg is shot up," I explained. "When he's in uniform, with all his old campaign ribbons on, the wound is like some sort of Old Heidelberg dueling scar. He doesn't limp. He practically swaggers. In his civvies, he's just a cripple."

Nancy nodded. "The strange ways we all compensate for our wounds and scars," she mused, studying MacCafferty, then turned to look intently at me.

Suddenly she jumped up. "Now, let's go see the rest of San Diego by night." I must have looked surprised, because she added, "I'm here to start a new life, Charly. Teach school and date attractive, eligible young men. It's not going to be the same way between us. But I won't be coy about it. You're fifty percent of the reason I'm here. You are still eligible, aren't you?"

Three weeks later I gave Nancy a sweetheart-sized se of Navy wings, and a month after that we were married The first year of marriage, they say, is the toughest. I must be. Nancy and I did not survive it. With aircraft op erations out of San Francisco and Special Weapons and gunnery training at Fallon outside Reno, I spent many more nights than not away from home. And a few more nights away than I should have.

Late at night at sea, the intimate disasters of my life loomed up to haunt me. The Pacific salt wind splashed in my face. Behind me, the attack planes on the flight deck strained and creaked at their tie-down wires. And all about me in the night, warships barreled along in task force, crushing the waves beneath their bulk, hellbent in a dark, relentless procession.

9

The aircraft carrier arrived at Station Zulu off the north
end of Taiwan just before dawn, some forty-five hours after we scrambled from Japan. As Aerology had predicted,
a thick thieves' mist surrounded the carrier, pressing in on
it, gray and dripping as the walls of a cave.

Daylight never really broke. Instead, a slimy, flat lumi-
nescence seeped from the low-hanging overcast. Even the
festival bunting of the aircraft carrier's signal flags and the
brilliant red, green, and yellow jerseys of the flight deck
crew were muted by the light so that they no longer
seemed primary colors at all, but merely tinted shades of
gray.

MacCafferty led the first patrol down the Straits himself. By the time I launched, it was midafternoon. I catapulted off the bow of the carrier, swooped up and was
enveloped almost immediately by a thick, smothering
cloud. I ducked my head and focused on the instrument
panel. An oily film of rain briefly battered the canopy, but
I kept my head down, too busy flying by the gauges to
notice the stratified layers of bumpy weather churning by.
All at once, the jet burst into the afternoon sun, and I was
blinded by searing red bolts. I yanked down my sun visor
and peered about.

A flat, boundless pasture of pure white cotton dropped
away from beneath the plane, flowing to the east in shimmering waves. But to the west and north, the clouds rose
up in abrupt, darkly threatening ranges and peaks, like
the Rockies approached through the flatlands of eastern
Colorado. Just beneath those dark peaks lay the mainland
of Red China.

Luke Alexander was already airborne and circling,
waiting for me to rendezvous. I moved into a loose com-

79

bat position off his right wing, and we banked and took off for the Straits of Taiwan.

We jinked to the north so that we wouldn't be approaching the Chinese coast directly from the carrier' position when our blips first materialized on the Reds' radar. Then Alexander contacted the Air Force radar control station on Taiwan, which took over radar control from the carrier, steered us to the south, and then passed the control of our flight to a U.S. Navy destroyer some where beneath us. The destroyer was a radar picket ship a vessel specially equipped with long-range air surveillance radar, back-up radios, and extra communication frequencies. It was one of a string of radar picket ship posted like sentries down the length of the narrow, churning sea between the island-nation of Taiwan and the coast of Red China. They kept track of all flights on both side of the Straits, monitoring the Red Chinese operations near the mainland and controlling American air patrols in the Straits. The radarman on the picket destroyer beneath u now gave Alexander a southwest heading to fly.

Our jets blasted down the Slot—the center of the Straits—above the unremitting landscape of clouds. The Crusaders' stubby, trapezoidal wings supported a long needle-nosed silver cylinder of a body that was more rocket than aircraft. The cockpit for the pilot was a blister of plexiglass that erupted from the streamlined nose, and from the side the cockpit looked as if it had been reluctantly added to the plane at the last minute by the Chance Vought designers.

Alexander and I had been flying about ten minutes when he suddenly hit the radio. "Tallyho, Charly. We've got company."

"What? Where?"

"About two o'clock. Five thousand or so feet below us."

I stared in that direction, but I could not see a thing except for those thick, dark shoals of weather over the mainland. "I don't see anything."

"They're there all right. I've been watching for a few minutes now."

Alexander radioed the radarman in the destroyer beneath us. "Are you holding a couple of contacts dogging us on our right, just over the mainland?"

The air controller must have been frantically examining his radarscope, for he took a long while to answer. Then the picket ship's transmission was very scratchy and garbled. "Negative. We're not holding any bogeys in that area. We do have some thick patches of weather around there to the west," he added, as if trying to assure us that he was on top of things.

"Oh, great," Alexander said dryly. "You guys are going to be a terrific help to us. I can see that now." Then to me. "Better keep your eyeballs peeled, Charly."

I anxiously searched the sky. "Luke, I'll be damned if ... *Hold it*. Got 'em." There, exactly where Luke had said they were, I saw a flash, and then another—the sudden flare of sunlight off silver wings. Without that flash to pinpoint their position, it would have been impossible to spot those fleeting dark spots against the clouds.

"Figure they're MIGs?"

"Well, they've been keeping right along with us," Alexander answered. "So they're too fast to be geese going south early for the winter."

"Charger Three, maintain your radio discipline," the controller on the destroyer ordered.

"Oh, bullshit," Alexander exploded on the radio. "We're supposed to let them know we're out here patrolling and loaded for bear. If *their* radar isn't any better than *yours,* they'll never see us. So they'd better hear us. You just keep us on track, and make good and sure we're outside their territorial limits, so they don't have any excuse to jump us."

There was a moment of silence, then the controller responded, "Roger, Charger Three. You are on track and well outside the twelve-mile line. Continue steering one-four-zero."

"Roger, steering one-four-zero," Alexander answered.

I felt as if there were a long, numbing icicle pressed along the entire length of my spine. But Alexander's voice was studiously casual. There was not the slightest hint of tension, as if there were nothing extraordinary about having a war party of MIGs now paralleling our path.

Our Crusaders were cruising at Mach .85, just below supersonic speed, and their formation was keeping up with us. They had to be MIG-17 Frescoes, the only plane the Red Chinese had at that time that could maintain

81

such a high speed. The MIGs were still about fifteen miles away, little more than a group of shining dots against the blue backdrop of sky. But I did not need a close-up to know exactly what they looked like. Since I had first climbed into a cockpit, I had been drilled to spot the distinctive features of that warplane from any angle at, literally, a fiftieth of a second flash. The short, thick, silver body, squared off at both ends like a clipped cigar. The towering, acutely angled trapezoid of the rudder with the high, brief pinfeathers of the stabilizer and the rounded, slender wings, swept back so sharply so that the MIG in flight always had the terrible swift beauty of a diving hawk. Under the gaping mouth of air intake bristled a 37-millimeter Nudelmann cannon and two 23-millimeter guns.

Alexander now caught my attention. He indicated with a hand wave that he wanted me to move in closer, and I crept up on his wing into a tight parade position.

Alexander pointed at the MIGs below and slightly ahead of us, then shook his head. Then he pointed above and behind us and shaded his eyes with his palm to indicate that I was to keep a sharp lookout in that direction.

Alexander was reminding me of fundamentals. The planes we could see below and ahead of us were not in position to be an immediate danger. If they were planning to hit us, they would probably be coming from high behind us, out of the sun. It was a principle as old as Eddie Rickenbacker and the Red Baron, and supersonic jets, radar, and rockets had not changed it.

I nodded and eased back into a loose combat echelon. My head was on a three-hundred-and-sixty-degree swivel. I checked the dome of sky ahead, below, behind, and above me, but especially, behind my right wing where I expected at any moment to see MIGs gun-barreling down at me. I was now drenched in perspiration, despite the cockpit's air conditioning.

Alexander's voice came up on the radio, calling the destroyer pitching and rolling on the angry seas somewhere below. "Are you holding any bogeys in our area?"

"Negative. The immediate area is clear except for you and that weather front."

"Well, you had better retune your radar, because they are *there*. You can believe it."

Once again, Alexander's voice was casual, almost good-natured. Then I remembered that first morning at sea when he had landed the crippled plane aboard the carrier. Listening to him over the speaker in Primary Flight Control, I had been struck by the same note in his voice. It was as if by regulating the mood of his voice, Alexander controlled his emotions and kept a tight grip in the hairiest of situations.

And it was a frustrating, gut-knotting situation. Our orders were not to engage the MIGs unless they fired on us first or were obviously maneuvering into position to make a firing run. Terrific! By then it would be too late. But the planes to the west were obviously keeping their distance.

Alexander and I flew down the Straits, keeping our own distance. I tried by dead reckoning to keep a crude track of our position on a chart on my kneepad. Past the Red Chinese coastal cities of Nanjih and Wuchiu and the harbor of Amoy. It did not take a very active imagination to conjure up pictures of flat, hostile faces down below squinting at radarscopes, antiaircraft batteries pivoting with our passage, and MIGs breaking from airfields just ahead of us.

I looked back over my shoulder, and the view of the Goshawk air-to-air missiles tucked boldly under my wing like a battery of lances was reassuring. I banked, weaving behind Alexander, checking out all quadrants, clearing our tail.

There was nothing there that I could see. But the MIGs at two o'clock had gained altitude and were ahead and above us at about 39,000 feet. Because of their increase in altitude, the vapor of their exhaust was being immediately condensed into a shimmering white wake of ice crystals, called a contrail. At the head of each telltale trail of condensation was a shining silver dot. They were ominously closer now, about ten miles away, as if they were flying on a gradually intersecting course. A ten-mile separation was no comfort. If we banked toward one another at our current speeds, we would close that distance in less than half a minute.

I eased up on Alexander's wing, pointed to the MIGs and indicated with a hand movement that they now had an altitude advantage and had crept closer.

He nodded.

Just then the controller came up on the radio. We were now south of Swatow, and he ordered us to make a one-hundred-and-eighty-degree turn to the east, right back up the Straits.

Alexander passed the lead to me, then maneuvered below and behind me into the combat wing position. He went into a weave behind me, clearing our tail.

After a while, I radioed, "I think we lost them on that turn. I don't see any contrails."

"Don't mean doodley squat, Tonto. It's an old bushwhack technique of Black Bart's from MIG Alley. He suddenly ducks below the contrail level to make the Mask Man think he's amscrayed. Then he bounces the Ranger and his faithful Indian companion from another quadrant. Savvy?"

"Right, Kemosabe."

Alexander was letting me know our radio was probably being monitored by the Reds, and there was no point in letting them know what we were doing. A Cantonese-born interpreter who had studied formal English would have had a headache trying to unscramble Alexander's message.

"Mark One Eyeballs peeled."

"Roger, eyeballs."

We hauled ass right back up the center of the Straits and, in turn, the radar control was passed to a second radar picket destroyer on station farther north in the Straits.

The radio suddenly crackled, and the new controller called us: "Charger Three, *bogeys,* two-six-five, eleven miles." I shot around and looked over my left shoulder and, Jeezus, I was staring into the glare of a blinding afternoon sun. Half the People's Red Air Force might be lurking there.

"Roger, bogeys, two-six-five, eleven. How many are there and what's their altitude?" Alexander came up on radio.

"I can't get an altitude reading on this radar," the controller responded. "There's just one big blip. It could be a cluster of planes."

"Roger, give me a range and bearing every minute."

"Roger, bogeys, two-six-five, ten miles."

"Think it's our old friends?"

"Probably."

84

"Can you spot them?"

"No, they're in the sun."

"I hope it doesn't give them false confidence."

"Bogeys, two-six-seven, nine," the controller reported.

Alexander eased up alongside me and, when he caught my eye, tapped his helmet to indicate that he was again taking over the lead. I was only too happy to pass him the responsibility for what happened next, and I swooped under his plane and back into the tail position.

"Bogeys, two-six-five, eight miles."

I could feel the hackles on the back of my neck rise. The MIGs were there, closing steadily, right over my left shoulder, and in a few minutes we would be in range of their big 37-millimeter cannons. Alexander had to make a move soon. They had us sitting ducks for a classic shot. With the altitude advantage, they could swoop down at us from high and out of the sun, with a deflection shot at our tails. A Red GCI (Ground Control Intercept) radar on the mainland had set them up perfectly.

But there was a vital bit of information that the MIG pilots could not get from their radar. They had no way of knowing which of a dozen different Navy or Air Force jet fighter-bombers they might be engaging, or how we might be armed. On a radarscope, the two Crusaders were just a shapeless blue-green blip cruising at an altitude of 37,000 feet at a speed of Mach .85. The MIGs were closing on an angle, and to catch up with us, they had to be pushing their top speed, which was a hair under Mach One. At any moment, we could slam our throttles balls-to-the-wall, kick in the afterburner, and just blast away from them. *But if we ran away, what was the point of our being in the Straits in the first place?*

"Bogeys, two-six-five, seven miles."

Alexander made a very gentle right bank away from the MIGs and, almost imperceptibly, increased his speed. Only his wingman, staying right with him, could have been conscious of that slight change in course and speed. It would be imperceptible to either the MIGs or the radarman.

"Bogeys, two-six-five, seven miles."

By slightly increasing his speed and turning away from the MIGs, Alexander had changed the relative motion between the two flights. The MIGs were no longer closing

85

us at an angle but were now chasing our tail as we both flew northeast, deeper into the Straits and away from the mainland.

"Bogeys, two-six-five, seven miles."

"Roger, bogeys," Alexander responded to the controller. "How far from the mainland are we out? Over."

There was a moment's pause while the controller made a measurement on his radar. "Charger Three, this is Blue Boy," he now answered. "You are twenty-five miles out."

"Roger. Are the bogeys squawking IFF yet?"

"Charger Three, this is Blue Boy. IFF negative. Bogeys are assumed to be hostile."

"Aaaaaaah, roger." Alexander's voice was languidly casual, practically a drawl.

IFF literally meant Identification, Friend or Foe. All American and Chinese Nationalist aircraft carried specially coded IFF radar transponders. They were the supersonic electronic equivalent of the ancient challenge, "Halt. Who goes there?" and the answering password. The challenge was a special electronic signal built into our shipboard and shore radar beam, which triggered the aircraft's IFF transponder. It then automatically flashed back the proper electronic "password" which appeared on the radarscope as a distinctly identifiable code of dashes. The flight of bogeys on our tail had failed the challenge.

Alexander signaled me to move in tighter under his wing.

"Bogeys, two-six-five, seven miles."

Alexander looked straight ahead for a moment, as if intently studying something in front of him, then turned to me and nodded.

Seven miles up, where the turbulent churning weather of the troposphere filters to the calm blue purity of the stratosphere, a man whose features are totally hidden behind a crash helmet and oxygen mask turns and nods to you over a brief void of airless space, and there is a tension and smug satisfaction in that gesture that is suddenly electrifying. Alexander was about to mousetrap the MIGs.

The orders for our patrol were very specific. We were not to tangle with Red Chinese aircraft unless we were attacked first, and only while flying over international waters well outside the territorial limits of Red China. It seemed clear enough, but there was a Catch-22 to those orders. Any Red aircraft aggressively closing on our tail quarter might be considered as attacking before the 37-millimeter shells actually began chewing up our planes. In the past, there had been cases of MIGs simply sidling over next to American patrols and flying along wingtip to wingtip. Other times, Red fighters had made threatening sweeps without ever firing. But then too, American patrols had been shot down by Red fighters as far as fifty miles off the coast.

Now our radar air controller on the destroyer had officially verified that a flight of hostile planes were closing on our tail. They came from high and out of the sun, confident that they had the advantage of position and could sweep in on us with impunity. Alexander, as section leader of our flight, had let them come closer and closer, all the while sucking them further and further out into the Straits and away from their sanctuary over the mainland. But he never let the MIGs get within cannon range or close enough to identify the type of plane they were attacking.

The Red pilots had no way of knowing that a new chapter in fighter tactics had been written by Chance Vought aircraft designers and Marion Electronics Corporation engineers.

In a moment, Alexander was going to signal me to arm our Goshawk missiles and burn on full power. The Red flight commander would be surprised to hear from his radar that the American planes were suddenly running away. If he were on top of things, the Red officer would realize that he had almost tangled with one of the new U.S. Navy Crusaders or Air Force F-104's for which his intelligence officer had briefed him to be on the lookout.

But Alexander would not be running—merely giving us turning room. The Crusader was a new generation of jet fighter, superior to the graceful, swallow-shaped but subsonic MIG Frescoes. Designed from the drawing board up to fly at supersonic speeds, the Crusader maneuvered more quickly and turned tighter the faster it flew. In a moment, the ChiCom radar would report to the MIG commander that the American planes were making a sharp, high speed turn back in the direction of the mainland. At first, the Red commander would be confused. But when he heard that we had reversed direction and were coming back at him at almost twice his speed, he would panic, suddenly realizing that his retreat to the sanctuary of the mainland had been cut off. He would have to face an obviously faster, superior but still unknown jet fighter in a head-to-head shoot-out in which the planes were racing toward one another at over sixteen hundred miles an hour.

But long before his booming 37-millimeter Nudelmann-Swianov cannons were in range, while the Crusaders were still silver specks in the sky ten miles away, his MIG would blow up in his face. A radar-controlled Goshawk missile would electronically home in and zap him. The entire procedure was a maneuver Alexander and I had each practiced in all its variations in a hundred dry runs.

"Bogeys, two-six-five, seven miles."

Now Alexander raised his fist and shook it at me, the signal to arm the missiles. Alexander was a MacCafferty pilot all the way. He was gunning for the first combat kill with the new Goshawk missiles, the first score in the Straits. His mind, humming like a computer, had been setting up the play since our first contact with the MIGs. Now he was springing the trap.

"Bogeys, two-six-zero, eight miles," the controller's voice read off. The MIGs' position had changed.

"Blue Boy. Charger Three," Alexander radioed excitedly. "What's happening? Their position's changing. What are they doing?"

"It looks like they are making a sharp left turn, back to the mainland."

"What? Why would they do that now?"

There was a long silence, and then the controller came back up on the radio. "They are definitely making a turn back to the mainland. You're coming up on Quemoy Island in a moment. The Red patrols we've monitored on radar for the past few days have avoided flying in the vicinity of Quemoy. They don't want to give us any excuses to increase our air cover over the island."

"Rrroger," Alexander responded, and there was a hollow, disappointed rasp in his voice. If the MIGs were turning back, he had no justification for bouncing them. The picket destroyer would report that they had already broken off their threatening approach on our tail.

I looked out across my wing to where Alexander now sat silent. His head was set straight ahead, but whatever electricity had galvanized his posture a moment before seemed to have dissipated.

I looked down, searching under my left wing, trying to spot Quemoy Island. There was a low overcast of broken scud covering the area, and through the gray-tinged breaks, I glimpsed water and dun-colored earth and the occasional demarcation of a white surf-line and sand. Then suddenly, the scud in one area took on a rose-colored glow that shimmered a moment then dissolved, then another red glow, and another. At a break in the clouds, I realized what was happening below. What I had at first thought were smaller puffs of clouds were actually columns of smoke, generated by flames that exploded beneath them and then went out.

10

News bulletins were radioed to the ship, mimeographed, stapled, and stacked by the wardroom coffee mess at breakfast the next day.

(TAIPEI)—QUEMOY ISLAND WAS ROCKED TODAY BY A DEVASTATING BARRAGE ESTIMATED AT 60,-000 ROUNDS FROM RED GUNS ON THE CHINESE MAINLAND. THE U.S. MILITARY ADVISORY AND ASSISTANCE GROUP HERE CALLED THE HAIL OF FIRE THE MOST INTENSE BOMBARDMENT EVER DIRECTED AT A SINGLE OBJECTIVE IN HISTORY.

(HONG KONG)—THE RED ARMY COMMANDER FOR THE FUKIEN DISTRICT OF SOUTH CHINA RADIOED A MESSAGE TO THE NATIONALIST GARRISON ON QUEMOY ISLAND: "NO MILITARY WORKS CAN AVOID COMPLETE DESTRUCTION UNDER THE ASSAULT OF OUR MODERN ARMY AND AIR FORCE. THE LANDING ON QUEMOY IS IMMINENT. SURRENDER."

When it came time for my patrol that afternoon, my bowels were in knots. The thick, threatening banks of weather over the Chinese mainland had heaved noticeably closer, and a very high milky film of cirrus now veiled the sky.

I sat scrunched down in the cockpit on the carrier's flight deck and nervously eyed the weather to the west. Swarms of Red bandits hovered in ambush in those darkening canyons and defilades of clouds, waiting to pounce on me. Methodically, I flipped through the procedures on my precatapult checkoff list, but again, my bowels surged alarmingly, threatening to erupt involuntarily at any moment.

Old war stories to the contrary, it is not fear that causes men to dirty their pants. It is instinct, an ancient mammalian mechanism. When the animal is in danger, it empties its bowels before fighting or fleeing so that it will not be poisoned by its own wastes if it is wounded.

I sat in my space suit squeezed in amid the electronic toggles, dials, switches, radios, radar consoles, and circuit breakers—attached by a half-dozen electronic and pneumatic umbilici to the systems of a supersonic Chance Vought jet fighter—but still my guts rumbled and contracted with paleolithic survival reflexes that had become an embarrassment.

Since my patrol the previous day with Alexander, CincPac headquarters had flashed new intelligence reports that the Chinese Reds were increasing the strength of their MIG squadrons and concentrating them along the coast opposite Taiwan. There were now an estimated three hundred aircraft in a front line along the Straits, another two hundred in a supporting line back of the coast, and one hundred planes guarding both the north and south entries to the Straits. Our schedule of patrols had been doubled immediately. My transverse colon was now making its own appropriate response to the intelligence estimate that there was a reasonable chance that I might have my guts ripped open within the next hour. I held my breath until the peristaltic heebie-jeebies passed. Then I goosed the plane's throttle, and the jet rolled onto the catapult ramp at the bow of the carrier.

Two crewmen immediately crabbed under the plane. Lying flat on their backs, they strapped on the catapult yoke, hooking the jet to the steam-driven catapult like an arrow to a giant crossbow. Then they scrambled clear, crawling out from under the fuselage and wings on their hands and feet.

I checked the catapult officer. He stood just off my wing, bracing himself against the gale that blew straight down the deck. Under his identifying yellow jersey, he wore a heavy foul-weather jacket, making his body thick and bloated. For protection, he also wore goggles and a red skullcap with enormous earpads from the top of which radio antennae stuck up like insect feelers.

Crouched into the wind, bent almost double, he looked more like a giant beetle than a man.

He suddenly stood straight up and made a whirling motion with his arm. I shoved the throttle all the way forward, braced against the backrest, and then flipped him a quick salute. Ahead, the carrier's bow dipped down into a trough. There was a splash of slate-gray sea, and then the bow heaved up again. At that moment, the catapult exploded, and I was jammed into my seat. The troughs of gray water and whitecaps were instantly beneath me and then melted together in a blur. I flipped the landing gear up. The air speed indicator hit 175 knots, and I reached down and threw a lever that adjusted the pitch of the wing for flying speed. The jet's nose came up automatically as if it knew instinctively that the deeper heavens above were its natural element. I eased back on the stick and steepened the climb, and in seconds I passed through 10,000 feet, sailing up through white islands of condensation.

Right away, the radio reception started breaking up. The carrier was loud and clear, but I had great difficulty picking up the destroyer in the Straits that was to be my radar control. It took several tries to make radio contact and then, right after we finally established it, the ship's transmission cut out.

I went into a holding pattern, flying a big circle over the northwest end of Taiwan. After a half-dozen more tries, the destroyer switched to another radio transmitter and came in strong. Under its radar control I flew out over the Straits, then banked south and began my run down the Slot.

I flew alone, without the wingman I had had on the first day's patrol. Just that morning, MacCafferty had called the squadron together. He had stood up in front of the ready room balancing a coffee mug in one hand and fingering a cigar the size of a fungo bat in the other, silently inspecting his pilots as we took our seats.

"Gentlemen, your attention," he said and the rumbling, gravel voice pierced the chatter like a bull horn. In the immediate silence, his hawk eyes swept the room, meeting his men's gaze. "Okay, we've all had a good look at what the playing field looks like. From here on out, we're buckling down to our mission."

Officially, the squadron's primary mission was all-weather and night nuclear attack. The squadron's F-8 Crusader jets were the first in the fleet to be equipped with a new integrated radar and missile system. With it, we could launch at night and in the dirtiest, zero-visibility weather, streak in at supersonic speed about fifty feet off the deck to avoid being detected by radar, pinpoint our target electronically, then let loose a Goshawk IV air-to-ground missile with a nuclear warhead.

But although nuclear war was what we were trained for, war had not yet been declared. As far as MacCafferty was concerned, our mission, for the moment, was to set the Pacific Fleet standards in operations. It was now Mac-Cafferty's doctrine that all of our patrols be flown as single-plane, all-weather, or night missions, whether or not the conditions actually prevailed. On paper, it made the squadron look like world-beaters. We would log twice as many sorties over the Straits as the other squadrons who lacked our radar gear and had to fly in protective coveys of twos and fours. But beyond that, any eventual nuclear strike into mainland China would be flown by single attack planes launching against individual targets. And Herr Squadron Führer MacCafferty assiduously prepared us for that day.

From that morning on, each man patrolled alone. After my near-miss with blood-and-guts Alexander the day before, the idea of a lone patrol of the Straits without the protection of a wingman had me in a state of terror. By the time I had been out for ninety minutes, the loneliness and silence were nerve-racking. I had not received a routine course or radio check from the destroyer controller for several minutes, and I now flashed him. "Hangman, Charger Nine, over."

There was no response from the destroyer. After a moment, I impatiently repeated the call. Again, no answer. I cursed into my oxygen mask, and my own voice sounded strangely distant and ominous.

I banked shallowly to my right and then to my left, weaving an *S* in the sky, checking out the areas all about me, then settled down to the tense drudgery of flying straight and level over a harsh, weary landscape of scud.

I nervously probed the clouds and sky over the mainland. Oh, Jesus. From the corner of my eye, I saw something glitter for a moment. I turned toward what I thought was a wing flash, but I could make nothing out against the glare of the late afternoon sun.

With an almost involuntary jerk of the stick, I banked sharply to the east to double insure that I was over international water.

"Hangman, Charger Nine, are you holding any bogeys in my area? Over, goddamn it."

There was still no response.

I cross-checked the radar against the chart on my kneepad, then double-checked it. I was overdue to switch control to another radar picket destroyer stationed to the south. I now tried several times to contact the ship, but again without success. Communications with the picket ships, flailing about like flotsam in the rough seas below, were at best unreliable. The lack of radio contact did not bother me. My immediate worry was MIGs.

I flew due south-southwest, giving a wider berth to the coastline, and when I dead-reckoned that I was about opposite Swatow on the mainland, I made a wide bank to east and gun-barreled right back up the center of the Straits.

After I settled back down on course, I tried to contact the Air Force ground control station on Taiwan. "Dogmeat. This is Charger Nine. Over."

This time the flat, remote sound of my voice sent a chill through my guts, as I suddenly realized what was wrong.

"Dogmeat! Charger Nine! Over!"

I screamed into the mike in my oxygen mask, but the sound came back to me unamplified, as if from a great distance. My radio receiver was dead.

For the next few moments, I just sat staring at the yellow and black eye of the oxygen feed regulator, which winked maliciously at me with every quick nervous breath. The radio was as necessary to my survival as that oxygen. Between me and the aircraft carrier was a barrier overcast as solid and murky as potato soup. Without a radio steer, finding the ship would be almost impossible, but making any sort of blind landing approach *was* impossible.

I panicked, then fought to suppress the panic. A glance

at my fuel indicator broke me out of it like a slap in the face. I had less than a quarter of a tank of fuel left.

In my nervousness, I had been flying the patrol route faster than the regular cruising speed, and now I was down to two thousand pounds of fuel. I had just enough to head directly back to the ship and set up for a normal landing. If I was jumped by MIGs on the way back, I would not have enough fuel to burn away from them. Every moment I sat hesitating, the needle of the fuel gauge fell lower and lower toward the tick mark that indicated EMPTY.

I inched back the throttle to the minimum power setting to sustain flight, and began to go through the established emergency procedures. I was aware that the procedures did not work almost as often as they did, but that was not the point. The point was to do something. I found in the emergency procedures a temporary refuge from my fears.

I tried to estimate my position. On a chart on my kneepad, I had kept a crude track of my flight, laying out the rough course and distances with a grease pencil. Now the smudged scribblings looked like a route followed by a blind man. As close as I could figure, I was over the middle of the Straits approaching the north end of Taiwan where the island's coastline curved away to the east. Each minute of indecision meant I was blasting away from the island, skirting the forbidden coast of China.

The airfield at Taipei was closer than the carrier. But finding either under that cover of clouds without direct radio contact was going to be pure witchery. Both the Taipei airfield and the carrier had omnirange stations for radio navigation. They transmitted a distinctive, very-high-frequency radio signal on each of three hundred and sixty degrees. Perhaps the breakdown in the radio was only in the earphones and not in the radio receiver itself. If that were the case, I would not be able to hear the signal but the omnipointer on my compass would still birddog in on the navigational signal and point me toward home. I dialed the carrier's frequency on the VHF radio. The needle did not move. I banged the dial to jar the needle loose, then cranked in the numbers again. Still the pointer did not quiver.

I shuffled quickly through several cards clipped to my

kneepad, found the approach chart for Taipei, and dialed its omnisignal. Again, the pointer never flickered from its neutral position.

I was running out of options fast. There was one other radio navigational aid, the TACAN. It was a backup system that operated from an entirely different electronic signal from the omni. It had a separate receiver on the plane that gave a direct digital read-out of the distance and bearing to the transmitter. But it was a short-range transmission. To pick up either the carrier's TACAN signal or Taipei's, I had to be within a hundred miles of it. Considering the smudged grease-pencil track on my chart, I could only pray that I was within a hundred miles of anything west of Hawaii.

By crude dead reckoning, I estimated that I would soon be passing west of Taipei. I had a terrifying vision of the hidden mountain peaks of Taiwan, jagged and malevolent, waiting silently in that shroud of low-lying clouds to smash the plane the moment I let down into the dark overcast. Instinctively, I banked away toward the carrier's estimated position. The ship was almost twice the distance away, the odds of locating it were slimmer, but out over the water at least I knew what lay waiting for me beneath the overcast.

Although my radio receiver was dead, there was an even chance that the transmitter still might be operating. I switched it to a special emergency frequency that automatically would come up on all aircraft radios in the vicinity, even those tuned to other frequencies. "Anyone, can you read me? Over." The voice sounded frightened and lost and familiar.

I repeated my call every few minutes, at the same time reporting my general position.

Had I forgotten anything? I quickly shuffled through the cards on my kneepad to the one that outlined the procedures for loss of communications. The IFF. I had forgotten to switch the Identification, Friend or Foe radar transponder to the EMERGENCY mode. I frantically groped for the IFF switch and flipped it. The IFF now sent out a coded signal that would appear visually as four short dashes right next to my blip on a radarscope. The dashes were a red light indicating that the anonymous yellow-green blip was in trouble, and they gave the radarman an exact fix on my position. But at that point, I had no way of knowing whether I was in range of anybody's radar. Even if I were, the radarman might not notice that silent tick—the size of an apple seed—gleaming faintly at the edge of his cathode-ray tube. The radar blip of my plane would be all but lost in the shimmering snow and blobs created by the heavy-weather clouds now looming about me. But my life now depended on that tiny pip on the face of a cathode-ray tube being spotted and identified as good old Charly Rohr in Charger Nine, overdue and in trouble.

Without radio contact, I could not even tell if the IFF emergency signal was operating. My dead radio receiver might be part of a wider electrical malfunction that had cut off all outgoing and incoming transmissions. Yet I kept calling, calling, calling, not knowing whether my calls for help were going any farther than my lips.

I checked the clock on the instrument panel, then roughly computed how far I had flown since my last mark, and scribbled the track line of my flight on the chart on my knee. That thick, smudged grease-pencil line ended on the X that marked the carrier's position. I should have been right over the ship.

I looked desperately at the TACAN read-out. Its digital spaces were blank. I flipped the switch on and off and pounded the face of the dial. The read-out space remained blank, giving me no indication of how far away or in what direction my only refuge lay. Either the TACAN was not working or my grease-pencil navigation was so far off that I was still more than a hundred miles from the carrier.

The omnirange navigational signal pointer on my compass remained frozen in the neutral position. I furiously redialed the omniradio frequency. The needle never quivered. I slammed the dial with the heel of my hand. Still nothing. The carrier's omnirange transmitted a very-high-frequency radio signal that had considerably greater range than the TACAN signal. If my radio direction finder was not picking it up and birddogging it, then the receiver was either totally fritzed or I wasn't even in the East China Sea.

That latter possibility was beginning to haunt me. I had not seen a single landmark since I had taken off from the carrier two hours before. Beneath me, in every direction, was the wispy, ceaselessly shifting upper surface of an overcast. For the last hour, I had flown without direct control, strictly by compass. If my compass was off, I might well have been flying over Goose Bay, Labrador, at that moment. I checked my radarscope. It was still working, but the radar was for target acquisition and it scanned only a short-range, narrow area directly in front of the plane. Ahead of me, the radar revealed neither land nor ships; there was nothing but the vague yellow electronic images reflected back by an empty sea and thickening shoals of weather.

The time and distance I had flown had stripped away all my options. I had only one play left. My fuel reading was critical. If I pushed down through the overcast, down to where the air was breathable but where the Pratt & Whitney J-57 turbojet consumed fuel three times as fast, and the carrier was nowhere in sight, I would not have enough gas to climb back to altitude and search elsewhere.

Instead, I banked to the left and, according to gospel, began flying a lost plane pattern. The specified pattern was a triangle with two- to three-minute legs. It was an SOS to any radarman who was plotting my track that I was lost, running out of fuel, and going down in that immediate area. For God's sake, it said, send help!

My eyes flicked from the clock to the fuel gauge to the radar to the fuel gauge to the TACAN to the fuel gauge. Neither the radar nor the TACAN indicator held out the faintest glimmer of a contact. Panic was building up, uncontrollable and insistent as anger. "Anyone, can you read me? Over," I shouted into the mike.

Not much air time was left. In a few minutes, the fuel-starved turbine would flame out, and I would have to eject. Trying to crash land a Crusader jet in the sea was suicidal. But even if I survived the bailout, the odds of one man adrift in the expanse of the East China Sea being found under that overcast were not to be computed. My only real chance was to stay in the air as long as possible, screaming into the mike in the faint hope that somewhere I was being heard on radio or tracked on radar. I inched the throttle back to the point where the engine almost flamed out, then banked gently, and began my second pattern.

Then, out of nowhere, another Crusader materialized on my right wing. Hallelujah! My eyes brimming with tears of relief, I immediately began babbling into the mike.

It was one of our squadron planes with the flaming Black Knight in armor insignia just below the cockpit. But I could not make out who the pilot was. His helmet, plastic visor, and oxygen mask presented a face as anonymous and inhuman as an android's. He nodded at me, tapped his helmet in the area of his ear and gave me a thumbs up. Evidently my transmitter was working okay. I anxiously gave a fuel report, and my silent wingman nodded again and made a series of dips with his hand, indicating that I was to join up an his wing and closely follow him.

The other plane immediately nosed down into the clouds. It became a silver ghost that gently dissolved and rematerialized in the mists swirling about it. I stayed as close as I dared, numb with dread when the other plane momentarily faded from sight. The other pilot, seemingly unconcerned, flew an exceptionally smooth lead even though he was flying entirely on instruments. He went into each maneuver gradually, carefully signaling beforehand. Relieved of the responsibility for my own fate, I settled down and concentrated on shadowing the other plane.

My shepherd had throttled his engine back so far that the turbine was just windmilling in a glide, providing a minimum of power. I glanced at the instrument panel. We were in the gentlest of glides, with the nose barely below the horizon, and we were slowing down. The other pilot was assiduously squeezing every foot of altitude, every knot of air speed, and every ounce of gas into gliding distance. Apparently, I was still a good distance from the carrier, and every drop of fuel was critical. I was already well below the minimum safety figure at which I should have been over the ship. Perhaps I didn't have enough fuel to reach the carrier, and he was merely trying to get me just that much closer so that the rescue helicopters or escort destroyers could pick me up quickly if I survived the ejection. I had no way of knowing whether he was leading me to the carrier or merely to a point in that gray, dimensionless void at which the turbine would suddenly flame out and I would have to jettison the plane's canopy, yank a dark hood down over my face, and fire the cannon shell set directly beneath my coccyx.

But I had no time to dwell on the possibilities. My life, or death, hinged on my making split-second corrections in my power settings, course, and nose attitude. At the speed we were flying, a second of hesitation would send me shooting a thousand yards ahead of the other plane, or leave me behind to be swallowed in the murk through which we flew. Each adjustment of the controls had to be immediate and instinctive.

I gradually became aware that the pilot whose every move I was shadowing had to be MacCafferty. The realization first came in my fingertips on the controls and then the knowledge moved through my arm and shoulder muscles to my consciousness. Every maneuver I mimicked had that hair-splitting control and fluid grace. Who else could it be but MacCafferty? No one on the carrier was his equal.

I concentrated so fiercely on following him that I did not realize we had broken into the clear. My shepherd unexpectedly tapped himself on the head and pointed, signaling the lead back to me. I looked up and found myself directly astern the carrier, perfectly set up for a landing. A big fat meatball, the red orb of the landing-signal lights, beckoned me to continue straight in.

My eyes flicked to the fuel gauge and I momentarily panicked. I was down to two hundred pounds. If I blew the landing, I would not have enough fuel to wave-off and make another approach. The carrier's blunt, armored stern loomed up and the postage-stamp-size landing area atop it grew steadily larger. The meatball held its position. There were no last-second corrections for me to make. My lead pilot had set me up so there was nothing critical for me to do. My position on the glide slope was perfect. I relaxed. I had only to aim at the meatball, and the plane rode down easily and caught a wire.

On parking, I immediately vaulted out of the plane and looked about eagerly for my savior. He was nowhere in sight, and for a weird moment, remembering that silver phantom silently floating ahead of me through the mists, I wondered whether he had really existed at all. But the hard steel deck under my feet felt real and solid enough, and I stomped on it with my boots, relishing its hardness, and, what the hell, I got down on my hands and knees and kissed the goddamn deck.

But it was not MacCafferty who had shepherded me back to safety. The squadron commander was there in the ready room when I charged in.

"What did you do, get lost?" MacCafferty asked, and his voice was barren of either concern or sympathy.

"My radio conked out."

"Yes, I know. We heard you screaming from two hundred miles out." He turned and hobbled forward toward the aircraft status board at the front of the ready room.

I could feel my jaw muscles knot. I glared at MacCafferty, and all the fear I'd experienced in the past two hours congealed into anger.

MacCafferty was slouched before the board, studying it, his weight shifted off his bum leg. He was revising his lineup. MacCafferty, the terror of two wars. To him, my patrol emergency was a routine operation.

Red Lucas was seated at the squadron duty officer's desk shuffling papers.

"Who brought me back?" I asked Lucas.

"Pastori. When the air controller reported you were in trouble, he was suited up and on the catapult in sixty seconds. I've never seen that skinny-ginny move so fast. You owe him a bottle of booze."

"I owe him my life."

"He'd rather have the booze."

"Where is he now?"

"Since he was already airborne, he stayed up and took the next patrol. Now I have to reshuffle the whole damn schedule." Lucas said it in the querulous voice of a chief bookkeeper whose careful ledgers have been loused up by the stupid error of a subordinate. He looked over to where MacCafferty was frowning at the board, then turned back to me.

"Anything else down on your plane besides the radio receiver?"

"The omnireceiver. And the TACAN only works within ten miles of the ship."

"Figures," Lucas said sourly. "Before you secure, get the avionics gang right to work on it and check it out. MacCafferty wants that plane back by tonight. The patrol schedule is getting hotter."

On my way out of the ready room, the mimeographed news of the day tacked on the bulletin board caught my eye.

(TAIPEI)—AN ARMADA OF TWO U.S. HEAVY CRUISERS AND SIX DESTROYERS TODAY ESCORTED A PAIR OF NATIONALIST SUPPLY SHIPS TO QUEMOY'S THREE-MILE LIMIT IN BROAD DAYLIGHT IN AN UNMISTAKABLE PARADE OF FORCE. THE U.S. SEVENTH FLEET HAS BEEN ORDERED TO BREAK THE COMMUNIST BLOCKADE AROUND QUEMOY. IN THE PAST WEEK COMMUNIST GUNSHIPS AND TORPEDO BOATS ATTACKED AND TURNED BACK NATIONALIST CONVOYS AND SANK ONE LANDING SHIP GORGED WITH SUPPLIES FOR QUEMOY.

(WASHINGTON)—THE STATE DEPARTMENT ANNOUNCED TODAY THAT THE U.S. DOES NOT RECOGNIZE COMMUNIST CHINA'S CLAIM OF SOVEREIGNTY OVER ALL TERRITORY UP TO 12 MILES OFF ITS SHORES. THE U.S. FLEET WILL CONTINUE TO OPERATE UP TO THREE MILES OFF THE MAINLAND, THE RECOGNIZED INTERNATIONAL BOUNDARY. HISTORICALLY, THREE MILES IS THE DISTANCE AN 18TH CENTURY NAVAL SHORE CANNON COULD FIRE A 24-POUND STEEL CANNONBALL.

(WASHINGTON)—AN AIR FORCE TACTICAL MISSILE WING OF NUCLEAR-ARMED MATADOR MISSILES HAS BEEN DEPLOYED TO TAIWAN. ACCORDING TO A PENTAGON SOURCE, THE MATADOR MISSILES ARE ALREADY SET UP ON LAUNCHERS

102

AND CAN DELIVER NUCLEAR WARHEADS TO
MAINLAND CHINA FROM THEIR POSITIONS ON
TAIWAN. THE CREWS ARE ON A 24-HOUR ALERT,
CONSTANTLY REHEARSING COUNTDOWNS.

11

The next morning, right after my game of Russian roulette with the erratic electronics of the Chance Vought F-8, I sacked in late. My first patrol was not scheduled until the afternoon, and there was no reason for me to hang around the ready room getting nervous about my rematch with the fates.

About ten-thirty, I finally eased my beef out of the bunk, gathered up my toilet kit, draped a towel about my ass, and headed for the showers. The officer's head was at the end of a corridor of staterooms, and my wooden Japanese clogs slapped on the steel deck, resounding noisily in the now empty passageway. At mid-morning, the head was deserted except for the black enlisted man whose daily misery it was to clean and polish the officers' stainless-steel urinals, toilets, shower stalls, and sinks. He eyed me resentfully as I clopped in. I ignored him, and took my own goddamn time shaving and showering, turning the water up just short of scalding and soaking long in the billowing steam.

Then I dressed and worked my way back through the gloomy, steel-paneled tunnels of the ship to the ready room.

I had just stepped through the hatch into the ready room when I froze. The hairs on the back of my neck bristled. How do I explain it? If the Reaper had been standing right there, scythe in bony hand, the skull grinning at me out of the shadows of his black hood, I could not have felt Death's presence more. Somebody had bought it.

The ready room was unusually crowded, but the men were either keeping to themselves or seated in pairs, whispering conspiratorially. Most just sat staring off into space, smoking. No one was playing cards or Acey-

Deucy. Red Lucas picked up a *Playboy*, started to leaf through it absently, then hesitated, as if questioning the appropriateness of what he was doing, and put it down.

Ernie Scholl sat by himself brooding at the rear of the room.

"What happened?"

"Luke Alexander," Scholl muttered. His voice was as listless as a sleepwalker's. "Power failure . . . flameout . . . on catapulting. Who knows what?"

"*Alexander!* Oh, Jesus. Did he . . ."

"Just dribbled off the bow and sank. The damn boat plowed right over him. I was coming up right behind him. I was the next one!" Scholl said it with a sort of shocked surprise.

"How long ago did it happen?"

"The tin cans and choppers are out searching for him, but there's not a trace . . . Nothing . . . Just sank," Scholl rattled on as if he did not hear the question.

I walked over to the coffee mess and poured a cup, mostly to delay the moment when I would have to move forward and join the others at the wake. I offered a cup to Scholl. He took it with a trembling hand. The cup rattled in the saucer in a little jiggling dance. I stared at it, fascinated, as it tap-tap-tapped in his trembling hand and then tipped, dumping its contents into Scholl's lap.

"I'm sorry," he sputtered, although it had not splashed anyone else. "I guess I'm a bit shaken up."

Pastori had come up behind me. He nodded sympathetically at Scholl, but his eyes, dark and troubled, were carefully watching me.

Scholl dabbed ineffectually with a handkerchief at the dark stain spreading over his trousers. "I guess I'd better go change," he stammered and bolted through the door.

"They were roommates," I said, feeling somehow compelled to excuse Scholl's behavior to Pastori. "He's taking it hard."

Pastori did not say anything at first, then looked directly at me and asked, "How *you* doing?"

"I'm okay. What exactly happened?"

"We'll never know. It looked like some sort of power failure on catapulting. The plane just shot off the bow into the water."

"Didn't he have a chance to get out?"

Pastori shook his head. "Even if he managed to eject through the water, he would have smacked into the bottom of the ship."

"What a lousy way to go."

"You know of a good way?"

Pastori took out a pack of cigarettes and offered me one. I accepted it and his light. "Who tells his wife?"

"Most likely one of the guys on the staff at Miramar. He'll probably go over with a chaplain. Everybody else is out here," Pastori said.

"I wonder how she'll take it?"

"How would your wife?"

I shrugged and shook my head. Now it was my turn to sprawl in a chair, smoke, stare at nothing, and try to sort out my thoughts about Alexander's death.

Alexander had flown combat in the Korean War and survived without a scratch. A week before, he had greased a crippled plane back aboard the ship on a wing and a prayer, and a few hours ago he had soared over the Straits of Taiwan hunting for the first kill of a war that had not yet exploded. Now he was dead, a casualty of a war that didn't exist.

The other men in the ready room, now grieving for Alexander and reflecting on the precariousness of their own lives, had flown with him longer and knew him better than I. But for me, his death ripped open old scabs. For I had known Alexander's wife too well.

I had met Maureen Alexander casually, in a bar and restaurant in San Diego called the Mexican Village. It was a place that people went to meet other people. She came in with another woman whose husband was also on a seven-month duty tour in the West Pacific. Maureen was a big brassy blonde who stood five-foot-ten in her stocking feet, yet swept her blonde hair up in a towering pile of curls, and wore spiked heels. Her eyes met yours at a level, not giving an inch. The other woman was uneasy about being there and glanced about shyly, whispering quietly to Alexander's wife. But Maureen looked around with frank, bold eyes, and when they met mine, she simply stopped and looked directly back at me. The look was open and candid, without any flirtation or sexual subterfuge. Her eyes and mouth were too wide and her nose too broad and thick for beauty, but she was attractive in a healthy, vulgar way. She weighed about ten pounds more than she should have for her height and the flesh was there in her breasts and hips. When you looked at her, it was not desire that she immediately provoked but the feeling that you rather *liked* her, and if the confident candor of her eyes did not make you look away, then you just grinned back simply in approval.

In the next several weeks, I saw her often, quietly, but seldom more than once a week. She, the older, married woman, was in control. The first night at the Mexican Village we had spoken and danced two or three times and then she had left—as she had entered—with her girl friend. Right from the start she had been quite open about the fact that she was married and that her husband was a Navy lieutenant commander. Where another woman might have felt hesitant or defensive, she seemed to derive authority from her status and the power to demand discretion and to decide when and where I would see her.

And it was she who declared, without fanfare or emotion one night, that it was over. "Luke's squadron will be back in a couple of weeks." She lay on the bed, propped up on a pillow—posed with one hand behind her now tumbled blonde hair and one knee lifted—totally naked. Her flesh, her breasts, her hips, her long moist thighs were a presence, a power she displayed self-confidently. She leaned back, smoking quietly, momentarily satisfied.

Reaching forward, I took a cigarette from a pack on the end table and lit it from hers. Then I sat down on the edge of the bed by her side. "What happens now? You being transferred?"

It was customary for a squadron to reorganize after it had completed a tour in the Far East and the officers were usually transferred to other duty.

Maureen shook her head. "We're staying in San Diego. Luke's been assigned as operations officer of a new squadron that's being put together."

"Not VA-219?"

"That sounds familiar. I think it is. Why?"

I started to laugh. Maureen stared at me, first in confusion and then startled. "Oh, Jesus Christ."

"I got my orders Wednesday."

"Oh, Jesus," Maureen repeated and snubbed out her

cigarette. She looked back at me with an expression of both disgust and worry, then shook her head and gave a brief, rueful laugh. "Oh, Jesus," she said again and leaned back against the pillow looking at the ceiling, deep in thought.

I had met Maureen shortly after arriving in San Diego, long before Nancy had suddenly materialized. As a normal procedure, I had been assigned to a reserve air group where I transitioned from the Korean War-vintage jets I had learned to fly in the Advanced Training Command in Texas to the higher-performance planes now in operation in the fleet. Now that I finally had been assigned to a fleet squadron, I found myself in bed with the wife of one of my commanders.

Maureen let out a long, deep breath. "Well, Charly, my boy, I don't know what to tell you. Except that you had better be cool and discreet and keep your mouth shut."

"That goes without saying."

"I hope so, Charly. I sincerely hope so. As much for your sake as mine. This isn't the first time something like this has happened in the United States Navy and it undoubtedly won't be the last. If you were to say something to anybody and Luke were to hear of it, I'd just deny the whole thing. There might be some rough moments, but it would blow over. Luke hasn't been wearing a chastity belt over in Japan, or anywhere else for that matter."

Maureen's eyes narrowed and her voice took on a tighter, tougher tone. "You're the one who would probably come off the worst. In cases like this, they usually transfer out the junior officer. Sometimes to places like Kodiak, Alaska."

"Don't threaten me, Maureen."

"I'm not threatening you, Charly." Her voice immediately softened. "I'm just telling you the facts of life. For both our sakes."

She looked at me with concern and then, as if to reestablish what had been our intimacy, reached forward to take my hand and bring my cigarette to her lips for a drag.

"Charly, please don't get any wrong ideas about Luke. Or about Luke and me. Luke's a hell of a guy. You'll find that out. He's all man, and I love him. This, between me and you, doesn't have anything to do with him. Or even

108

him and me. It's just me personally." She put her hand lightly on my leg for emphasis.

"Do you understand that, Charly?"

I didn't really, not then, but I nodded "yes" because it was important to her.

Then I smiled and said, "Well, Maureen, it's far, far better to have loved you and lost, than never to have loved you at all." I slid my hand up her thighs to caress the wet hair and quick flesh between.

She looked startled, but not displeased, then smiled and placed her hand insistently on the back of my neck and pulled me down on top of her to kiss her. "This is going to be the last time, Charly," she whispered.

Later, when I got to know Luke Alexander, I found that Maureen had harbored no illusions about her husband. He was, in fact, a tough, professionally capable, attractive man. He did indeed play around with other women whenever we left San Diego. But then I understood something of how making love to a big, dominant, self-possessed woman like Maureen Alexander drained a man and how they both, in their separations, sought others to fill the voids they left in each other. Now death was his final infidelity.

"He isn't worrying about Luke or the widow Alexander."

The sharp intensity of MacCafferty's voice broke me out of my reverie. The squadron commander and Frank Pastori were standing at the front of the ready room a few feet away from me, conferring in tense, quiet voices.

"They were roommates," Pastori said. "It's tough on him."

"They weren't that close," MacCafferty said in a low growl. "He's just psyched out about taking a cold catapult shot off the bow or the fantail coming up and smacking *him* in the face."

"Well, aren't we all?" Pastori said. "A couple of stiff drinks, and he'll be all right."

"He can't even hold a glass," MacCafferty said. He frowned contemptuously and looked as tough as an old lanyard knot.

I gathered that they were conferring about Ernie Scholl. The squadron commander's face suddenly softened, and he rubbed his forehead as if trying to massage out the tension. "I don't know, Frank. Go talk to him," he said in a softer, more sympathetic tone. "But you know the signs as well as I do. You've seen it happen often enough before to know there's not much you can do. Talk to him as long as you want, but until one of you convinces me differently, Scholl is not to suit up. We'll keep it in the family as long as we can."

Pastori nodded solemnly. "Thanks, Tom." Then he turned and left the ready room.

I did not hang around much longer myself. The whole atmosphere was depressing, and the time for my afternoon patrol was approaching. I headed back to my stateroom to gather up my gear.

As I passed Ernie Scholl's stateroom, I could hear the muted voices of Scholl and Pastori through the door. Something in their fervor stopped me for a moment.

"Well, what are you going to do?" Pastori insisted.

"I don't know." Scholl's voice was almost a whine.

"What are you going to be? Who are you going to be? What are you going to do, reject your whole life and start over as a shadow?"

"At least I'll be alive."

"Alive at what? Some desk job where you'll walk around hangdog like you had your balls cut off?"

I was eavesdropping on an intensely private conversation and, embarrassed, I moved on quickly to change for my flight.

I still had a few minutes, so I lit a cigarette and sat back, trying to unwind. But my mind was in turbulent riot. The first thing that hit my eye was the big Kodacolor photo of Nancy on my bureau. The inscription—"With all my love, Nancy"—now had a mocking echo to it.

My marriage was all but ended, without my ever really knowing why. Those last few months in San Diego, on the nights when I was home, Nancy and I silently stalked So I escaped to the car. I drove the Chevy to nowhere, each other about the house. That tract home was like our marriage itself—its walls and ceilings crowded in on me. just around San Diego on the intertwining grapevines of freeways, sometimes with Nancy huddled silently beside me. She did not even protest when the speedometer hit 80 ... 85 ... 90 ... as if she had lost interest in keeping either one of us alive.

That last futile ride together, I pulled off the freeway onto the road used for sports car races at Torrey Pines. I played with the course in the dark for a while, watching the headlight beams lose the road as it dipped and fled about hairpin bends. Then I turned off onto a deserted plateau at the top of a cliff overlooking the Pacific. In the day time, local glider pilots used the cliff as a launching site, taking off into the strong steady offshore breeze and then soaring back inland on the steeply rising thermals. At night, there was a spectacular starscape and a view of phosphorescent surf that suddenly materialized out of the blackness below, thundered forward in a thickening line, and then evaporated again into the darkness. Nancy and I had made love there in the car, before we were married.

Now I sat sprawled in the front seat looking straight ahead, but I could feel Nancy's eyes on me, waiting.

She smoothed her skirt. "When do you leave?" she asked finally.

"A couple of weeks."

The night air teased her hair, and it shimmered in the moonlight like an amber waterfall. But in spite of the wind, I had the feeling that everything was perfectly still. Waiting. Even the boom of the surf seemed to have faded. The silence hung in the air like a soap bubble waiting to be popped.

"Well, what do we talk about next?" Nancy said, her voice shrill with a falsetto note of cheer. "I know. Let's talk about the divorce."

I didn't say anything for a long while.

"Is that what you want?"

"That, as you like to say, is the play the situation calls for."

"What game are we playing?"

"You tell me, Charly. Just what are you doing?"

"Look, this is all pretty senseless now. I mean I'm taking off in a couple of weeks, and I'll be gone six, seven months."

"And where does that leave me?"

"In San Diego." It didn't come out right.

"Just what the hell am I," she snapped back bitterly, "your girl in this port? I'm your wife!"

"I'm sorry. I didn't mean it the way it came out. I don't know what it is you want from me."

111

"For openers, fidelity would have been nice."

"Nancy, for Chrissakes . . ."

"I hope things are a lot less complicated for you in Japan, or wherever the hell it is you're going. I understand that all you have to do there to make out is hand out a few Hershey bars or something. That should be just about your speed."

Women. They are natural street brawlers. When they are hurt, they instinctively go for the groin. But there was nothing I could say to her. No way I could explain it to her. She was my wife, and she wanted me to be hers. There was nothing wrong or laughable in that. She had a wounded and desperate look in her eyes, and it touched me. I reached out to stroke her hair, to try to tell her by touch that it wasn't that I just didn't give a damn, but she shook off my hand with a brusque movement.

"I don't want a divorce," I said.

"All right then, I'll become a WestPac widow. I'll sit and I'll stare at the walls for a month or two and go half out of my mind imagining what Oriental orgies you've got going. Then one day, when I've had it, I'll just shower and sprinkle myself with My Sin and toddle down to the O Club or the Mexican Village and hoist myself onto a bar stool next to Maureen Alexander. Just buy one Daiquiri and wait until someone else offers to buy the second."

"You do that, and I'll . . ."

"You'll do what? Beat the hell out of me? But what makes you think you'll ever know about it, Charly? What's good for the gander is good for the goose, baby."

I could have killed her. But I didn't do anything. I didn't say anything. I couldn't even look at her. I just stared straight ahead.

"Well, forget it. I'm not a cheat," Nancy said in an infinitely sad and depressed voice. "I want a divorce. I'm going to be another one of the gay divorcées who doesn't give a shit what anybody says or thinks. Especially you. Jesus, I'm sick of San Diego. I wish the hell the school year were over. I'd move tomorrow. I don't like you or our life here very much anymore. You've changed."

"We all change."

"Yes, but you've grown cold. Detached. Even brutal. I

don't know, maybe it was always there, and I just didn't see it before. Maybe I've been kidding myself about you all along. When Bob got killed in Pensacola, you cried. You felt it. But then you went on to do what you had to do. And I loved you for it. I thought, there's a man whose strength I want to live with for the rest of my life. I know the thing between Bob and me has always bothered you. But what I felt for you was another whole dimension compared to the thing between Bob and me."

She paused, but I had nothing to say.

"But last month when that sweet blond kid from Iowa got killed at Fallon, I don't think you gave it a second thought."

"I felt bad about Jerry," I protested. "But you can't afford to think about it too much and still do your job."

"When is it all right for you to give a damn, Charly? About me, for instance?"

"What the hell does one thing have to do with the other?"

"I don't know," Nancy said quietly. "They just involve the same stranger."

In my stateroom aboard the carrier, I conjured up Jerry Dahl's death in the puffs of cigarette smoke that rose to the ceiling. We had been playing war games in the Nevada desert. In a loose column we had streaked over the sands on a low-level attack, weaving through the ridges and closely hugging the ground contours. The bleak hills flowed beneath the wing edges in blurred brown waves. Over the earphones crackled the excited calls of the cover fighters as they scrambled the Red Group harassment.

"There they are. Jump them. Bend it over, bend it, damn it."

"Roger, Black Leader, will handle ... What happened to the bogeys?"

"Bogeys now crossing left to right. Go get them!"

"Rog. Hold many bogeys at seven o'clock. I'm still heavy. I can still burn. We'll chase them off."

"Go get them, then."

Suddenly, a ridge line just ahead of me burst into a silent orange blossom of flame. Dahl had flown too low. That's all there was to it. Men like Dahl and Alexander

113

were often killed playing war games, and the justification was that someday there would be a real war to fight.

I checked my watch, then snubbed out my cigarette. It was time to suit up for my patrol over the Straits of Taiwan.

12

Once in the plane, I was nervous and taut as a violin string. On my patrol, I flew very badly. I fought to concentrate, but my thoughts kept short-circuiting. Two days before, Alexander and I had soared together above the storm clouds. Now he was drowned or crushed to death—trapped in a titanium and aluminum coffin identical to the one in which I was strapped—while it sank down into the black ooze at thirteen hundred fathoms. Yesterday I had come close to preceding him.

At the end of the patrol, I made an erratic landing approach. First I was too high, then I overcorrected and came in too low. The red landing signal lights on the carrier fantail suddenly flashed on and off, and Hooks Lewis shouted at me over the radio to wave-off and make another approach.

The second time around was only slightly better, and I crunched down onto the deck too heavily and too late. I caught the last wire by a lucky hair.

When I returned to my stateroom, my roommate, Marty Cullen, was there propped up in his bunk, reading *Playboy*. I grunted a greeting, and without a word, stripped down to my shorts. I dropped to the floor and pumped out thirty push-ups the hard way, with my feet up on a chair, trying to work out the knots of tension in my neck and shoulders.

Cullen was used to my sudden bursts of calisthenics and ignored me until I was through. Then he asked, "Did you hear about Scholl?"

"No, what?" I panted, heaving back to my feet.

"He turned in his wings."

I didn't say anything, but just stood there absently massaging my arms. My shoulder and pectoral muscles were bloated and vaguely ached from the exertion. "I didn't

115

know we still could," I said finally. "Well, what happens now?" I put on a pair of pants.

"Pastori's spent the whole day trying to talk him out of it, but no go. Scholl's really psyched out, I guess. I hear MacCafferty is going to high-line him by bosun's chair to a supply ship as soon as one comes alongside and ship him back to San Diego."

"What the hell's the rush? MacCafferty doesn't have to do that," I said reproachfully. It bothered me. "He could keep Scholl aboard in some ground job if he wanted to. Just ground him temporarily. Or give him some sort of leave so he'd have time to work it out. For Chrissakes, they do it all the time. MacCafferty's just being a son of a bitch."

Cullen shrugged. "Things are too tense. They could push the button at any moment, and the skipper doesn't want Scholl fidgeting around getting the rest of us nervous. He's a rotten apple in the barrel."

I started to gather up my flight gear, which I had dumped in the middle of the floor in a sweat-soaked, foul heap. I picked up my helmet, then I exploded and slammed the hard hat into the metal dresser. "What the fuck is he trying to prove?"

Startled, Cullen sat up and stared at me. Then after a moment he settled back. "He's just bucking for his own air group," he said, as if that excused everything. Cullen was Annapolis, and like all Annapolis men he was himself plotting to become chief of naval operations some day. At heart, he was totally sympathetic with MacCafferty's zeal. Even his overzeal.

"I warn you," I said to Cullen, "Peg-leg Pete the Pirate won't be happy until he finally kills us all."

"Hey," Cullen responded cheerfully, "maybe we'll see some real action, huh."

"You guys are dangerous, you know that."

Cullen got his Commodore Oliver Hazard Perry look. "If running up and down the China coast at all hours of the day and night is going to make them stop and think twice about starting anything, then that's what we're going to do, Mister."

"Don't Mister me. I'm not some fucking plebe."

Cullen's homely Midwestern features grew stern, the line of his jaw taut. He glared at me, as if mimicking one

116

of the J. W. Jarvis portraits of Perry or Stephen Decatur
strung along the walls of Annapolis' Bancroft Hall. I
started to laugh, but the sound came out as a short, nervous bark. "Once more into the breach, lads," I exhorted.
"Sheeit." Shrugging into a clean shirt, I stalked out of the
stateroom and headed for the squadron ready room to
drum up a game of Acey-Deucy.

But the place was deserted, except for Chubby Harris,
who had the squadron duty.

"Where is everybody?"

"Crapped out. Trying to get some sleep."

"Everybody?"

Harris waved his small, fleshy paw at the flight
schedule board. "Read it and weep."

I followed his hand and read the chalked-in schedule
with a growing sense of panic.

Pilot	Plane	Estimated Time of Launch	Estimated Time of Landing	Mission
Tallman	213	2330	0130	Patrol
Lucas	204	0030	0230	"
Rohr	209	0130	0330	"

"Oh, Jesus. That's all I need." We were each scheduled
for patrols that night, flying straight through until morning.

I had never flown patrol at night. If I had been edgy
before, now there was the hollow ache of fear in the pit of
my stomach. I wandered about the ready room, ostensibly
checking out the new notices and bulletins, but really trying to settle down.

The squadron ready room was set up like a small classroom or theater with rows of upholstered chairs and an
aisle cutting down the center. On the front wall was a
large blackboard, now entirely covered by an aerial navigation chart of the Taiwan Straits and the Chinese mainland.

The side walls were paneled with cork bulletin boards
tacked with mimeographed watch bills and plans of the
day, recognition charts with the black silhouettes of Russian and Red Chinese aircraft, and instructions for

117

survival at sea and, in case we crashed on the Chinese mainland, escape and evasion.

An air-safety poster pictured a pilot intently studying a map while through the cockpit windshield another plane was seen flying head-on into him. The caption read:

A MID-AIR COLLISION CAN RUIN YOUR WHOLE DAY.

Tacked just below the poster was a mimeographed

News of the Day.

(MOSCOW)—THE RUSSIAN GOVERNMENT TODAY WARNED THE UNITED STATES THAT THE SOVIETS INTEND TO GIVE RED CHINA ". . . NECESSARY MORAL AND MATERIAL AID IN THE JUST STRUGGLE FOR THE LIBERATION OF TAIWAN." THE RUSSIAN COMMUNIQUE ADDED THAT ". . . ANY AGGRESSION BY THE U.S. IN THE FAR EAST WILL LEAD TO SPREADING THE WAR."

(WASHINGTON)—SECRETARY OF STATE JOHN FOSTER DULLES TODAY RESPONDED TO ADMINISTRATION CRITICS, WHO CHARGED THAT THE UNITED STATES WAS RISKING A MAJOR WAR OVER TWO TINY ISLANDS. "IF YOU ARE SCARED TO GO TO THE BRINK," DULLES SAID, "YOU ARE LOST."

When I got back to the stateroom, Cullen was already bunked down asleep and snoring like an asthmatic horse. I stripped down and crawled into my own rack to catch a nap before my night patrol. I tossed back and forth for about fifteen minutes and punched a pillow a dozen times, then gave it up. I turned on the bedlight above my head and reached for a cigarette. But I did not relax. Finally I climbed out of bed, dressed, and fled up to the afterbridge of the ship to gulp in the sea air and watch the night operations.

The flight deck at night was eerie, evilly lit by dim red lights. Two disembodied hands waved a pair of fluorescent light sticks, and they floated over the deck like will-o'-the-wisps, beckoning a taxiing aircraft forward toward the catapult area. Beyond was the pitch blackness of the sea itself.

Kkkrrrrrrrreeeeeeeeeeeeeee. The banshee shriek of the heavy bomber directly below me drilled into my brain, the noise of its twin jet turbines so shrill it made my very skullbone ache, and I squeezed the heels of my hands into my ears to shut out the scream. The ponderous A-3 Douglas Skywarrior, twice the size and thicker-bellied than a fighter, rolled onto the starboard catapult. The shriek from the two jet engines thickened to the *carooooommm* of sustained thunder. There was a sudden belch of steam that shimmered red like the smoke of an intense flame, and the big aircraft shot forward. Thirty-five tons of machinery exploded from a standstill to one hundred thirty miles an hour in seventy yards, and then dropped abruptly off the bow, suddenly disappearing from sight as if it had plunged right into the sea. In a moment, the exhaust fires of the twin jet engines reappeared a hundred yards ahead of the ship, rising swiftly in the black sky like a pair of flaming arrows.

"Is that you, Charly?"

That hour of the night, I had expected to be alone on the afterbridge, but now a tall figure in a canvas foul-weather jacket materialized on the rail next to me. In the noise of the bomber's blastoff, I had not heard him approach.

"How ya doing, Stan? Just blowing the cobwebs out before I have to take off."

"Yeah. What are you doing up?"

"Just got off watch."

"You qualify as officer of the deck yet?"

"Last time out."

"Terrific. I'll sleep easier at night knowing that you're up there on the bridge conning us through the darkness."

The other man laughed politely and then fell into an uneasy silence. There was always that awkwardness between us that no amount of chatter could dispel. Stan Haverman was a deck officer on the carrier, but in advanced flight training in Corpus Christi, Haverman had been one of the four students in my flight. On a strafing run in gunnery training, one of the other wingmen had frozen on the target and dived straight into the Texas sagebrush. The three of us remaining had returned imme-

119

diately to the field. Without a word to the other man and me, Haverman had parked his plane and, still in his flight suit, had walked directly to the administration building and resigned from flight training. At the time, we had been flight students over a year and a half and were all just a week away from getting our wings. It was a coincidence that Haverman had been reassigned as a deck officer aboard the same carrier to which my squadron was now attached. The dropouts and washouts of Pensacola and Corpus Christi, the disturbing casualties of the selection process through which we had passed, were, as often as not, immediately transferred to nonflying billets on aircraft carriers or Navy air bases as if to be waiting there when their classmates later flew in.

During a lull in the flight operations Haverman and I both leaned on the railing and looked out to sea. A few hundred yards to port, the running lights of a destroyer bobbed and flickered in the darkness. Its blinker lights suddenly turned on and off, flashing dots and dashes of yellow light directly toward us. Almost immediately, I heard, rather than saw, the metallic staccato of our blinker answering from the signal bridge on the level just below where we were standing.

Haverman turned to me in the dark. "The guy who bought it today, Alexander, was he a close friend of yours?"

"Yeah, Stan, fairly close."

"I'm sorry. That's rough." There was another silence, then Haverman said, "I had the con when it happened."

"Did you see it?"

"Yeah, he went off right below me. Right off the starboard catapult."

"What happened?"

"It looked like his power quit just as he shot off the catapult. The plane just dove for the water and went in like a lead shot. That plane doesn't float."

I nodded. "The low jet intake under the nose just sucks the water right in."

Beneath us on the flight deck, the aircraft were being respotted for the next day's operations. It was like watching a team of men work a giant puzzle—one of those plastic gadgets in which numbered discs, mixed up and locked tight in a frame, have to be endlessly slid back and forth and up and down to arrange them into proper numerical sequence. An ancient propeller-driven Spad now in the rear of the hangar bay was to be launched first. It had to be moved up onto the forward flight deck, adjacent to the catapults, but first room had to be made for it by lowering an A-4 Douglas fighter down below on the elevator. It would be stored on the hangar deck and moved back up later. A fat twin-jet A-3 bomber now blocking the middle of the upper deck was hauled down the elevator and then shoved out of the way into the spot left vacant by the Spad. While all this was going on, an occasional night patrol was launched or landed.

The crewmen working on the flight deck moved about cautiously, constantly looking over their shoulders, stepping softly. A tangling, foot-clutching undergrowth of cables, tie-down rings, and parking chocks, hidden in the shadows, constantly tripped them. In the darkness that enveloped the crewmen as they scurried about the aircraft, shoving the planes into place, the dangers were invisible but deadly. The whirling propeller blades of the taxiing Spad had sliced and quartered a careless man the month before on that deck. The hot jet blast of another plane had seared the skin off one man who had stayed too close and blown a third man overboard. Yet in spite of the hazards and interruptions, the flight deck was set up with impressive coordination and speed. While Haverman and I watched, the job was done and the majority of the flight deck crew secured, leaving only the teams that manned the catapult and arresting gear.

"Tell me, Charly," Haverman said suddenly, "do you ever feel vulnerable?"

"What do you mean, vulnerable?"

Haverman did not answer right away, then said, "I remember in Pensacola, in one of our preflight classes, one of the instructors telling us that if we stayed on as Navy fliers, statistically, two out of three of us would eventually be killed."

"He was just trying to scare you."

"Maybe. But I remember kidding the guys on both sides of me. Telling them how sorry I was about it. Was there anything I could do for them afterward. But, you know, I was serious. I really believed that I was going to be the one that survived. I would do one tour of duty and then get out. If anybody got his ass busted, it was going to be the other two guys. I guess that's what I mean by being vulnerable. Have you ever lost the conviction that it was always going to be the other guy that bought it, Charly? That it could be you?"

I didn't answer. Instead, I asked, "Is that what happened in Corpus Christi?"

"I tried to explain it to you."

"I wasn't listening, Stan. I didn't want to hear it."

There was a sudden roar of a formation returning to the ship. Haverman and I both looked up instinctively as two planes broke through the overcast just ahead of the ship. In the opaque darkness only their jet exhaust fires and lights were visible. They looked like two shooting stars hurtling down, brighter and brighter, and then they were suddenly extinguished in the blackness of the sea. The two planes simply plunged right into the water, one after the other. One, two. Like a string of closely placed bombs, they burst in two quick explosions of white, phosphorescent foam that immediately settled, leaving no crater in the dark, implacable surface.

"My God," Haverman turned to me, stricken and confused, as if to confirm what he had just seen. "What the hell happened?"

"I don't know. It looked like they just flew right into the water," I said incredulously.

"Oh, my God." Haverman turned back to stare at the spot where the two planes had disappeared, but there was nothing there to indicate that a formation of two jets had just crashed.

"I've got to get to the bridge. I don't know if they even saw it." Without another word, Haverman sprang forward, running along the catwalk.

His feet clanged on the metal plates. Then a hatch creaked open and slammed shut, and there was silence. I was left standing alone in the night on the afterbridge, gripping the railing with both hands. There was a tremor in my knees, and I couldn't control it. It rose in shuddering waves up through my legs, shaking my whole body in a violent spasm. I squeezed the steel railing with every gram of my strength and fought to hold on.

13

I fled from the bridge to my stateroom. I stood just inside the door in the dark, breathing deeply to quiet myself down. I was still very shaky. I was sweating heavily and the inside of my mouth was dry and cottony, as if I had just landed after a tense, hairy patrol. Only now I had to begin suiting up for a flight. It was a hell of a state of mind to be starting out in.

Cullen's bedlamp suddenly switched on. "Whataya doing, coming or going?" he moaned. He rubbed his eyes and then peered at me groggily, his eyes slowly opening and closing as he tried to figure out if it was time for him to get up for his flight yet.

I quickly told him what had just happened. "The lead pilot must have misread his altimeter," I said, still excited. "It's the only way I figure both of them would have deep-sixed like that."

"He sure must've had his head down in the cockpit," Cullen nodded. He swung his feet onto the floor and sat huddled on the edge of his bunk, worrying about it. "But what the hell was the other guy following him so closely for at night?" he said belligerently. "It sounds to me like it was both of their damn faults."

Cullen, only half awake, was already performing the litany. The other guy augered in because he screwed up. He made a mistake, when there was no room for error. But it will not happen to me, Cullen silently recited the incantation. It just won't. It can't.

I turned away from Cullen and began setting up my flight gear. Dressing for a high-altitude flight in a jet fighter is a ritual, like suiting up for a bullfight or football game. It is the mental preparation by which the mind is focused and the loins, limbs, and groin girded against the impending violence. The procedure is part superstition—

123

the right sock goes on first for good luck. And it is part realistic safety precautions—the CO_2 cartridge that inflates the flotation belt is unscrewed and checked to make sure it has not accidentally punctured. But that night, the equipment that I checked and donned did not focus my mind on the nuts and bolts of flying. Instead it conjured up nightmare images of the dangers awaiting me.

My hands were moist and shaking badly as I tugged on the black rubber suit. It was like the outfits that skin-divers wear for plunges into freezing water, and I wore it for the very same reason. The rubber suit was stifling and foul as a sweat sock from my previous flight. Over it, I pulled on a pair of flight overalls, the cloth of which was stiff, musty, and reeking with the sharp, acrid smell of fireproofing chemicals.

"He must have had his head down in the cockpit and misread his altimeter," Cullen repeated, still worrying the accident. "That's where he screwed up. If he had kept double-checking his position visually, he wouldn't have augered in."

"It wouldn't have made any difference," I said. "You can't tell your altitude over water at night. Hell, I can't even judge it in the daylight most of the time unless I have a reference like the ship."

"Well, maybe you ought to be grateful for all the night and instrument flying we're getting in, instead of bitching about it. It puts us ahead of the game," Cullen said, as if trying to reassure himself.

I didn't say anything. I was having trouble just getting dressed. Each piece of equipment I put on brought me that much closer to the time when I would have to step onto that black flight deck and crawl into the plane. I became increasingly paralyzed, and each movement became an act of will. Inside the clammy rubber exposure suit, I was soaked. But it was not a hot, healthy sweat. It was a nervous perspiration that oozed through the skin—greasy as oil—and left my muscles chilled and tight.

I struggled and wriggled into my G-suit, an arrangement of thick, pneumatic bands that wrapped around my waist, thighs, and calves and were all connected with narrow, rubber tubing. It looked like some sort of orthopedic girdle and garter belt, and it was, in a way. It would keep me from blacking out by pushing back the suddenly sagging flesh and blood during seven-G pullouts and turns. Over it went the sleeveless, legless, nylon torso suit, which attached at the shoulder and hips to the plane's ejection seat.

I moved like an automaton, while my mind ricocheted from one terrifying image to another. The intricate details of preparing for my own night flight only reinforced the memory of the two Skyhawk jets plunging into the sea, the second pilot blindly following the first like a lemming. It too vividly reminded me of my first night flights while I was still a student in Pensacola.

The first time any of us were aloft at night, we had simply circled the field in a nervous pack, following each other's tail lights, the strange lights and vague shapes of the aircraft blurred and out of focus as though seen through heavy rain.

The second time up at night, several weeks later, we had to navigate about a triangular-shaped cross-country route, supposedly checking our courses and positions by radio signal bearings. I had had little confidence in the radio signals or in my own ability to navigate by them, and for the most part I had again simply followed the tail light of the plane ahead of me, hoping that he knew what in hell he was doing. It had worked out. But the next day, I had heard that another student, doing the same exact thing, had mistaken a bright evening star for the plane ahead of him and unhesitatingly followed it far beyond the field and deep over the forests and swamps of Alabama. Behind him, one after another, had trailed a line of planes. An instructor finally realized what was happening. But I always wonder what would have happened if the instructor had not caught them. How many of them would have followed that leader pursuing his false beacon until, fuel exhausted and beyond refuge, they had all crashed into the wilderness.

Over my torso suit, I strapped on my shoulder holster and the single bandoleer of .38 caliber bullets that wrapped across my chest, Mexican-bandit style. Every other bullet was a tracer, the noise and flare of which was to attract rescuers if I went down at night. The regular .38 slugs were for hunting small game, if I came down over land, or shooting it out with hostiles until a rescue chopper could take me out. We were not at war with anyone, but that was a situation that might change momentarily. I checked the safety catch on the Smith & Wesson revolver and shoved it back into the shoulder holster.

Stitched to the leg of my coveralls was a fancy leather sheath and a heavy deerhunter knife. The knife was to cut the parachute shroud lines if I got hung up in a tree or church steeple. The survival training officers recommended always carrying the knife as a basic tool, and they told the parable of the pilot whose landing gear jammed. While flying a landing approach left-handed, he slipped the blade between the cockpit floor plates and sprung the jammed hydraulic mechanism that released the gear. The possibility of my ever using the knife always seemed to me as remote as, say, using fishhooks that were part of the sea survival kit. And in the back of my mind, tucked there *just in case* like the fishhooks in that para-raft, were exotic, perilous lessons in survival: kick vigorously when threatened by sharks stand still when threatened by wolves; and, if down in the Arctic, don't eat the liver of a polar bear or ring-neck seal, since they both contain poisonous concentrations of vitamin A. Previously, I had viewed the survival precautions half jokingly, as a sport. That night, they all foreboded terrifying possibilities.

I buckled the flotation belt about my waist, then straightened up and shook myself like a wet dog to settle all the equipment in place. I was as ready as I was going to be.

"I'll see ya," I told Cullen.

He was still slumped deep in thought on the edge of his bunk, hands clasped between his legs. He looked up, as if startled that I was still there. "Hey, well, take care," he said.

I forced myself to move toward the door, out of the sanctuary of my stateroom and toward the flight deck.

"Hey, and don't forget," Cullen shouted after me. "Keep your head up in the cockpit. Don't get fixed on the instruments."

14

I was in about as much shape to fly as a stumbling drunk.
I stood by the black mouth of the jet intake and stared
first at the open cockpit and then at the dripping opaque
wall about the ship, and I could feel my facial muscles
twitch.

There were demons hiding in the black shadows just
beyond the ship. They had already killed three men that
day, yanking them suddenly out of the sky into the depths
of the sea and trapping them in an agonized tangle of
shattered plexiglass and aluminum until their lungs burst.
Now the same demons waited for me in the dark at the
edge of the flight deck.

I thought about waking one of the flight surgeons and
getting myself grounded. But what would I tell him? That
I was exhausted just like everyone else? Or the truth?
That I was terrified. I had a mental picture of the contempt on MacCafferty's face when he heard that I had
grounded myself. It was a contempt that I shared, and for
an instant, self-disgust went deeper than fear and drove
me right up the side of the aircraft and into the cockpit.

From that point on, practice and muscle memory took
over. The sudden shriek of the turbines startled me. I did
not remember having gone through the starting procedure. A pair of glowing hands clutching red and green
wands of light materialized directly under the plane's
nose, beckoning me forward. I knew it was a taxi director,
but it seemed like one of the demons of the night leading
me over the cliff edge of the flight deck into the black
water fifty feet below.

I taxied forward in nervous fits and starts, jamming on
the brakes each time I thought the darkness ahead appeared a mite blacker than the other areas, until the air

boss in primary flight control called down impatiently, "What's the problem down there, Charger Nine?"

Then I was on the catapult being strapped down. But I might as well have been inside the tunnel of a coal mine. In front, overhead, and on both sides of me, the darkness pressed in, black and solid as anthracite. The catapult shot suddenly jammed me against the cushions, and I hurtled toward the black wall. I was airborne.

The plane was immediately swallowed up by the clouds. The world about me exploded into flames, as the jet's tailfire was mirrored in millions of droplets of moisture. But I kept my eyes glued to the glowing dials eighteen inches from the end of my nose, not looking up until I leveled off above the weather.

An exceptionally high veil of cirrus hid the stars and moon, denying me a horizon to fly on, and I had to go back on instruments immediately. At 41,000 feet, I could see neither sea nor sky. Outside the cockpit, there was only the jet's pointed nose and wing tips hanging motionless, without reference, in a darkness of infinite loneliness. I gripped the stick so tightly my knuckles ached.

The tops of the clouds dimly visible below were like an upside-down sky, and I had the vague impression I was flying inverted. I wasn't at all surprised when vertigo hit me. In my state, I expected to look out and discover the Four Horsemen of the Apocalypse flying wing on me. The plane fell out from under me, tumbling to the left in a spin. I clutched the seat with one hand and the stick in the other. Every muscle in my body braced against the spiraling dive that the instruments insisted was not happening. I was still flying straight and level, according to the dials. Now I sat back and leaned to the right because the seat of my pants said I was in a climbing bank in that direction. I wasn't really, but my spasmodic jerks on the stick were causing the plane to fly along in porpoiselike dips.

I fought for control, concentrating on the gauges, trying to cut off my mind and hand from the false signals coming from the cochlea of my inner ear. I breathed deeply to relax, but the excess of oxygen combined with the sharp, chemical smell of metal and rubber made me nauseous. At 41,000 feet, when your life depends on an oxygen mask, vomiting can be terminal.

Most of my previous instrument flying had been in the back of a trainer with a tentlike hood over the cockpit bathing me in a quiet sepia twilight, while up front another pilot kept lookout. I never really suspended my basic disbelief in the instruments. There was something unnatural about trusting your life to the flickering hands of those dials. But now, flying between two overcasts at night alone above the sea, I had to believe the dials. There was nothing else to believe in.

After a while, I settled down. I contacted the control station on Taiwan, and under its direction once again turned south over the Straits, and then was relayed to a picket destroyer somewhere below. I was grateful for the sound of a human voice, no matter how remote, telling me what to do.

I was on the long straight leg of the patrol, paralleling the Chinese coast. Suddenly, off my right wing, red blossoms of flame burst open then immediately disappeared. Soundlessly they appeared, flared brightly for a moment, and then were quickly smothered in black again. I checked the position on my chart. It was Quemoy Island.

"Hangman, this is Charger Nine. Over."

The phones crackled. "Roger, Charger Nine. This is Hangman. Over."

"You holding any contacts in my vicinity? Over."

"Negative. Crystal ball is clear except for you. Over."

"Roger. Out." I didn't want to end it, but I could not think of anything else quasi-official to say. For the moment, an anonymous metallic voice talking in brevity code was my solitary contact with the world.

The destroyer was supposed to confirm my course every few minutes. In the interminable lapses between contacts I wondered if anyone was really listening to or watching me. Did the ChiCom radar have a fix on me? The primary reason I was streaking through that muck loaded with weapons like a French buccaneer was to make the Red Chinese aware that we were there.

For the moment, there was nothing to do but fly along straight and level. An idle mind is the devil's rumpus room, and for no reason at all, I remembered an all-night Los Angeles disk jockey, an old-timer on the job who in the dark, doubting hours between the closing of the bars and dawn had had a nervous breakdown right on the air, screaming into the microphone, "My God, is there really anyone out there listening to me? Answer me! Is there anyone out there listening?"

I was sweating heavily. I could feel it pouring down my spine, coursing between the ridges of my back muscles and collecting in a sopping pool in my seat.

Radio static started up, crackling like a remote broadcast of a forest fire. The controller came on again, overriding the static, and ordered me to alter course to the west. The prevailing winds from the northwest were apparently stronger than Aerology had anticipated and blowing me too far off the Chinese coast. I banked to right and settled down on the new heading. To keep busy, I fiddled with the radar, tuning it finely, and then stared at the pale yellow-green pattern.

"Hangman. This is Charger Nine. Hey, I'm getting too close to the coast. Over."

"Negative. You're right on course, Charger Nine. Continue present heading."

I checked the radar again. "Hangman. I'm going to be over the mainland in a minute. Over."

Static grated in my ears. The controller came up, "Negative. We hold you well clear. Continue present heading."

It simply did not check out. Something was wrong, and I could not quite put my finger on it. I suddenly had a chilling suspicion.

"Hangman, *authenticate* your last heading. Over." By that word, I had ordered the controller to put his directions in code and identify himself. The authentication codes were secret and changed daily. I reached down and flipped through the cards clipped to my kneepad to that day's code.

"R-r-roger, Charger Nine. Continue heading two-six-zero."

"Authenticate that heading, Hangman," I barked back.

"R-r-roger, Charger Nine, I will have authentication in a minute. Continue on course two-six-zero." The voice overriding the static was confident and well modulated as a radio announcer's.

That was it. It was not the sullen, bitchy, tired voice of an overworked radarman. I was being bushwhacked by a ChiCom controller.

I banked violently to the east, recoiling and fleeing from the coast of Red China.

"Charger Nine, this is Hangman. We will have authentication in a moment. You are ordered to heading two-six-zero."

"You lousy yellow sons of bitches!" I screamed into the mike. "What the hell are you trying to do?"

I kicked in the jet's afterburner and blasted like a rocket due east, until the mainland and the offshore islands disappeared from my radarscope. My head was swiveling frantically, searching for the squadron of MIGs I was expecting to burst on me at any moment.

I did not cut north again until I was well over the midfield stripe in the Straits. Then I got on the radio. After several calls I finally contacted Dogmeat, the Air Force ground control station near Taipei, or someone who said they were Dogmeat. I made them authenticate their directions in code twice before I swung onto the bearing that pointed me back toward the carrier.

When Dogmeat, in turn, passed me onto the carrier's control, I again demanded the code, and the irritated let's-knock-off-this-bullshit tone of the ship's controller was more reassuring than a dozen correctly encoded authentications.

The carrier gave me a penetration heading. I pushed over and dropped into the suffocating, soot-black mists below, flying blind and knowing only one thing for sure—that I was plummeting toward the sea. I had no sooner dropped into the overcast when a wave of dizziness sent me reeling. I felt as if the plane had rolled over three hundred sixty degrees and then the false signals from my middle ear tumbled me into a drunken spin.

"When you have the meatball in sight, commence a normal rate of descent," the approach controller droned in a mechanical voice.

I started shouting to myself—exhorting, cursing, pleading. "Fly the gauges, Charly. Fly the instruments."

The plane did another imaginary whirl that did not register on the dials. But what did register was trouble enough. My altitude was too high. My airspeed was excessive. It was partly due to the jet's unusually heavy load of weapons and partly to my own confusion. I glanced up anxiously, hoping to catch a glimpse of the ship's landing lights, but outside there was only a carbon blackness, as if I were boring through the very center of the earth.

At a thousand feet, I finally broke clear and spotted the carrier about a mile and a half ahead coursing straight through the water, low waves phosphorescent with plankton sweeping off the stern like the barbs of an arrow and the long shaft of the wake glowing faintly with white feathers of foam. On a night like that, there could not have been a lovelier sight in the world.

I adjusted my altitude to the landing lights, centering on the bright red eye of the meatball, and lined up on the carrier for a straight-in approach. Then I scanned back to the instruments. I was still much too fast. I hacked off power and raised the nose just as Hook Lewis' voice came up on the radio with the order. Ahead, the meatball dipped, and I pulled back on the stick to lift the plane back on the glide slope.

Now it began, the instinctive, intricate interplay of forces that no mind can consciously calculate fast enough. The plane decelerated rapidly. To keep it on the landing glide slope, I yanked back on the stick. The sharper angle of the wings increased their drag, and the plane's speed and altitude dropped quickly. I desperately rammed on power. But it was too late. I was now at the point in the equation where the falling plane's need for power to stay airborne was increasing faster than the turbines could accelerate.

There was that moment when I knew I was going to crash. The carrier's deck disappeared above me, and the enormous crushing stern suddenly loomed up before my face like a mountain. There was nothing I could do. It was all inevitable. The only thing I remember thinking was, "Oh, shit!"

The midsection of the aircraft hit first, crashing on to the ship's fantail just where it curved down to form the stern. The plane ricocheted off the blunt steel round-down and pancaked onto the deck. Both landing gears sheared off but, by raw momentum, the plane careened across the deck on its belly, bounced over the side, and with the turbines now firing at full power the jet blasted back into the air.

"You're exploding! Get out! You're exploding! Get out!" Hooks screamed over the radio.

I was stunned by the crash. And awed by the fact I was still alive. Behind me I felt, rather than saw, a blast of flames from a giant blowtorch. I stared at the instruments, but nothing came into focus. I blindly kicked my feet into the stirrups of the ejection seat and yanked at the face curtain. There was a roaring whoosh of air . . . a strong thrust upward . . . a flash . . . a whirlwind ripping at me . . . and then a quick deceleration. For a long moment, I seemed suspended in space, weightless, and then I began to tumble head over heels, but slowly, as if in a dream.

The opening snap of the parachute abruptly jerked me back to consciousness. I was hanging from my parachute harness, rocking slightly. I could not breath freely. I felt as if I was suffocating, then realized my oxygen mask was still on. I ripped it off and took off my helmet and dropped them both. They fell away from me in slow motion, sinking out of sight into the blackness below.

I thought I heard water splash. In a sudden panic, I fumbled around trying to release the parachute clips before I hit the water; in the next moment I plunked in and went under. I groped back to the surface and flailed about to free myself from the parachute harness before the billowing canopy overhead settled on top of me. The parachute that a moment before had saved my life was now a trap that could smother and drown me.

In a blind panic, I thrashed and kicked clear of the chute. The air and water were the same dimensionless black ink, and only the fact that I was choking and coughing told me I was on the surface. I treaded water frantically, groping to locate the toggles for the CO_2 cartridges. I tugged, and the flotation belt inflated with a pop, snugly buoying me up under the arms.

Then I just hung there, panting and coughing. My stomach surged, and I vomited up all the sea water I had just swallowed. Even after my stomach ceased its violent heaving and my breathing quieted, I still hung there with only my head out of the water, not moving, a wounded animal. I do not know how long it was before I started to act with a conscious effort. From the beginning of the landing approach until now, I had reacted automatically, in a combination of panic and procedures. Now I had to stop and think what to do next. It was very strange. I was still alive, and that consciousness of existence gave me a great sense of wonder. It was about the only sense that was operating. I could not see or hear a thing.

"But I'm alive, and that's a fact," I said it out loud, and the timid, strained sound of my voice confirmed the statement. "Alive and kicking," I shouted.

Something grabbed me about the legs like the tentacles of an octopus.

I yanked and thrashed furiously until, sobbing and exhausted and terrified, I just hung helpless in my life belt. Nothing happened. I reached down and felt around and then, line by line, methodically freed my legs from the tangle of parachute shroud lines.

"Okay, now what did you do with the para-raft?" The lanyard was still attached to my life belt, and it, in turn, was attached to the seat pack floating nearby. The raft packet was in the seat, and it easily pulled free with a tug on the lanyard. Working strictly by feel, I located the inflation toggle on the raft and yanked. The raft only partially inflated and sagged limply in the water.

"For Chrissakes, don't panic again. John Wayne never panics. The oral inflation tube. Find the oral inflation tube. . . . Who's hiding the fucking oral inflation tube? Don't panic!"

I panicked. In a frustrated fury, I ripped at the toggle again. With a pop, the raft inflated fully.

The para-raft was little more than an oversized, oval-shaped innertube with a rubber sheet across the bottom. It barely held me afloat, and after trying to bail and splash it out for what seemed like an hour, it still held two inches of water. With my head hanging over one end and my feet propped over the other, I bobbed along in a soft, fragilely buoyant rubber tub.

I now began to shudder violently. I was soaked through and chilled, and when I settled down after the first frantic efforts to stay afloat, I became aware I was in pain. I had hurt my back somehow during the ejection, and now it ached very badly. I considered slipping back into the water where it was warmer, but then I thought about sharks and I just huddled over like a man in grief, hugging myself tight with both arms, knowing in every throbbing cell of my body that I was going to be cold, wet,

134

frightened, and in pain until I was found or died of thirst and exposure.

There were no lights visible, no signs of a ship or a plane. All I could make out were dark patches of gray suspended in a void of deeper black and the vague shapes of my two feet propped up in front of me. I talked out loud to my feet.

"Okay now, men. There's no sense in my trying to kid you. You all know the score. We're in a tough jam. But just remember, when the going gets tough, the tough get going. These are the times that separate the men from the boys. And we're not going to let that Big Red Machine stop us. Right? Right! We're going to go out there and win this one for the Gipper and Mom's apple pie. The apple pie would have wanted it that way."

My pep talk was interrupted by the chattering of my teeth. After a moment, I continued talking to myself, with an occasional involuntary seizure of shivers. "You, Rohr, that big buck linebacker that's working you over. You're not going to intimidate him by trying to sneak in an elbow or punch at his head. Go for his guts. You can't hurt a nigger hitting him in the head. The next time there's a pileup, I don't want to see that boy jump to his feet and jog back. Any questions? Okay, then, let's settle down and get organized. Everybody empty their pockets. We're going to inventory everything in the raft."

I groped about until I found one of the raft's pouches of survival equipment, and my fingers closed on a small cylinder. "Ah-ha, flares!"

I held it right up to my nose and studied it intently in the darkness, then struck the fuse. The flare sputtered briefly and fizzled out.

"Shit!" I screamed and hurled the dud out over the water. "Shit, shit, shit!" The words lashed out but were smothered in the night like blows in a pillow.

Next, my rooting fingers seized the small, one-cell emergency flashlight. I shone it all around the craft, but the pathetic beam reached no further than a healthy piss. The sluggish light on the dark sea surface reflected back the impression I was floating on a thick black pool of oil. Christ, the beam was so weak it didn't even travel with the speed of light.

With the flashlight, I picked out the packet of shark repellent and peered at it. Scuttlebutt was that the stuff did repel sharks, but it attracted barracuda. God knows what sort of man-eating sea monster it might attract in these Asian waters.

I shoved the repellent back down to the bottom of the para-raft emergency kit and dug out a water dye marker. I poured it out all around the raft. It was too dark to see any color change in the water.

"Ah-ha, Wrigley's Juicy Fruit! And a whistle!"

I blew the whistle so fiercely my ears ached and then sat back very still, listening intently for some answering sound. There was nothing except the soft lap of the water against the raft.

I still had my thirty-eight. I broke out the gun, blew into the barrel, and spun the chamber to shake out the water. Then I loaded it with tracer bullets from my chest strap and popped off six fast shots. The tracers streaked off and dissolved immediately in the night like timid meteorites.

When the last tracer died out there was nothing. Not a sound or speck of light. A lone astronaut marooned on the dark side of the moon would know what I felt in the pit of my stomach at that moment.

To keep busy, I plunged back into my inventory, rummaging through the raft's equipment pockets.

"Ooow! Goddamn fishhooks." I slumped back, sucking on an injured finger. Blood, salt water, and Juicy Fruit. Those were the flavors of my misery, and there was nothing else to do but crouch fearfully in the dark and taste them.

The space about me was black and dimensionless as death. I toyed a moment with the thought that I might, in fact, really be dead. But no, I gasped for air, shuddered with cold, my back ached, my finger throbbed and bled, and I moaned and cursed aloud, very much alive. At the moment, no one in the whole world knew for sure whether or not I was alive, but I knew; for the moment, that was enough.

Hanging in a black void with your ass in sea water, brooding over half-baked existentialist thoughts, you can go a little nuts. Cramped up in a sort of embryonic curl, I stoked the spark of that one thought into a roaring fire. I began to chant to myself, "I know I'm alive. I'm Charly

136

Rohr. I know I'm alive. I'm Charly Rohr." And the chant built and gathered steam like a locomotive. "Charly Rohr. Charly Rohr. Charly Rohr."

I tried to stand up and shout, damn near swamped the raft, and pitched onto my hands and knees still shouting.

Once, in a high school football game, I had gotten clobbered and was being carried off the field when the cheerleaders started the chant, "Charly Rohr. Charly Rohr. Charly Rohr." The rooting section picked it up and blew it into a huffing, puffing football locomotive, the sound and the energy filling my head and charging me up so that I couldn't feel the pain anymore, and I tried to tear away from the trainers and run back into the game.

"Charly Rohr. Charly Rohr. Charly Rohr." I was on my hands and knees in a swamped raft in a fathomless night, and three feet from me and beyond, out for miles where the absence of light had the thick black texture of soot, there was nothing, not a flick of light, nor a faint teasing ripple in the sea's surface, nothing to give any acknowledgment of my life, except my own voice bellowing and shattering the silence. "Charly Rohr. Charly Rohr. Charly Rohr."

After a while I fell asleep, or rather passed out, and dreamed that the uneasy sleep into which I was descending was death itself. I broke out of the nightmare and woke with a violent shudder. It was much colder now. My bladder was full and cramped, the need to urinate painful. I tried to raise myself, but even getting up on my knees bucked and rocked the raft dangerously. I twisted around to the stern—if an oversized innertube can be said to have two ends—which was lower than the head so that the survivor could crawl in out of the water more easily. My concentrated weight shoved the end under water, swamping the raft and almost flipping me out. I tried stretching out and hanging over one of the long sides, but again I almost capsized. The raft was about as stable as a unicycle in an earthquake.

I was completely soaked again, but I did not want to go back into the water. The bladder pressure was now red line. I reached under flotation belt, bandoleer of bullets, and torso and G-suits and pulled down the zipper of my coveralls, then knelt down in the thick bow of the raft. I leaned back and, balancing my weight with one hand be-

137

hind me, attempted to urinate in a trajectory up and over the bow. Most of it just splashed back into the raft. I washed down the bow section with sea water and splashed as much as I could out of the raft. Then I sat back down, thoroughly miserable, worrying if it was my fate to end up pickled to death in a brine of sea water, dye, piss, and shark repellent.

At that moment, I spotted the lights. I watched them in confusion for a while. Then I realized they must be search-lights of a destroyer looking for me, and I started shouting. I jumped to my feet, swamped the raft again, and tumbled down. "Hey! I'm over here. Here! You blind, tin-can bastards, I'm over here. Here!" I yelled my throat raw.

The searchlights came nearer but were moving at an angle that would soon carry them past me. I dug the last flare out of the emergency kit. It was a dud. I hurled it in the direction of the destroyer.

I blew the whistle furiously and then took out the thirty-eight and emptied it over my head. I reloaded fran-tically with numb, wet, fumbling fingers, dropping bullets into the raft water.

The ship behind the searchlight was invisible in the dark. I took direct aim at the light and fired the whole chamber.

"You sons of bitches. Here I am!" I reloaded and fired again at the light.

One of the beams swept in my direction, passed, then immediately reversed and settled on me and began blink-ing. A second light trained in, suddenly thrusting me into blinding daylight. In that isolated stage of light in the middle of nowhere, I sat ass-deep in the sea, blinking painfully, alternately shouting and blowing a whistle, and wildly firing a pistol over my head, celebrating my own deliverance.

15

As soon as I was hauled aboard the destroyer, I began trembling violently. At the first morning light I was transferred by helicopter to the carrier. The flight surgeon waiting on deck took one look at me as I staggered on board, cramped up with shivers and hugging myself for warmth, and he hustled me below to sick bay, where they gave me a shot and put me to bed under four blankets. The sudden warmth made every nerve end in my body twang like a toothache, but the drugs took hold and gradually I stopped shaking. The long, raw, black-and-purple bruise that the doctor discovered on my buttocks and side slowly ceased to throb. I fainted into a dreamless, downlined sleep.

I woke once during the night. Sick bay was dark, and the hush of the sleep-breathing and soft snores of the other patients lulled me right back to sleep. When I woke again, it was morning and they were serving breakfast. I had slept around the clock.

I was having a second cup of coffee and looking around for a cigarette to go with it, when MacCafferty appeared.

"How do you feel?" he asked. The question was not a formality. He wanted information.

"Terrific!" I said. "Especially when I consider the options I had."

MacCafferty gave me a half-smile and nodded. "I heard you tried to sink the tin can with your thirty-eight," he said.

"It was either them or me."

He smiled and nodded again, but there was something numb and automatic about his response. It was more conditioned reflex than humor.

A medical corpsman came up to clear the tray away. "Well, Mr. Rohr had quite an adventure, didn't he?" he said, carrying on like a bright, cheerful nurse rather than a sailor.

"Oh, yeah," MacCafferty said in a flat, toneless voice.

The corpsman had been staring at me almost admiringly. I looked around the sick bay and saw that several of the other patients and corpsmen were looking my way. They smiled and nodded when they caught my eye. To them, I was apparently some sort of hero. I had screwed up, almost killed myself, wiped out half the flight deck, destroyed a jet aircraft, and cost the taxpayers of America several million dollars. But the other patients—whose humdrum lives were now only punctuated by the flu, appendicitis, or galley burns—had twisted my fuck-up into something heroic. Well, MacCafferty was under no such illusion. He was here to give it to me straight.

He took out his cigarettes and offered me one. I shook my head.

"That was quite a landing," he said exhaling.

"That it was."

"What happened?"

I shrugged, moved to get into a more comfortable position, and winced at the sudden pain. My side and back were still tender as a stubbed toe.

"What really happened?" I said. "I guess I was just thinking."

"Thinking?"

I nodded. MacCafferty did not say anything but just sat watching me, waiting for an explanation.

His stare made me nervous, so I talked fast. "When I was a sophomore in high school, I ran the two-twenty in track. We had a pretty strong half-mile relay team. I was the youngest man on it, but the other three were really strong, and we had a good shot at the state championship. I was the lead-off man. But not because I was the fastest. I had a way of elbowing and bulling my way out of the bunch up at the start that gave us an edge. I didn't deliberately spike anybody, but it was up to them to get out of my way. "I paused.

MacCafferty nodded to indicate he was still listening. "Go ahead."

"But at the state championships, I had never been in competition that strong before. With so much riding on it, I was nervous as a long-tailed cat in a room full of rocking chairs. At the gun I got jostled, and I dropped the goddamn baton and had to run back and pick it up and, Keerist, we came in almost last. The coach was madder than hell. He stormed over to me all red-faced and shouted, 'What the hell were you doing out there, *thinking?*'"

MacCafferty still didn't say anything. Maybe he knew I was trying to con him. He just sat there silently studying me, and I got the definite impression he was only half interested in any explanation of why I crashed. There was something else he was there to do.

"Skipper, what's up?"

MacCafferty was silent a moment, then let it out like a sigh, "Cullen bought it last night."

I immediately remembered my last sight of Cullen, sitting on the edge of his bunk, still half-asleep but worrying about keeping his head down in the cockpit. He must have been almost as frightened of that first night patrol as I was. I started to say something to MacCafferty, but I had difficulty speaking. I had to swallow hard several times to loosen the vise around my throat. "I . . . I'm really lousy luck as a roommate."

Then, because it was the expected question, I asked, "What happened?" Not that it mattered a rat's ass. One secret of life I had learned out on the raft was that one of the least important details of existence is how your ticket to this planet is canceled.

MacCafferty shrugged. "Who the hell knows really. They had him on radar one moment, and the next he was gone. There was no radio transmission. Maybe he had a low-altitude flameout and didn't have a chance to get on the horn. Or maybe he just misread his altimeter or had vertigo. We'll never know. Sometimes, these birds just blow up. A wingman of mine once disappeared in a puff of smoke just doing a tight turn. They figure one of the fuel cells ruptured, causing an explosion, but they don't really know."

MacCafferty rubbed his eyes and then massaged his cheeks with his fingertips in a gesture of infinite weariness. "It happened last night. The helos and tin cans searched all night and this morning, and we didn't find a trace of Cullen, even though we had his position pin-

141

pointed on radar," he said. His voice fairly croaked with fatigue.

For the first time since he had sat down, I took a good look at MacCafferty. I was shocked. His eyes were sunk in his skull in deep shadows, as if heavily mascaraed with sleeplessness or grief.

"When was the last time you slept?" I blurted out.

He shook his head and smiled, the first real smile I had seen, as if the mention of sleep were the first genuine joke I had made. He obviously had not slept either that night I was lost or last night when Cullen was scratched.

"What happens now?" I asked.

"About what?"

"About me, the fact I creamed a plane."

MacCafferty sat slumped in his chair, his shoulders hunched with fatigue, his hands dangling loosely between his legs. The two fingers that held his cigarette were nicotine-stained to the color of burnt umber. Again he did not say anything.

"Will I get a review board?" I prodded him.

"Do you want one?"

"No."

"Then I suggest you get back into an airplane. Look, Charly, you know and I know you ought to get a board of review and be grounded. If this had happened a couple of weeks ago, your ass would be in a sling. But we're playing by combat rules now. Cullen is dead, and so are three or four others. You're alive, and that practically makes you a goddamn hero. And the guys who fished you out of the China Sea are all goddamn heroes too. You get back in the ready room and suit up, and no one is going to have time or the inclination to drum you out. We need every pilot we can get right now."

"What's the situation?"

"No one is saying for sure. The word is that if the ChiComs move on either Quemoy or Matsu, we launch an attack on the mainland."

MacCafferty got slowly to his feet. "There's nothing else I can tell you," he said. "It's your decision." He started to leave, then stopped and turned at the foot of the bed. "You know, Charly, you're still basically a civilian. You can finish your tour any way you want, and still get out of the Navy and go to work on Montgomery

142

Street and make a million dollars, or go back to school and become a lawyer. You can even become an airline pilot and ball stewardesses from coast to coast. But keep in mind one thing. Today, tomorrow, the next day, some other poor bastard who's just as scared and exhausted as you are is going to have to fly that patrol in your place. Because one way or another, it's going to be flown."

I nodded. "Cullen would have wanted it that way."

There was a cutting, sarcastic edge to my voice, and MacCafferty caught it. "What the hell is that supposed to mean?"

How could I explain it to MacCafferty? As a seventeen-year-old plebe at Annapolis, Cullen had taken his oath of allegiance in the marble-vaulted pantheon of Bancroft Hall under Commodore Perry's original battle flag, "Don't Give Up the Ship." The faded blue banner with the crude hand lettering had made a deep impression on him, and not a week went by but somehow he would refer back to that reference point of his life.

"Marty always saw himself as Commodore Perry standing on the flaming deck of the stout brig *Lawrence*," I told MacCafferty. There was still that edge to my voice. "He sincerely believed that it was an honor to die for one's country."

"Then Cullen was a fool in a long line of fools," MacCafferty snapped. "No one ever won anything for his country, or himself, by dying. Dead men are always the losers."

The sharpness of MacCafferty's outburst surprised me into silence. MacCafferty stared at me a moment, then smiled humorlessly. "Annapolis likes to build monuments and make heroes out of dead men, but I'm here to tell you that it's all horseshit. There is only one honor in war and that is to stay alive and kill before you are killed. That's the first and only law. Everything else is a perversion of nature. A lie.

"I'm going to tell you one more thing and then I'm going. It's something the statisticians found out in Korea. Only ten percent of the fighter pilots accounted for ninety percent of the kills and the damage to the enemy. Only ten percent."

MacCafferty looked hard at me, and I nodded. He did not have to say the next line. Either by transfer or attrition, MacCafferty was honing his pilots to that ten percent.

With that, he turned and hobbled off. He pitched from one side of the aisle to the other, occasionally bumping into a bunk. His game leg was apparently giving him a great deal of trouble.

After MacCafferty left, I lay back in bed with my eyes shut. The corpsman who came to take my temperature thought I was asleep and left me alone. I was awake, but I was trying to reach down into myself, searching deeply for some ultimate recognition of who and what I really was. I had to look beyond all the conditioned reflexes and the uniforms and the costume jewelry—through the John Wayne movies, recruiting posters, and barroom bravado—and walk past the dead men that no longer shocked or frightened me. I plunged through all that I had fabricated, or forgotten, to the memory of a red-eyed college boy sitting at a wake, numb with horror and bourbon.

The afternoon Ferrara was killed, I sat in Olson's BOQ room downing straight shots of Old Crow, when suddenly I closed my eyes and saw again the charred hulk hanging by shoulder straps in the wreck. I began to feel sick and sweat heavily.

"What the hell are you going to do," Olson shouted at me. "Sit around and think about it until you get the shakes and wet your pants? We're alive and you're going to get through The Program now. We're going to fly and forget the whole thing. We're really going to forget the whole thing," he swore and pounded his fist on the table.

I had not forgotten. But I had learned that bravery, or at least the control of fear, was simply a well-disciplined lack of imagination. Nancy had accused me of being insensitive. Of being callous. She was always muddling things up with her own hurt feelings, wanting me to shoulder all that emotional baggage women constantly haul about. I was insensitive; I was callous. I admit it, and not without pride. Those traits are the warp and woof of cool nerves. They were a discipline that I had once mastered, but in the past several months, with my heart in constant riot, I had lost it.

In Corpus Christi, the afternoon when Stan Haverman

144

had resigned immediately after the crash, I had simply walked back to the ready room, taken off my flight gear and hung up the equipment for the next day's flight. The nightmare images that festered in the dark outbacks of my mind were forced back, locked there, and never allowed to emerge into the realm of consciousness. And by exercising that discipline, I had gone on to complete The Program.

As far back as I can remember, it had always been referred to as "The Program." It was The Program that I had signed up for in college, and in the end, it was I who had been programed. Looking back, it had been done in ways so seemingly absurd that they were jokes at the time.

PSYCHOLOGICAL TESTING

Answer *yes* or *no:*
1) Would you like to be shipwrecked on a desert island with an interesting companion?

Multiple choice:
2) How would you prefer to spend a free afternoon?
    a) Tinkering with an automobile engine.
    b) Watching a baseball game.
    c) Learning landscape painting.
    d) Attending a symphony concert.

I was checked out enough to know that an All-American jet pilot should prefer baseball, and I marked accordingly. There was a platoon of studious men in Pensacola figuring out correlations between how many MIGs a pilot bagged and how he played Ping-Pong.

The instructor in my first preflight physical training class looked like an anatomical chart for pre-med students, an ancient Greek Olympic champion with the trapezius, pectoralis major, and abdominal muscles jutting and sharply etched as if the skin had been stripped away. He had stood in front of the class, torso bared, dressed only in a pair of white, skin-tight, gymnast's tights, and informed us, "You gentlemen are here because you have demonstrated an aggressive, mesomorphic psychological profile. For the next month, and periodically throughout your flight training, we are going to further test and develop these tendencies."

After some routine chin-ups, push-ups, and sit-ups, we were all given the Step Test. Keeping strict time to a loud, fast metronome, the preflight students had to step up and down a high bench on one leg for five minutes. At first it seemed silly, and I lightly bobbed up and down. But by the third minute, with the drum of the metronome as insistent as a heartbeat, the leg began to tire and then cramp. I finished in agony, the blood pounding in my temples, sobbing for breath.

I vigorously kneaded my thigh to get the cramp out, and looked around. About half the class had dropped out. They were simply assigned to an extra physical training period each day in which they repeated the Step Test. It surprised me how many of the young officers who had trouble with that exercise decided that they really did not want to fly after all and resigned from The Program although their other grades were excellent. It was the same with the obstacle course.

As physical conditioning, its value was questionable. We were allowed to scramble over the knobby log barricades, rope climbs, mazes of pipes, and rough plank walls any way we could, as long as we did it within a certain time limit. I stumbled through the ankle-deep sand at the finish with my shins and forearms skinned and bleeding. Jim Brannon—a slightly built, wiry student with a dark, weasellike head—wrenched his knee so badly jumping from one of the barricades he had to be carried off the course and was on crutches for weeks.

"What the hell does climbing over a goddamn wall have to do with flying a plane?" one of my classmates complained. He was a tall, good-looking athlete who had played varsity basketball at Cal, but he couldn't get over the wall.

There were two ways to do it. The first was simply to stop at the bottom, leap up and grab the top edge, and shimmy, kick your legs, horse up with your arms, and generally wrestle yourself over at the expense of a great deal of skin and a painfully mashed groin. The second method—which I used—was to run at the wall full tilt, hit it high with a foot, and spring up, awkwardly vaulting and scrambling over.

Driving off base after classes late one afternoon near the end of the preflight course, I spotted the basketball player in his sweatsuit working out alone on the obstacle course. The track was laid out in a grove of Southern pines, and the setting sun slanting weakly through the trees silhouetted him. Something in his stance caught me, and I quietly stopped the car to watch.

He charged the wall as if to vault it, but somehow misstepped and, instead, crashed right into it. He didn't appear hurt. In fact, he almost seemed to have expected it. He stood off from the wall a moment, studying the top, and then jumped up to grab it, struggling to pull himself up. He managed to throw one foot over the edge, but apparently did not have enough strength in his arms to pull himself all the way over. His spasmodic thrusts just made his body swing out and back into the wall of planks with a hollow thud. He hung on a little while, arms spread, with one foot hooked over the top and the other dangling, as if some giant hand had simply flung him against the wall. Slowly the foot came down, and he hung on by his fingertips until they too slipped and he slid off and just sat in the sand at the bottom. I drove off, for some reason feeling uncomfortable and embarrassed, without his being aware I had been watching. I was not at all surprised to hear, a few days later, that the basketball player had resigned.

The last week of preflight course, Brannon, the weaselly little guy with the wrenched knee, wrapped it tightly in an Ace bandage, took four Bufferin to ease the pain, and ran, hobbled, and lurched through the obstacle course on sheer guts. He made it in the time limit and collapsed at the end.

After preflight, the physical training stopped, and the last trial came as a shock, almost an indignity. We had moved on to Saufley Field by that time, and we had all successfully soloed. We were pilots at last, in our own estimations at least. But the Navy had always demanded more than just the ability to fly. Out of the blue, the base commander ordered all the flight students on a five-mile run about the base the next day. There had not been any sort of organized physical training for months.

The evening of the announcement a large group

gathered in the officers' club after dinner to bitch over their beers.

"It's sheer stupidity. It doesn't make any goddamn sense."

"I'll bet someone has a heart attack. In all this heat."

"I'm not going to do it. I'm just not going to show up. What can they do to me?"

"How about a court-martial?"

"They can't force a Navy officer to run like that . . . can they?"

But there was a current of resignation underlying the chatter. I saw more than one man pull out his cigarettes, study the pack a moment, and then put it away without lighting up.

"Another round?"

"Thanks, but I think I'll just nurse this one for a bit."

The morning of the run was the sun-searing start to a blazingly hot, merciless Florida day. The officers all lined up on the baking runway in a rummage sale of sports clothes and athletic gear. The one who was planning to have the heart attack and sue the Navy wore a pair of defiant red madras Bermudas. We had to run around the entire perimeter of the landing area, and as I looked across that vast plain, the distant boundaries of the field melted and swirled in the heat waves. "I'm definitely going to have a heart attack," the madras Bermudas assured me. He seemed to relish the thought with a sort of malevolent cheer.

On impulse, I sought out the weasel, Brannon, and decided to follow him. He started off in an easy, determined trot. Most of the runners dashed out ahead of us, but by the time we hit the first turn at the corner of the field, they began to fall behind, and several had already begun to walk.

The weasel stuck to his relentless pace, which at first had seemed so casual. By the halfway marker, the salt sweat scaled my eyes and a bone-deep fatigue had set in. I concentrated on the small soles unremittingly turning up and down ahead of me. The momentum and the hypnotic effect of the rhythm kept me moving. My lungs were burning and the cramps in my calves made each stride a shock, but if I stopped to walk a while I felt I would never be able to lift those leaden legs and start running again.

It was not a race, but at the finish I sprinted past the weasel and came in just behind the ex-Ivy League boxing titleholder and a Marine first lieutenant who both made a fetish of staying in shape. Close behind me came an officer who a decade later did his jogging on the moon. Once I stopped, I could hardly stand up, and for the next two weeks could not walk without stabbing pains in my calves. Behind me, like the stragglers and also-rans at the tail end of a Boston marathon, staggered the others. All of them—the boozers, the heavy smokers with cigarette hacks, the ones who bitched like draftees, and the ones who were going to refuse to run out of principle—all had made the run and somehow or other completed it in the time limit. Which was all the Navy had ever really wanted from us, now or then.

At the moment, a great many of us were poised on carriers at launch stations surrounding Red China and Russia. It seemed as if all the games of my youth had unerringly escalated to this contest in the Taiwan Straits. At some point, perhaps after Ferrara's death, I might have said the hell with it and walked away. But at some unannounced moment, I had passed a personal point of no return. If I turned my back on the man I had striven to be, then who was I? No, I had to play the game out.

That was how I made my decision—not out of fear, or courage, or patriotism, or morality. It was a simple matter of identity.

I eased out of bed and hobbled to the head. There I showered, soaped, and shampooed every millimeter of my body as if performing a purification rite. Then I soaked long under the smoking water—working to loosen up the aching bruise of my back and buttocks in the steam heat—until my flesh was as red as watermelon meat.

When I demanded my clothes, the medical corpsman looked startled and immediately trotted off to summon the head flight surgeon, a burly captain with the bedside manner of a boatswain's mate.

"Absolutely nothing doing. Get your ass back in bed. I want you flat on your behind for a week."

"I'm as rested as I'll ever be."

"Forget it. Back in bed."

149

I stood my ground. "Captain, last night my roommate Marty Cullen got killed flying my patrol. Tonight, someone else who is already punchy from flying too much is going to have to double up and take my flight if I don't."

It was not exactly the truth, but the surgeon nodded solemnly. He stood silent a moment, then asked, "How's your back feel?"

"It's stiff and it aches, but I can move around. It's not going to heal faster sitting on my ass in a bed than in a cockpit. But I'd appreciate something for the pain."

The surgeon nodded solemnly again, then turned to the corpsman. "Get someone to bring the hero here his clothes," he said in a tough voice. "I'll get you some pills to take," he added, and walked back toward his office.

The corpsman looked at me quizzically, and I winked at him.

Red Lucas brought down my gear, waited while I dressed, and together we went up to the ready room to face MacCafferty.

16

Did medical clear you?" MacCafferty asked.

"Yes, sir."

MacCafferty stared at me, his face stiff and expression-ess, the whites of his eyes yellowed with fatigue. Finally e asked in a hard voice, "Do you think you can remem-er that the proper approach speed for the Chance /ought F-8 Crusader is one hundred and thirty-five nots, not one fifty-five?"

"Yes, sir, I'm not about to forget it."

"How soon will you be ready?"

"As long as it takes to suit up."

MacCafferty examined me silently for a moment and 1en turned away toward the schedule board. "Okay. ake the fourteen-thirty launch instead of Tallman. Two-ero-seven should be up by then."

"Yes, sir."

That was all that was said.

I was, quite frankly, something less than confident bout that first rematch with the Fates. I suited up, rapped in, and took off with butterflies in my gut the ze of pterodactyls.

Above the overcast, it was bright and clear. The tops f the clouds below were like a snowy mountain plateau, eeply shadowed and etched with secret caves, overhangs, nd ravines. Beneath that overcast, off my right wing, the ed guns on the Chinese mainland were pouring 50,000 ounds of high-explosive shells a day on Quemoy Island. line of supply ships convoyed by American warships eamed in and out of that circle of flames, and off my left ing in the Pacific just east of Taiwan the whole Seventh leet was now gathering. But above the clouds I found, 1at day, a fragile peace. No Red Chinese phantoms ap-

peared to haunt me, and for once I managed to keep m
own personal spooks in check and concentrate on flying.

By the time I approached the ship, the butterflies in m
stomach had settled, and I swooped down to buzz th
Russian trawler.

The trawler had materialized in the carrier's wake th
previous evening as a greasy smudge of black diese
smoke, hull down on the horizon. In that troubled sea
hard and dark as obsidian, the converted tuna boat fishe
for information. It wallowed in the carrier's overboar
garbage, scooping up the floating gobs of creame
chipped beef as if it were ambergris. The Russia
crewmen poked through the slop, tin cans, and potat
peelings for any paper scraps of intelligence inadvertentl
discarded. Special electronic equipment aboard th
trawler eavesdropped on the carrier's radio and radar sig
nals and tracked each flight as it launched and returned t
the carrier. There was nothing to be done about it. A
long as we were not at war with Russia, its ships enjoye
the same freedom of the high seas that our warships did.

That morning, however, the game quickened. When th
carrier wheeled about into the wind to land aircraft, th
Russian trawler suddenly changed course to a collisio
heading, forcing the carrier to abort the recovery. Th
next time the trawler positioned itself on a collision cours
with the carrier, one of the destroyers peeled off from th
carrier's starboard quarter and unflinchingly placed itsel
between the trawler and carrier to take the collision. Th
Russian ship backed down and cruised back to its positio
in the carrier's wake, collecting garbage.

Now, as each plane returned from its patrol, it made a
low-level, mock strafing run on the Russian. In the read
room, a betting pool started. Everyone would kick in ter
dollars to whomever buzzed closest to the Russian ship
although we never specified who would judge the winner
It was a dangerous game, and thoroughly illegal, but no
word came down to knock it off.

I made a strafing pass at the trawler, swooping in a
masthead level at a right angle to the ship. Then I imme
diately made a three-quarter circle ahead of the ship so
that when I leveled out I was flying head-on at th
trawler, flat-hatting just off the waves. I came in at th
ship below the bridge level like a kamikaze, and only a

the last possible moment did I touch the stick to swoop up and past the bridge. As I blasted by the deck, I saw several Russian crewmen waving their hats at me.

When I plunked aboard the carrier, Hooks Lewis radioed me, "Now that's the way ah taught ya. That's a good ole boy."

When I got back to the stateroom, Red Lucas was stretched out on his bunk. I had moved in with Lucas, rather than bunk with Cullen's ghost.

"How'd it go?"

"I'm back in the saddle again."

"Back where a friend is a friend." Lucas hauled himself out of his bunk. "How's about a drink to celebrate before dinner?"

"Terrific."

"Martini?"

"You got ice?"

"I got everything aboard here but women." Lucas slid open a drawer underneath his bunk to reveal a modest bar from which he selected a bottle of Beefeater and two old-fashioned glasses. Then he opened the steel wardrobe locker on the floor of which, cached among his boots, shoes, and flight equipment, was a small refrigerator.

Lucas broke out an ice tray and a small jar of olives.

"Hey, I really buzzed that trawler."

"Yeah," Red said absently, as he mixed the drinks.

"What I did was, I flat-hatted straight down his throat right off the waves. That Russian captain was looking *down* at me when I finally peeled off right in front of him."

Red handed me my drink and eyed me questioningly. "That's a little hairy, isn't it?"

I nodded. "Yeah. But I'll tell you something, Red. After the past couple of days, it just felt good to be in control again."

Lucas raised his glass to toast. "Welcome back, Charly," he boomed.

"Thanks, Red." I drank, winced, and thumped my chest. "Now that's a martini," I said appreciatively. "The thing is, welcome back to what?"

"It's a weird operation, that's for sure."

"Lot of guys getting killed."

"It's going to happen whether they actually shoot at

153

you or not in an operation like this," Lucas said offhandedly. He sipped his drink. "Hell, in Korea we lost more men and planes in operational accidents aboard carriers than we did to the gook gunfire and MIGs."

"Is that a fact?"

"That's a fact."

We knocked off our drinks and went to dinner. The pilots flying the patrol now lived in their flight suits, and we were segregated in an auxiliary wardroom, aft of the formal main dining room where dress blue uniforms and ties were still being required at dinner.

But among the pilots all military formalities were being dropped as the patrol wore on. Around the pilots' tables, the strain of round-the-clock flying was increasingly visible. Several of the faces opposite me had, in just the past few days, become noticeably tense and haggard. A few were sitting down to dinner still unshaven. The men flopped wearily in their chairs still wearing their sweat- and grease-stained flight coveralls, each with the inevitable knife scabbard stitched to the right leg. Many still toted their thirty-eights and their chest bandoleers of bullets. In all, we looked like a gang of bandits breaking bread.

Chub Harris looked up at me and frowned, "Hey, Charly, I'm trying to run a nice peaceable-type saloon here. You're supposed to check your gun with the girl at the door."

"That's no girl. It's the Filipino steward. You've been out at sea too long, fellow."

"Haven't we all."

On the table were a stack of mimeographed, stapled sheets with the latest news bulletins. Lucas picked one up, studied it intently, and then suddenly read aloud in his deep, kettledrum voice, "In Peking, the Supreme State Council had an emergency meeting and ordered a general mobilization of China's 600 million people for, quote, the struggle against war provocation by the American imperialists, unquote."

Lucas looked up to see if we were listening, then glanced down at the paper and read aloud the next item, "The official Soviet government newspaper *Izvestia* reported yesterday that if the United States attacked Red China, Russia would assist Peking with, quote, everything at its disposal, unquote. Sheeit. We're going to get our-selves into an ay-tomic war over those two-bitty gook is-lands."

"They just wiped out another one of Chiang's landing ships on the beach. A total loss," someone volunteered. "It's just a matter of time before their artillery *accidentally* pops one of our ships and then all hell will break loose."

"It may anyways. Chiang wants to bomb the main-land." Everybody looked up. Steinberg, our air intelli-gence officer, sat down at the end of the table. He was wearing washed khakis as if he had just come from a briefing, and was using that as an excuse to eat with the pilots rather than in the formal main wardroom.

Steinberg arranged his silverware, then picked up the mimeographed sheet and glanced at it, as if he already knew in detail what was on it but was merely checking to see if anything new might have been added. Everyone waited for him to finish and elaborate. Steinberg was a lieutenant junior grade and no older that I was, but his tall, thin, slightly stooped figure emanated an air of tough intelligence. He had been a graduate student and teaching assistant in political science at Stanford when he dropped out to join the Navy and see the real world. But he had already mastered a good professor's way of capturing a group's attention. He looked up and gave Red Lucas a sardonic smile. "The Generalissimo is an impatient man. He does not believe we can hold Quemoy with bigger and better convoys. He argues the convoys can never be made big enough to get through the Red barrage and keep Que-moy supplied. The old Kuomintang war lord is insisting to Washington that the only solution is to knock out the Communist guns with planes. He claims the Nationalist Air Force can do the job by themselves. He doesn't need our help . . . just our permission."

"Why?"

"Well, that's the schnitzel. If the Nationalists bomb the mainland, then the Communists are perfectly within their rights to retaliate and attack Taiwan. Of course, we are, by treaty, committed to defend Taiwan. And our policy now is if Communist aircraft attack Taiwan, U.S. planes are to follow in hot pursuit all the way to the mainland, even bomb their bases. The air bases in Red China are not to be sanctuaries anymore, as they were in Korea."

"Well, that'll be it then, won't it?" Lucas said gruffly. His thick face and heavy jaw were solemn, and his eyes never left Steinberg's.

Steinberg nodded.

Jack Tallman spoke. "Well, goddamn it, the Reds have said all along that the shelling is just the build-up to an attack on Quemoy and Matsu, and then on Taiwan. Maybe we ought to believe them. I don't know what in hell we're waiting for. For the Russians to drop on us first? Then it'll be too late. We ought to launch right now and wipe out their military capability while we still have the edge on them. That's what MacCafferty thinks we should do. And you can bet that a lot of the top brass thinks so, too. I don't know why we're stalling around. Goddamn politicians is what it is."

"Tallman, spare me your war-mongering on an empty stomach," I snapped irritably.

Tallman looked startled, then angry. He was a senior lieutenant and junior officers did not snap at him.

"Who the hell do you think you're talking to, Mister?"

"Tallman. Shut up," Lucas broke in with a voice that rumbled like faraway thunder. "Just shut up." Lucas did not look up, but kept his eyes on the table, both thick, mottled hands lying quietly on either side of his plate, not touching his utensils.

Tallman stared at Lucas a moment. "Well, that's what they said they were going to do," he said, then looked around the table importantly. He got no response and fell to eating his soup.

After dinner, Lucas and I both headed back to our stateroom. Lucas immediately stripped to his shorts, then sat on the edge of his bunk and reached down between his legs to the bar drawer beneath the bunk. He pulled out a new bottle of Scotch and broke the seal.

"A shot?" he asked.

I shook my head, "No, thanks," and began pacing back and forth like a caged cat.

"What time's your patrol?"

"About one this morning."

"You must have the one right after me."

"I'll wave when I pass you in the Straits."

"They're packing us boom-boom one right after the other, all right." He poured about two fingers of Scotch into a glass and began sipping it straight.

Just then the compartment shook as a catapult fired on the flight deck above us.

"You planning on getting any sleep before your flight?" Lucas asked.

"I might try." I picked up a magazine on the bureau, glanced at it, and threw it down.

Lucas took another sip of Scotch. "Bucko, there ain't nothing you or I can do about it, one way or the other. Big wars, little wars, it all boils down to whether you get your personal ass blown off or not. The ticket is not to think about it."

"What do you think about?"

"Your family, women, anything else but flying and little wars and big wars." Lucas took another sip of Scotch. "Everything go okay today, Charly?"

"Terrific. No problems."

Lucas nodded. "At night. That's when it gets to you. Not up there. You're too busy then to think about it or feel it. It hits you when you're alone at night, ready to drop off to sleep. This *fear*. That's the only word for it. And it builds and builds and builds. That's what happened with Scholl. MacCafferty did the right thing. He saved Scholl's life by grounding him. I saw it happen that way with a roommate in Korea and sure enough, bammo, two days later he was killed."

Lucas took another slow deliberate sip of Scotch, and then looked up directly at me. "What you do, Bucko, is live one day at a time. You fly, you eat, you sleep, and you drink."

Lucas raised his glass to me. "You do a lot of drinking. Because if you don't, you are not going to sleep. All the goddamn news and the scuttlebutt and all the goddamn bad flights you ever had and the guys you knew ever had are all churning around in your head like a cement mixer."

"I know what you're saying, Red, I've just been there."

"Have you now?"

"Oh, yeah."

"What happened?"

"Everything I was afraid of happening happened. I
157

spun, crashed, and burned. Had to eject into the black-ass night in the middle of nowhere and damn near drowned and froze to death. And now I'm here to tell you about it with nothing but an aching bruise on my behind."

"You going to make it okay now?"

I shrugged.

"I'll tell you what you do now, Bucko. What you do is take two, three good belts of Scotch, then sleep like a baby, and you'll be up in a few hours ready to go for one more day."

I nodded. "You're right, Red. You got enough booze to get us both through a war." I took the Scotch he poured for me.

"Hell, I always come aboard a carrier with a combat load. It's as vital as the ammo and the bandages."

I stretched out in my bunk with an ash tray balanced on my chest, smoking, sipping my three fingers of Scotch as Lucas had done, quietly courting sleep.

The crash and clamor of the carrier now booming full steam ahead with the twilight launches kept me from dropping off. From the pillow, my eyes settled on the big Kodacolor photo on my bureau. Nancy the WestPac widow. The letter with her formal request for the divorce came with the first mail upon our arrival in Japan, but still I did not take down her picture. The lush sunburned look of her, the swarm of copper hair and the laughing, green-flecked eyes, haunted me, and made other women seem as if they belonged to a lesser, drabber strain.

The image of Nancy's legs about another man's thighs, his hairy paunch heaving on her silken belly, had often come to me at night like a fever, making my blood throb with anger. And once in that anger, I had almost killed a man in Japan. Now as the Scotch seeped through my veins, the memory of it was just another sordid fact of my life, and death.

17

Just across from the main gate of the U.S. Naval Base at Yokosuka, Japan, a kaleidoscope-colored neon arch announcing "Broadway Avenue" spanned the width of a side street like an electric rainbow. Square in the center, at the highest point of the arch, snapped, popped, and crackled a red and blue neon Statue of Liberty.

Hooks Lewis and I, already three sheets to the wind from our dallying at the base officers' club, sailed under the arch into "Thieves Alley." The narrow street was no wider than a carnival midway, and bars crowded in on both sides. They had names like amusement park rides— The H-Bomb, The Jet, The Playmate Pen, Heaven & Hell, San Diego. From all sides hand-lettered sandwich boards pitched "Biggest Drinks and Biggest Bosoms in Town," "Hot Sexest Girls," or "Brown Baggers, Come In and Suffer!" Sailors jammed the street, wandering from concession to concession. Hur*ray,* Hur*ray,* Hur*ray.* Step right up there, sailor. There was a frantic, carnival pulse, as if the whole street would be taken down in the dark, quiet hours before sunup and loaded aboard trucks, leaving just a windy, paper-strewn vacant lot in its place.

An enormous red and blue neon sign bawled out "Cabaret Black Rose." Hooks and I lurched in. A group of glossy bargirls in cocktail dresses sat at several tables near the entrance, preening themselves and cooing in quiet coveys like pigeons waiting to be fed.

As I leaned against the bar, looking the girls over, I heard my name called out from across a great reach of time. "Rohr! Ensign Rohr! Hey Rohr, front and center."

There were several Marine officers in uniform at a nearby table, and one of them was waving excitedly at me. I could see the Marines clearly but nothing about them registered, and then gradually, as if looking at some-

159

one a good distance away through binoculars that slowly focused, I recognized Olson, my old flight instructor from Pensacola.

"Hey, it *was* you," Olson yelled in that high-pitched adolescent voice of his. "Goddamn. I thought I recognized you. How about that!" He was pretty excited about running into me, and insisted that Hooks and I join them, scurrying around pulling over chairs. There were two other Marines in Olson's gang, with three of the Japanese bargirls seated among them.

"How about that!" Olson exclaimed again, after we were all seated. "It's funny. I was just thinking about you the other day." He nudged one of the other Marines, who was talking in a low, intimate voice to one of the girls. "Hey Vinnie, this is that student of mine I once told you about. The one whose best buddy creamed in, and I got him drunk and back up in a plane before he had a chance to think about it."

Vinnie glanced up at me, looking slightly annoyed at the interruption, and mumbled, "Oh, yeah," without much interest.

"Hey, what're you doing now?" Olson asked eagerly.

"I'm laundry and morale officer on a tanker," I said.

"Hey, come on," Olson scoffed and jabbed me in the arm. "I ran into somebody who told me you were flying F-8's."

I grunted an acknowledgment.

"Way to go! Goddamn!" Olson exclaimed, puffing up with a certain pride. He jabbed Vinnie. "I taught this son of a gun how to fly formation."

Vinnie, whose girl had just lit his cigar, turned and squinted at me through bursts of cigar smoke. His face was brutal: a thick, hooked poleax of a nose, dark, narrow eyes, and a complexion pocked with the acne scars of an ugly adolescence. His jet-black hair was clipped so short that his head showed more white scalp than hair, and his ears jutted out like thick jug handles. Yet there was a dangerous tension that held all the features together that made him striking, possibly even attractive to some women. He looked at me across the table with an even, entirely impersonal expression of faint challenge.

"Hey, you remember Ferrara's old gal friend?" Olson suddenly asked. "Cute little gal with big boobs."

"Nancy?" I turned back to Olson.

"Yeah, that's the one. I ran into her in San Diego. Goddamndest thing. She knew all about me. I mean she knew that I had been your instructor and Ferrara's and she was all over me." A knowing, carnal smirk twisted Olson's features. "A real pretty piece, but she was a little drunk that night."

"She doesn't drink," I said, suddenly very confused.

"She talked about you and Ferrara quite a bit. Funny thing though, I mean strange, half the time she was mixed up about which of you was which, like even who was dead. She seemed pretty screwed up. But, you know, really a nice girl. I mean to talk to and to look at." Olson frowned, his pale eyebrows knotting in puzzlement.

"San Diego and Pensacola are full of cunts like that," Vinnie snorted. "They don't remember who they're sleeping with half the time." He reached around and gave the girl next to him a hug that was at once possessive and contemptuous.

The faces and sounds kept moving in and out of focus as if someone were playing with the adjustment of the binoculars through which I was observing things.

"Where y'all stationed at?" Hooks asked, and his voice startled me. I had forgotten he was there. I kept thinking we were all back at Trader Jon's in Pensacola.

"Kaneohe, Havahii," Olson answered. "We just got scrambled out here on this here alert. We're headed for Okinawa, but we're holed up here waiting for the weather to break. It's socked in around there thicker 'n shit. Hey, what do you guys hear about what's going on in the Taiwan Straits?"

"Not one helluva lot," Lewis said, shaking his head.

"Goddamn!" Olson broke out excitedly. "Maybe we're really going to see some real action, huh? Combat maybe. I tell ya we're going to lose face with these gooks if we don't quit playing games and screwing around. The only thing they understand for sure is force." He punctuated the sentence with a hard rap on the table with his knuckles.

I stared at him a moment, then said, "Inside all that gyrene bullshit, there really is a mean little kid who dreams of being a killer, isn't there?" It came out nastier than I had meant it.

Olson looked back at me with a puzzled, almost hurt expression.

"That's what we've been goddamn trained for," Vinnie snapped. He leaned forward, facing me head-on, his face flushed and his black eyes thickly veined with blood.

Suddenly all the confused anger roiling around my guts focused and zeroed in on a target. I smiled at Vinnie, then laughed. *"Sheeit!"* I turned to Hooks. "Harry Truman was one hundred percent right about the Corps. The gyrenes got bullshit coming right out their ears."

Vinnie leaned in closer to me, half rising out of his chair, the muscles of his jaw knotting big as walnuts.

"Hey, for Chrissakes, knock it off, huh?" Olson beseeched us. "Let's just have a good time. He's one of my old students," he appealed to Vinnie.

"He sure as hell has a hell of a lot more to learn," Vinnie growled, not taking his black, hooded eyes off me.

I grinned back at him and said, "Sorry, no offense," and at the same time reached down and deliberately overturned a drink into Vinnie's lap.

He sprang up, almost knocking over the table, and lunged at me. I was up, feet planted, waiting for him, and I drove my fist right between his eyes. All my weight and mean-drunk anger behind that fist collided head-on with the full momentum of the Marine's charge.

He stopped cold, he staggered, his feet tangled in a tumbled chair, and he went down in an explosion of furniture, glasses and beer bottles.

The other Marine with Olson came at me, and Hooks grabbed a chair and swung it between us, thrusting it first at me and then at the Marine like a panicky lion tamer. "Now break it up, you guys, ya hear? Break it up!"

Suddenly, Vinnie was on his feet, looming at me. *Jeezus*, he was big. I hadn't noticed before, but he was half a head taller than me. He flung a table out of the way and charged me. I backed up and managed to block a right and then a left, and he drove me right into a wall. I bounced off and tied up his hands, but he slammed me back into the wall, crashing me against it as if he were trying to beat me to death.

His size and his wildness panicked me. I brought both hands up and clapped them hard over his ears. The concussion of the air exploding against both ear drums stunned him. It was the dirtiest defensive blow I had been taught in football. It is seldom used, because it can burst a man's eardrums. Now I did it instinctively, in desperation.

Vinnie reeled back, letting me go. I hit him, one two, with everything I had. The son of a bitch hardly flinched, but crouched down covering up with both arms, weaving as if he were about to explode into me again.

I stepped back and groped around for a chair to hit him with. But Vinnie got his hand on a long-necked beer bottle first and swung it like a club right at my head. It caught me on the thick muscle at the base of the neck. An inch higher, and it would have split my skull; an inch to the left, probably shattered my collarbone. A searing paralysis shot through my left shoulder and arm, and I went down.

I caught myself on my hands and came up fast, bringing my right fist up hard and low, like a lineman does when the game has gotten vicious and dirty and the referees have lost control. My fist caught the Marine square between the legs.

Vinnie let out a horrible animal noise, as if his bowels were coming out his throat, clutched at his groin and dropped to his knees.

"Are you crazy? Are you out of your fucking mind?" Olson screamed at me.

"Good God, boy, what you go and do that for?" Hooks shouted and grabbed me from behind, locking his skinny arms around me.

"That fucker was going to kill me," I shouted back angrily, trembling but not struggling in Hooks' restraint.

Vinnie was sprawled on his hands and knees sobbing for breath. Even then his arms and legs were struggling to push him up, but the muscles did not quite have the strength.

"Did you have to hit 'm in the balls?" Hooks blurted out, genuinely shocked.

Over our shouting back and forth now rose another voice, high-pitched and insistent as a siren. A Japanese man, apparently the club manager, stood behind us yelling about the Shore Patrol and then took off for the door.

"Man, we all ought to get out of here," Hooks said to the other two Marines. "Afore we find our ass in the brig." He helped them get Vinnie to his feet. "He shouldn't have hit Charly with a beer bottle," he said placatingly. "He oughtn't of done that in a friendly fight."

Vinnie was still in pain, gasping for his breath. It had all happened so suddenly that the other customers and the hostesses were staring at us in a stunned silence. The two Marines headed for the door, supporting Vinnie who jelly-legged between them.

Outside, the manager was screaming for the Shore Patrol. The three Marines tumbled into the only cab in sight. At the end of the street, there were two uniformed figures coming toward us, and Hooks and I started walking fast in the opposite direction.

We turned the first corner we came to and, without a word between us, broke into a run. We ran for two blocks, ducking around each corner we came to, until Hooks started stumbling and giggling, and then we stopped and collapsed against a brick wall, both of us panting. I was soaked with sweat, and there was blood trickling down my neck from a laceration in my scalp where the Marine had banged me against the wall. I moaned and sank down to the sidewalk and leaned against the bricks.

"You okay?" Hooks asked anxiously. "You break anything?"

"All the National Collegiate Athletic Association rules."

"Ah swear, Charly boy," Hooks gasped. "Y'all gonna be the death of me yet. Thazza fact."

"I believe it. Goddamn. Whorehouses and knock-down-drag-out barroom brawls. I'm really coming up in the world."

18

The carrier steam-rollered through a foam-flecked sea, effortlessly crushing beneath its bow the blue-gray waves that themselves looked cold and hard as steel. Overhead, great rags of clouds flapped southeast, harbingers of the dirtier weather now blowing down from Siberia.

In late afternoon, a light cruiser and four destroyers rendezvoused with the carrier. The destroyers immediately deployed ahead in a screen, their sonar pinging for submarines.

A few miles to the south, invisible in a squall, the carrier *Princeton,* with its squadrons of antisubmarine hunter-killer planes and a task force of six destroyers, moved into stalking position.

That day, a few days after my crash into the East China Sea, MacCafferty chose to test me. Ostensibly, we were on a test hop to check out the missile systems on two planes that had been repaired, but it was really me that MacCafferty was testing.

In the ready room, the squadron commander briefed me in a dry, bored voice without removing the cold cigar butt clenched in his teeth. "Okay, you take forty thousand feet, and I'll play at forty-two. Keep that separation until you have a position eyeball on me. Remember to set your altimeter on the deck. After launch, just head west and let the controller set you up for the attack run. The ship is your target. I'll play the interceptor for the first few runs. After a while, we'll switch roles. Just concentrate on checking out the radar and missile system in the air-to-ground attack mode. Make sure you get positive locks on target. Then when we switch roles, do the same thing in the air-to-air mode, using me as the target."

I nodded my head.

He glanced at the aircraft status board at the front of

the ready room. "You take two-zero-eight. I'll be in two-zero-four," and he was through the door without waiting for an acknowledgment.

I caught up with him on the flight deck and fell into step on his left side. MacCafferty strode across the deck and, in spite of his pronounced gimp, the thick heels of his boots rang on the armor plating like horseshoes. He rolled heavily from side to side with his hands swinging out as if to fight off interference.

My plane was parked alongside the island, tied down, its wings folded overhead, out of the way. The jet had just been topped off with fuel, and the plane captain was completing his check. I yanked a small cloth cover off the plane's Pitot tube and threw it to him. "What are you trying to do, kill me!" I shouted over the whining and roar of the aircraft all around.

"I'm just finishing up," the crewman shouted back. "I was just getting to that."

"I hope the hell you were," I yelled back and ducked under the jet into the landing gear recesses to check the hydraulic lines. But the covered Pitot tube still worried me. The air-speed indicator worked off the pressure in the Pitot tube, and with it covered the gauge would not work. Without exact air speeds to fly, it is fatal to try to land a jet aboard a carrier. The flight deck crew was getting punchy from the day-and-night grind of the patrol. They were starting to make the little mistakes that kill men. I made a slow methodical walk around the plane to check for anything else inadvertently plugged, misplaced, or bent that might conceivably kill me.

I glanced over toward MacCafferty's plane. The squadron commander had already mounted, and now stood one foot in the cockpit, gripping the canopy with one hand, cradling his helmet in the other. With squinty eyes he seemed to be searching among the clouds, wistfully, for the contrails of an enemy he could engage in battle.

I scrambled up to the cockpit and squeezed down into the thicket of hardware. I attached the clips of my torso suit to the ejection seat and then plugged in the rubber tube from the G-suit, which dangled from my waist like a severed umbilical cord, and the oxygen and radio lines.

Then, with a sharp pronging gesture, I signaled the

crewmen on the flight deck to plug in the auxiliary power unit. A shrill, electric whine thickened to a howl as the turbine fired.

I went about the cockpit flipping switches, wiggling controls, setting dials, knocking off the long list of post-starting procedures engraved on a plate on the instrument panel. A flight deck director, using hand signals like a traffic cop, guided me out of the chocks, and I taxied gingerly through the maze of aircraft and tractor equipment to a position right behind the catapult. The wings unfolded and stretched out taut, trembling in the gale that whipped across the deck. I rolled forward onto the catapult.

Once airborne, I banked west in a steep, almost perpendicular, climb. On the radio, I could hear the ship's controller directing MacCafferty into position.

"Homeland. This is Charger Eight," I called, keying my mike button. "Airborne and climbing out on a heading of two-eight-zero degrees . . . Passing through twenty thousand . . . Over."

An immediate answer rasped through my earphones. "Roger, Charger Eight. This is Homeland. Take Angels four-two. Over."

I leveled off at 42,000 feet. As the plane quickly built up speed, the noise of the engine receded farther and farther back until there was only the hum of the cockpit compressor and the shush of the air friction on the canopy. At that point, flight becomes silky smooth, the plane responds to a touch of the controls, and the turns are quick and tight. A Chance Vought F-8 is designed for the upper ranges of sky and speed, an in-between world this side of outer space and on the other side of sound. There it floated that day, without a quiver, as if it were mounted in the deep blue interior of a diamond. Up above, beyond earth, that fathomless blue deepened to absolute night, and down below, it faded to the dirty, gray, curving line of scud smothering the horizon and most of the sea.

A metallic voice suddenly crackled in my headphones, directing me to turn toward the carrier. I threw the Crusader into a bank and switched on the missile guidance system to the air-to-ground attack mode, then adjusted the radar scan. I flew with my face pressed to the hooded scope. The yellow-green wand of light flicked

167

restlessly back and forth, illuminating the screen but leaving no telltale blip to indicate my target—the carrier. I was still out of range.

Over the radio, I could hear the controller maneuvering MacCafferty to intercept me. "Bogey at two-four-five degrees, sixty-five miles. Turn left to two-three-five."

"Roger. Turning left to two-three-five," MacCafferty responded crisply.

An anonymous controller, who saw MacCafferty's jet and mine only as yellow-green blips on a cathode-ray tube in a gloomy steel-bound compartment of the ship, now maneuvered our planes as a child moves toy cavalry across a game board.

MacCafferty was still a great distance away, completely out of sight, but we were intimately connected by the thick, rasping sound of each other's breathing during the heavy pauses between words, sucking up and exhaling oxygen past the mikes built into our face masks. The noise of it roared in my head.

"Your bogey at two-four-zero, sixteen miles," the controller said. "Continue turn to two-three-zero." The shipboard controller was pointing MacCafferty toward my attack until the interceptor's own radar, more limited than that of the ship, could pick up the plane.

I was busy working my own radar to locate the ship, and both of us flew head down with our eyes glued to the scopes and instruments.

"Contact at two-three-zero, twelve miles," MacCafferty reported.

"Roger, that is your bogey," confirmed the controller. MacCafferty now had my plane on radar and could work out his own intercept.

Almost simultaneously, a blip, shimmering like a drop of ectoplasm, developed at the top of my scope. It was at the range I estimated the carrier and, with the toggle switch, I maneuvered the target cross hairs on to the blip.

"Judy!" MacCafferty called out. His missile control system was locked on, automatically tracking me and computing the kill. "Bird away!" shouted MacCafferty.

But I was now also locked on target. "Standing by to release," I reported. My finger hesitated a moment over the button, and then jammed down.

But neither MacCafferty nor I were carrying missiles

that day. And after several more mock runs, in which I pulverized the carrier and MacCafferty annihilated me, we switched roles. I played the interceptor, while MacCafferty—on the attack—feinted, jinked, made tricky, sharp turns and sudden, porpoising changes of altitude to confuse my radar. He was a beautiful runner. But his elaborate maneuvers could only delay the inevitable outcome. In the end, I—or rather the hardware—nailed him every time.

After we had shot each other down a half-dozen times—I had not actually seen MacCafferty's plane once except for the blip on radar—the squadron commander called for a change in tactics. "I have you in sight, Charly. I'll pull up on your wing, and we'll joust by ourselves a little before we head home."

He was telling me to turn off the radar, the computers, and the automatic target-tracking system and brawl with him in a classic, head-to-head dogfight in which the kill is scored by outmaneuvering and foxing the other plane into your gun sights at close quarters.

I was about to answer that a dogfight would slice it dangerously thin on fuel, but, as if anticipating me, the controller asked for our fuel state. MacCafferty answered up immediately. The figure he reported was several hundred pounds more than my own gauge reading. I turned and looked at him in surprise. He was hovering just a few feet away off my right wing. His sun visor was up, and over his oxygen mask his eyes glared at me, bright and contemptuous with challenge.

MacCafferty always allowed himself smaller margins for safety than other men, and now he was challenging me to accept them also. He was pushing me to the raw edge of skill and nerve. I was to dogfight him and then, win or lose, make a landing aboard with no margin for error. It was a stupid and dangerous game, and I could get out of it simply by stating that I was low on fuel.

I keyed my mike. "Roger, fuel state ..." and I repeated the figure MacCafferty had given.

MacCafferty nodded and slammed down his sun visor, and across that soundless gulf of speed and space between us, I swear I heard the snap.

He immediately banked away, his wings cutting perpendicular to the horizon. I broke sharply in the opposite direction. A moment before we would have been out of sight of one another, we each turned back. We charged head-on, one high and the other low, at such a tremendous closing rate—over 1,200 miles an hour—that his plane was blurred and distorted as it passed under me, bending and elongating like a fish flashing by underwater. The joust had officially begun.

Both planes immediately banked back, cockpit to cockpit, to crisscross each other's paths. Then we reversed to cross again in a series of scissor maneuvers. Our trails weaved about one another like the strands of a rope, and on each tight turn, the G-forces squeezed me like God's fist. The two jets Yo-Yoed up and down, converting a temporary altitude advantage to the next moment's speed advantage, and at each pass MacCafferty seemed to gain a little.

Banking back on the fourth or fifth scissor, I lost sight of him. Then there was a quick flash of sun off silver as MacCafferty, further back than usual, turned toward me. There was now something definitely ominous about our relative motion. MacCafferty was closing in on me, and a cold chill of panic seized me, as if death were really drawing inexorably nearer.

In a dozen subtle tricks I had yet to learn, MacCafferty had played his altitude for speed, and speed for tighter turns. Now he had me sucked into position for an angle shot as we closed. If I turned away, he would pounce right on my tail. I didn't analyze the play. Like a desperate halfback who suddenly sees a two-hundred-pound defensive end about to cut him down, I instinctively knew that I had to turn inside the other man faster and sharper. I dove frantically and banked as steeply as I dared. MacCafferty turned and dove with me. As the plane picked up more speed, I tightened the turn, threading the plane along the boundaries of a high-speed stall that would tumble me right into MacCafferty's line of fire.

But as each aircraft's turning rate increased with speed, irrevocable laws of physics also multiplied the G-forces, torturing both MacCafferty and me to the limits of physical endurance. In a plunging vertical bank, I was being racked by seven, eight times the force of gravity. The flesh of my face felt horribly distended, as if it were smeared clay. Lifting my arm was like raising a lead

170

weight. The blood was being sucked from my brain, and a gray mist surged up past my eyes. I grunted like a pig, squeezing my gut and thigh muscles in on themselves to force back the cloud. What had started as a contest of highly refined tactics and skill now became one of brute muscular endurance. And MacCafferty was just too old to meet the limits set by the thicker, younger slabs of muscle that squeezed the blood back into my brain. Gradually, painfully, MacCafferty had to ease his bank to maintain consciousness, as we closed to within gun range. Through my hazy, blood-starved tunneled vision, I watched his plane slide outside from its initial advantage right into my gun sight cross hairs. I bored in straight at MacCafferty, flashing under and by him, and then swooped up, whirling into a series of ecstatic victory rolls.

"Okay, let's knock it off and go home," MacCafferty ordered, and not even the tinny sound of the radio blunted the sharp edge of rage in his voice. He turned and headed for the carrier without circling a moment to let me join up on his wing. I had to chase him halfway back to the ship before I caught up.

"Let's tighten it up," MacCafferty ordered sharply as we swept down toward the ship. It was the only thing he said on the flight back. Angry or not, he was still pushing me. "Tighter." I eased in, inch by inch, until our wings overlapped only a few feet apart. I had to concentrate totally, blocking out everything else, on an area on MacCafferty's aircraft only a few inches wide. I had to keep my mind focused in that spot, totally detached from the reality that I was flying a few feet away from another aircraft at over six hundred miles an hour.

Locked together like that we blasted down the starboard side of the carrier just above mast level and then swooped up. A few hundred yards ahead of the carrier, MacCafferty broke off, sweeping into a sudden vertical bank into the landing pattern. At interval, I followed him. Turning into the final approach, I checked my fuel. It was low. Very low. If I did not make it down on the first shot, things were going to get hairy. The red landing signal light on the fantail indicated that my approach was too high. I started easing off power a moment before Hooks' voice came up on the radio. The hulking stern rushed up toward me and disappeared somewhere beneath, as I came crashing down on top of it. The hard landing and the violent slam of the stop stunned me.

"Goddamn it all," I heard Lewis reprimand me. "You dove for the deck. You oughta have taken it around again." I could never tell him that was an option I did not have. MacCafferty had denied me that margin for error.

I parked the plane, and then I just sat there in the cockpit, totally wrung out. I was sopping wet from the physical and mental strain of the flight, and the effort to unstrap and climb out of the cockpit seemed, for the moment, beyond me. Yet, slumped there, exhausted, hot, wet, and itchy in my junior spaceman suit, I felt good, almost triumphant.

Once, at the beginning of our training as a squadron, MacCafferty had told us: "You don't know what you can do. You don't really know your limits."

Now, man by man, he was forcing us to them.

19

The next morning, right after breakfast, there was a memorial service for Cullen, Alexander, and the two other pilots who had been killed. The service was held in the forward hangar bay, directly below the flight deck.

It drew a large crowd, almost entirely officers, and they sat quietly on metal folding chairs set in straight ranks between the parked aircraft in the cavernous bay. In the Navy, deaths and change of command ceremonies are always formal occasions, and the neat somber dress uniforms sparkled irreverently with shining brass and colorful arrays of medals and ribbons. A few of the senior officers wore swords, gleaming, improbable weapons used only for ceremony, and they sat there looking vaguely anxious and uncomfortable, like movie extras waiting to be called for a parade scene.

Yet it was an attentive audience. In the recesses of his heart, each man knew he was there to grieve for his own mortality as well. None had to be told for whom the chaplain's voice tolled.

> Yea, though I walk through the valley of the shadow of death, I fear no evil; for thou art with me; thy rod and thy staff they comfort me. Thou preparest a table in the presence of mine enemies. . . .

I sat brooding, picking at a nagging feeling of guilt as if it were a dry scab. I felt guilty because I did not deeply feel a great loss at this tragic death of two close friends. My lack of feeling was due, in part, to the mobility of my life. Friends came and went so readily that I hardly registered whether they had gone on to graduate school, military service, other jobs, or eternity. But there was more to it than that. Certain of my nerve endings had been cauterized in the blaze of Ferrara's crash in Pensacola. My sense of horror seemed to have been permanently affected. Looking at the faces about me, I wondered in what fires each of their souls had been similarly scarred and desensitized.

The chaplain haltingly read a summation of the four pilots' lives and careers, and then, in a doleful voice, launched into the eulogy. "We share the puzzlement, the grief and pain of their families over their tragic loss, for it is our loss also. We pray to God their loved ones will understand the real sacrifice they have made. Their loss is beyond expression of words. In each, we have lost a close friend, a comrade at arms, a shipmate. But they shall always be part of this ship. . . ."

The chaplain was a tall, slender man with fine bones and sharp, prominent cheekbones. This potentially ascetic appearance, which would have been quite impressive in a clergyman, was unfortunately smothered by an extraordinary softness of flesh, a hint of effeminacy that was verified as soon as the chaplain had spoken a complete sentence. He said the word *shipmate* in a way that made the men squirm a little in their seats. But they sat, heads bowed, in deep, respectful silence through the meditation and then the benediction: "Bless the Lord, all ye works of the Lord."

The immediate departure of the captain with a starched Marine orderly in his wake yanked the mourner from the edge of the grave back into the Navy. Trailing behind the captain came the senior officers, including MacCafferty and Pastori. I was dazzled by the squadron commander's display of medals. It made me suddenly self-conscious of the bareness of my own blouse. MacCafferty's chest looked like a full-page color chart in an encyclopedia of Decorations and Orders. There was the Air Medal, the Purple Heart, the Distinguished Flying Cross, the Silver Star, and, in the upper centermost position of honor, the blue and white swatch of ribbon suspending the Navy Cross. I glanced at the squadron executive officer Pastori as he passed by me. The display was identical, except that the last spot was vacant.

As if he had been following my eyes, MacCafferty

turned and examined Pastori's decorations. "Where's your Navy Cross?" he demanded.

Pastori looked startled, then vaguely embarrassed. But then he regained his composure and answered evenly, "I seemed to have misplaced it."

"You'd think more of that medal," MacCafferty said, "if it had cost you your leg."

Pastori did not say anything, but continued to look MacCafferty in the eye. He was half a head shorter than the squadron commander, and next to MacCafferty's looming beef the slender Pastori seemed frail and easily broken. But as if unable to withstand Pastori's level stare, MacCafferty abruptly turned and hobbled away.

Now what the hell was that all about?

When I got back to the stateroom, Lucas was changing from his dress blue uniform into his olive greens. The olive green was an optional working uniform that could be worn only by airmen. Lucas assiduously cultivated all the distinctive fashions and accessories that immediately identified him as a Navy pilot. He was a real dude. His shirts were tailored, tightly body-shaped, and the customized, heavy brass buckle of his belt was engraved with his name and Navy wings. And he wore soft, casual half Wellington boots instead of the plain-toed, laced-up, regulation shoes.

He reached into his wardrobe locker and pulled out the olive green uniform jacket. Lucas' uniforms were also custom-made, the jackets flared with side vents. He examined the blouse a moment, his coppery, freckled face in a frown, then carefully hung the uniform jacket back in the locker and took out his blue nylon flight jacket. The jacket was a patchwork decorated with a small American flag and the emblem of every squadron and air group that Lucas had ever flown with, almost a dozen in all. It had a dozen shiny zipper pockets, as if the number of pockets stuffed with jackknives, bullets, pads, pens that write underwater, navigation computers, Wrigley's gum packs, and cigars were in itself important. Lucas slipped into the jacket, brushed the crinkly nylon smooth with a sigh of satisfaction, then put on his squadron ball cap, emblazoned with the Black Knight coat of arms.

"What did Pastori get the Navy Cross for?" I asked finally.

Lucas checked himself in the mirror above the sink. "You mean MacCafferty."

"No, Pastori."

"I didn't know he'd won one. I've never seen him wear it."

"He has one, okay."

Lucas shook his head. "I'll take your word for it, but he's never worn it while I've been in the squadron. I'd have noticed it. I'm just a country boy, and things like that impress the hell out of me."

The personnel records for each officer aboard the aircraft carrier were kept in the ship's administrative office below Hangar Bay Three. The duty yeoman, an acne-spotted kid about nineteen, sat hypnotized by a paperback, a James Bond thriller, *Casino Royale*.

I mumbled something about having to make out a squadron training report. The yeoman glanced up only long enough to register an officer's uniform, and then shuffled over to the filing cabinet where the air group records were kept. He located the two folders with one hand, keeping his place in the book with the other. He never looked at me, just held the records out in my general direction as he settled down again, his eyes already drawn back to "Chapter 20—The Nature of Evil."

I hefted MacCafferty's folder in my palm a moment, glanced back guiltily at the yeoman, whose mouth hung open stupidly in his absorption, and then I flipped to the section with MacCafferty's citation for the Navy Cross. It read:

> For extraordinary heroism as a member of Attack Squadron 77 during action against the enemy forces in the vicinity of Hoengsong, Korea, on March 5, 1951. Returning from a successful fighter sweep, he sighted a heavy concentration of hostile ground forces and executed a daring bombing and strafing attack in the face of heavy enemy antiaircraft fire. Although without sufficient fuel to return to his carrier, and despite a serious wound and damage to the aircraft, he furiously continued the

attack, inflicting heavy destruction to the enemy in troops and equipment. The action disrupted an enemy build-up and contributed significantly to the success of subsequent action by allied ground forces. . . ."

I then went through Pastori's jacket. His citation was identical, except for the mention of the wound. He had been MacCafferty's wingman.

Curious, I thumbed through the rest of the entries in the file. Both had earlier decorations for actions around Okinawa and the Philippines at the end of World War II. MacCafferty and Pastori had been in different squadrons aboard different carriers then, but they had been thrown into many of the same battles. It seemed an extraordinary coincidence that these two men, who were not really friends, had now come together a third time in almost the same spot. But perhaps such a reunion was inevitable as the sharp attrition of their profession took its toll over the years. In what future Asiatic wars might I be called back to fly again with Lucas and the other Black Knights? Standing there with MacCafferty's and Pastori's service jackets in my hand, the battles of the future, present, and past all seemed to flow together into one inexorable combat mission.

I handed the jackets back to the yeoman, who reluctantly glanced at the name tags for filing.

"Hey, this is that commander with the bad leg, ain't it, sir?" he asked, holding up the folder as if MacCafferty himself was represented by that thick sheaf of typewritten personal data forms, orders to new duty posts, and citations in stilted prose.

"Yeah."

"I always wondered about that. How come they still let him fly jets and all? Sometimes he comes in here for something, it don't seem he can hardly walk at all."

"It doesn't interfere with his flying a plane."

"Yes, sir, maybe so," the yeoman said, cocking his head doubtfully, "but I always thought you pilots had to be perfect specimens or something."

"He got his leg shot up almost single-handedly destroying a Red army in Korea, and he got a Navy Cross for it.

You know of a flight surgeon who's going to ground him for that kind of wound?"

The yeoman shook his head. "No, sir, I guess not," he said, and bent back to the adventures of 007.

20

A great storm exploded on the task force. It came swiftly, with torrents falling straight from the heavens, then gale winds driving the rain into blue-gray sheets so that there was no longer a surface between the pummeling sky and the heaving sea. With the wind came a dark, frightening sky and savage rapiers of lightning and world-smashing thunder. Great ragged black clouds whipped by the carrier like evil galleons, and the other warships surrounding us disappeared. The carrier trembled amid violence, chaos and darkness.

With the storm came the darkening news. It circulated from the Joint Chiefs of Staff to the Commander in Chief Pacific Fleet to the Commander Task Force 77 and then to the commanders of the individual carrier air groups, the squadron commanders, and finally filtered down as specific orders to the Black Knights.

Our fighters, armed with Goshawk air-to-air missiles, were to be kept on the catapults at all times, with the pilots in the cockpits ready to launch in an instant to intercept incoming raids.

In the ready room, Steinberg, the intelligence officer, rubbed his long nose where his glasses pinched, sipped coffee and fielded questions. "Essentially, what's happened is this: Chiang Kai-shek's position has hardened. The Nationalists are taking a terrible beating on Quemoy and Chiang insists on bombing the guns on the mainland. Apparently, the last advocates of restraint among his advisors now agree with him, or, at least, are silent, and, reading between the lines, he has probably picked up support on the Joint Chiefs of Staff. The decision is now Eisenhower's. Unless, of course, Chiang takes it upon himself to bomb the mainland without Eisenhower's approval. The Nationalists have been sending out increasingly heavy war parties of Saber Jets over the Straits, deliberately looking for trouble. They are going out in group strength trying to suck the ChiComs into a fight. And now we're committed. The Air Force's Tactical Air Command fighters and medium bombers have been ordered from Okinawa to Taiwan itself." Steinberg gave one of his tight, sardonic smiles. "I presume to reinforce the Navy."

But I did not have time to digest the geopolitik of Chiang Kai-shek. The storm rolled past, spewing its fury elsewhere, but in its wake were the thick, poisonous night-flying conditions that had become our squadron's meat. With planes and pilots now tied up on the catapults, unavailable for routine flights, I had two patrols. Wham, bam. After the first, I slammed aboard, had a cup of black coffee and a Dexedrine, and blasted off again.

Apparently, the weather was so bad in most areas that everything was grounded. There were no bogeys reported, and the patrols themselves were uneventful. Still, it was with enormous relief that I finished the run down the Slot and banked away from the forbidden coast of China and back out to sea.

Suddenly, in the corner of my eye, there was a dark, ominous movement. I turned toward it, but whatever it was disappeared, dissolving into the blackness of the sky like a phantom.

To the south, there were sharp, jagged reefs of clouds. The storm activity had tossed the cumulo-nimbus clouds high into the air, and the thunderheads thrust up like snow-capped peaks. The constellations overhead were retreating westward, gradually being overtaken and dissolved in the dawn now spreading out from the eastern horizon.

Again something moved on the periphery of my vision, elusive and indefinite as smoke. Again it disappeared when I turned to look directly at it.

In the witchery of that hour before the sun rises, all bets are off on what is real and what is not. I was punchy from too many hops that day and too little sleep and, at the same time, revved up on amphetamines. On an impulse, I zoomed the plane and shattered a silver shoal of clouds with my wings and whirled away, pirouetting off through the puffs in a series of dizzying aileron rolls

Then I leveled off well above the clouds, tuned in the carrier on the TACAN receiver, and as the closing miles clocked off on the digital display—89 pause click, 88 pause click, 87 pause click—I settled back.

There it was again. It was larger and closer now, hovering in the sky at the edge of my field of vision. But it was real. The acrobatics had cleaned my head, and now I got cagey.

It is a quirk of night vision that one cannot look directly at an unlit object. Because of the arrangement of the rods in the retina of the eye, the object will disappear from sight as soon as its image falls in the center of the retina. One of the tricks in which night fighter pilots are drilled is how to perceive things out of the corners of their eyes, which are more sensitive to light. In this oblique way, I focused my attention, but not my sight, on the apparition and banked toward it, intentionally not looking directly at it. I maneuvered to silhouette whatever it was against the paling eastern sky.

At first, because of the aircraft's size and configuration, I thought it was a Lockheed Superconstellation, one of the huge Navy early warning radar planes. But then the aircraft went into a leisurely turn, and its sharply swept, high midwing and attenuated, fountainpen-shaped body hung in a distinct black silhouette against the bluish-gray backdrop of sky.

There was that chilling moment of recognition. Then I reached down and broke the safety wire on the toggle and flipped the switch that armed my guns.

In a few more seconds, I was going to overrun the plane. I chopped my power and dropped down, keeping my distance for the time being, watching it. The other plane continued its graceful turn. I could just make out the dark outline of a radar dome, like a blister under the plane's nose. It was time to yell.

I hit the radio button: "Homeland, Charger Seven. Over," I called excitedly.

After a delay, the phones crackled and the half-asleep monotone of the ship's controller responded.

"There's a bandit up here. Are you aware of that? There's a Soviet bomber circling the task force."

The controller was confused. "Charger Seven, repeat your last."

181

"There's a Soviet bomber up here circling the task force," I called, now thoroughly alarmed. "Don't you hold it on radar?"

The controller came back with an irritated edge to his voice. "There's a great deal of heavy weather return on our scopes. Are you sure there's a Russian bomber up there?"

"I'm looking at it right now. I can't make out the markings in this light. Maybe it's Red Chinese." I studied the other plane, whose profile against the lightening sky was now unmistakable. "It looks like a Badger-class-Soviet-built-medium-jet-bomber," I bit off into the mike. "You better notify the captain and the Flag immediately."

The controller started shouting to someone before he unkeyed his mike. After a moment, another voice came up on the radio: "Charger Seven, this is the CIC watch officer. I understand you believe there is a Russian or Red Chinese aircraft currently circling the task force. Is that correct?"

I was starting to get pissed off. "Roger. I'm dogging the plane right now."

"Are you sure it's a Russian plane?"

"I can't see the markings. But it's one of theirs. It is not one of ours. I'm sure of that."

"Well, what is it doing?"

"It's flying around."

"It's flying around," the watch officer repeated uneasily, as if weighing the significance of that particular maneuver. There was an infuriating pause, then he said nervously, as if he were not quite sure himself whether it was an order or not, "keep watching him . . . but don't take any provocative action."

"Roger." I dipped my wings to maneuver due west of the Soviet bomber and below it, putting the darker water and sky behind me and the other plane against the now pink-gray sky, so that the Badger could not readily spot me.

The controller contacted me again and ran me through an IFF signal check to distinguish my radar blip from that of the other plane.

After that, there was silence. As it grew increasingly light, I grew more nervous. I rummaged in my mind to remember what type of armament the Russian TU-1

182

bombers were supposed to carry. A stinger! They had automatic, radar-controlled tail guns. With sudden alarm I realized that I had automatically been drifting into the tail position, and I banked wide, now putting the Soviet plane off my wing.

Just then I heard another flight check in with the controller. The ship had launched the two ready fighters on the catapults.

I could hear the two pilots rendezvousing, and then the controller steered them toward me.

"Circle them around so that they join up on me from the west," I told the controller.

"That you, Charly?"

"Yeah, who's that?"

"Red Lucas. I thought I told you to stay out of trouble."

In a few minutes, Lucas reported that he had me in sight. I looked to the west, but there were no planes there, only the thick, black night.

Then, suddenly, magically, two Crusaders materialized on my left quarter out of the gloom.

"Who's that with you?"

"Stovall. Where's your bandit?"

"Over there, about two o'clock. Just above the horizon."

There was a break, then Lucas said, "Oh, yeah, you found one, all right."

Just then another voice broke in. "Charger Seven, this is Flag. Can you make out any markings yet?"

"Negative."

"Are there any other bogeys in the area that you can see?"

I scanned the sky all about me quickly. "No, sir. Nothing that I can see. This one seems to be a loner." I did not know whether Flag was the admiral himself or one of his staff. There was a long silence, as if a decision were being made at the other end, then Flag asked, "Is there enough light yet up there for the Peter planes to take photos?"

"No, sir, not yet," I answered, then added, "but by the time you wake those guys up and launch them, there will be."

"Roger. Thank you. Flag out."

Apparently, we were not going to be ordered to shoot. At least not at the moment.

I glanced down and noted with shock that I was low on fuel. I reported my state to the carrier, and a minute later was ordered to return to ship. I broke away from Lucas and Stovall, leaving them to ride herd on the Red Bomber.

MacCafferty and Steinberg were waiting for me in the ready room. "It's got Russian markings," the intelligence officer reported. "Lucas just identified it."

I nodded. "Would we shoot it down if it had Red Chinese markings?"

Steinberg shrugged. "I don't know. What does that mean? Is it a Chinese plane with a Russian crew or is this a Russian plane with a Chinese crew?"

Steinberg pulled out a long, legal-sized form and began filling it out. He had to formally debrief me. "What type of aircraft was it?"

"A Badger."

Steinberg put a finger to the bridge of his horn-rimmed glasses, as if focusing his thoughts at that point, then pulled out a deck of playing cards. He turned one up, flashing the black silhouette of an aircraft at me. "This plane?"

"No." We played the game with a dozen cards, before I stopped him and fingered the Badger, a twin-engine jet bomber.

Steinberg nodded. "What was his altitude and air speed?"

I gave my estimates, then added, "It's probably their setup for maximum cruising for patrol or electronics spooking."

"Why do you say that?"

"Just the way he was hanging around. He wasn't on a set course, as if he were on his way somewhere."

Steinberg again nodded. "Did you see anything unusual about its equipment? Were there any sort of special antennas or pods?"

"Just the radome." I pointed out the housing for the radar scanner under the nose on the identification card.

"Anything else?"

"I really couldn't get that good a look at him. It was

still too dark. Lucas and Stovall will have a better shot at him."

"By then, we'll hopefully have photos. What about missiles?"

I shook my head.

Steinberg referred to the notes on the back of the picture. "The Soviet Navy TU-16's carry air-to-surface missiles under the wing."

I shook my head again. "Maybe. But it was still too dark."

"What were you showing him?"

"The Goshawks. But he might not have seen me at all. As soon as I spotted him, I kept below and on his dark side. Always put him against the light," I said, rather proud of my heads-up ball on that play. I looked over at MacCafferty, who nodded and grunted approvingly.

I was still in battle dress, the sweat-soaked yellow scarf hanging limp about my neck and the heavy bandit bandoleer of bullets across my chest, sitting there with my Day-Glo orange and black helmet in my lap.

"Yes, but if Lucas got close enough to get a good look at their markings, then they probably photographed him—if it's a reconnaissance plane like Charly thinks it is. And it probably is."

"Shit!" MacCafferty exploded. It was the first word he had said since I had entered the ready room. "Did you have your radar on?"

"Not at the time. I didn't need it."

Steinberg looked curiously at MacCafferty.

"What about Lucas?" MacCafferty interrogated me.

"Probably."

"What do you mean probably?"

"He probably used it to find me in the dark and home in on me."

MacCafferty took a deep breath and blew it out with a loud sound of exasperation. "Well, that's it then," he said, his voice heavy with disgust. "If the plane is equipped for electronics snooping and their operator is on the ball, then they may have gotten the fingerprints on the plane's radar. It's not going to take a genius to put together the electronics data with the photos of the missiles on the plane and figure out we're here with a new radar missile system, and this is how it works."

"If they are alert enough and are able to get all that data," Steinberg interjected.

"We ought to shoot them down and make sure they don't."

"I thought it was part of the game to impress on them that we *were* out here with all-weather fighter-bombers with a new missile system."

"There's such a thing as giving them too much information," MacCafferty said in a heavy voice. "If they can jam the radar frequency, the missiles won't home."

"I'm sure the Red Chinese would like nothing better than to have us shoot down an unarmed Russian reconnaissance plane operating over international waters," Steinberg said evenly. "They've been deliberately trying to provoke an incident. Make the United States look like the aggressors. That's why they tried to bushwhack Charly here the other night. They've been sending out false directional signals, trying to lure American planes over the mainland and shoot them down and make it look like the American planes were on an attack."

"They don't need an excuse to shoot down American patrols," MacCafferty snorted. "They've shot down nearly a dozen out here since the end of the Korean War."

"Most of them weren't exactly over international waters."

"What does that mean?" I asked, looking from Mac-Cafferty to Steinberg.

"Are you about finished up with Charly?" MacCafferty asked.

Steinberg nodded. "Yes, sir. I'll have to get the rest from Lucas."

MacCafferty looked at me thoughtfully as if he were going to say something, but apparently changed his mind and just nodded and growled, "Get some sleep," and then careened out of the ready room. At the door, he stopped and looked back. "You're a smartass, sharp intelligence officer, Steinberg. Maybe you do know what the game is. But I'll be goddamned if I do." With that, he heaved through the door and was gone.

I turned to Steinberg. "What's this about all those patrols shot down?"

The intelligence officer studied me a moment, his lips pursed, then said, "Where do you think we get all that skinny you get in your strike briefing? The locations and types of their radar, the antiaircraft guns and missiles, the target information and their exact coordinates?"

"You tell me."

Steinberg gave me his mysterious smile. "We have regularly scheduled weather patrols all around the perimeter of Red China, North Korea, Siberia, Russia."

"Weather?"

Steinberg nodded. "At certain strategic points of interest, they'll dart inland to check the weather there."

I whistled. "What kinds of planes are we using?"

"A variety. The CIA has special planes I don't even know about. But the Navy uses specially equipped A3D's."

"The same plane we now have parked over the Special Weapons bay."

"It takes a jet bomber to carry all the electronics and photographic gear. And it has to be fast enough to get in and out without getting caught."

"Then what we're doing is making dry-run attacks into Red China and Russia."

"That's the whole point," Steinberg nodded. "To get them to scramble and test their radar and defense installations."

"Jesus Christ." I shook my head in awe. "What would happen if they tried to do the same thing over the United States?"

"Probably start a war," Steinberg said phlegmatically.

I waved him away. I had had as much intelligence as I could handle for the moment. I stumbled to my feet and toward the door. At the bulletin board, I glanced at the latest news flashes.

(TAIPEI)—THE INTENSE U.S. MILITARY BUILD-UP CONTINUES THROUGHOUT TAIWAN AT A CRISIS PACE. NUCLEAR-ARMED NIKE-HERCULES ANTIAIR-CRAFT ROCKETS HAVE BEEN AIR LIFTED HERE AND ALREADY SET UP ON CONCRETE LAUNCH PADS ALONG THE WEST COAST FACING MAINLAND CHINA. THE NUCLEAR WARHEADS OF THE GIANT RADAR-CONTROLLED MIS-

SILES CAN INTERCEPT AN INCOMING COMMUNIST AIR RAID WHILE IT IS STILL 100 MILES AWAY OVER THE TAIWAN STRAITS.

(MOSCOW)—RUSSIAN PREMIER NIKITA KHRUSHCHEV TODAY WARNED THE UNITED STATES THAT ITS SHIPS OFF THE SOUTH CHINA COAST "CAN SERVE AS TARGETS FOR THE RIGHT TYPES OF SOVIET ROCKETS."

My mind was battered. I couldn't absorb the news, let alone all its ricocheting alarms and intrigues. I lurched out of the ready room.

21

Hooks Lewis stood at the front of the ready room, conversing with Jack Tallman in a subdued voice. Hooks was apparently laying down one of his broadsides on faulty landing techniques. His left hand, dramatically high and trembling on the verge of a stall, banked and swooped down toward the firm platform of his right hand.

As the air group's landing signal officer, it was one of Hooks' chores to regularly critique all the pilots aboard the carrier on their landings. He glanced up and noted that most of the squadron had assembled. "Is that everyone?" he asked Tallman, who was the squadron duty officer that day.

Tallman looked over the ready room for a moment and then nodded. "Everyone except Hillyard, who's in the air."

"Okay, troops, y'all settle down now and tend to business. We've got a lot of ground here to cover, and ah've got other hawgs to slop this afternoon," Lewis shouted, by way of calling the squadron to attention. The few pilots still standing took their seats and looked up expectantly, like students in a classroom.

Hooks leaned against the desk, his normally flushed and mischievous face now somber and deeply preoccupied, as he thumbed through a black notebook. Something about his features always made me think of one of those editorial cartoons in which a definite human personality has been superimposed on an animal. In Hooks' case, the animal was a wild turkey. A gobbler's beak of a nose hooked over his petulant lips and when he talked his Adams apple bobbed nervously up and down his scrawny red neck. "Mr. Harris here crunched his gear the other day, so let us begin with the spectacular and work our way to the mundane. The landing was a replay of the one that Luke Alexander made the first day out. Ah mean no disrespect for the dead," Hooks solemnly intoned. "I think y'all know me better 'n that. But those here who do not learn from the dead are destined prematurely to join them."

He paused and looked about the ready room with a long mournful face, then fixed his gaze on Chub Harris. "Okay, as y'all came down into your final approach, y'all were a scosh fast in there. Normally, it's better to have a little cushion rather than get *too* slow. But the day before yesterday, the wind was blowin' in dribbles and squirts. It conked out just as y'all were about to slam down and the aircraft was just that much too fast in relation to the ship. Then the deck pitched up a bit and yore gear just couldn't take the added stress. It crunched. It was a combination of a lot of marginal things, two of which were not yore doin'. But, here agin, if yore approach speed had been right on the money, it might have made the difference."

Hooks referred back to his notebook. "Well now, Charly Rohr. For a fella who was trying to kill himself just a week ago, you've settled down real fine." He nodded his head appreciatively, studying his notes, then added, "*Except* for the day before yesterday, on that daylight hop. Y'all were high all the way on yore final, Charly. When Ah told ya, y'all took off your power, but not quite enough. Then ya tried to compensate for all your little mistakes by making one big one. Ya dove for the deck. Don't do that again!" Hooks said, jabbing out each word. "If yore too high, go round again. Don't be ashamed to take a wave-off or bolter. That's what, at great expense to the American taxpayer, they have built the canted deck on this carrier for. But for the grace of the good Lord, y'all should have been in the same boat as Harris here, probably worse."

I nodded gravely, but did not say anything. It had been the test flight with MacCafferty in which I did not have enough fuel left to make another landing approach. Hooks quickly reviewed two night landings in which I had displayed the same tendency to dive for the deck, but to a lesser degree.

The LSO then went to the next pilot, and the next each time breaking down the landings into their sequence of errors and corrections. One pilot tried to offer an excuse. "Ya don't fly the deck," Hooks railed at him, suddenly vehement. "Ya folla that signal mirror, ya listen to me, and ya do what ah tell ya. The deck, the ship, they'll take care of themselves then."

Hooks took a long, deep breath. "Gentlemen, there's a great day a-coming very soon when these here eelectronic engineers are going to put a big black box in all our planes." With a nod, Hooks indicated a bespectacled civilian who stood at the side of the room furiously scribbling notes on a large clipboard. "And thcse little black buggers are gonna take off the planes, navigate them to the targets, fire their missiles or whatever, and come on back aboard. And then we can all forget this here in-humane business of trying to get you jokers back aboard in one piece. But until that happy day, unless you become a cagey old ace like yore skipper there," he said, winking at the group and indicating MacCafferty, "or a cool calculatin' test pilot like Professor Pastori, it's gonna pay y'all to lissen to me."

The debriefing was over, and the civilian, a systems analyst for the firm that made aircraft computers, buttonholed Lewis. He was one of a dozen or more civilians attached to the aircraft carrier. They were the tech reps, the technical representatives of the companies that built the squadron's hardware. Bodies by Chance Vought Aircraft, turbojets with afterburner by Pratt & Whitney, and Goshawk missiles with interchangeable conventional and nuclear warheads by the Marion Electronics Corporation. The tech reps were the jet-age camp followers of the military-industrial complex.

Hooks stood, one hand on his hip and the other alternately scratching his behind and pulling the tip of his nose, listening politely to the systems analyst's long detailed questions. He tried to answer, but evidently the two men were on different wavelengths, and the computer man kept interrupting impatiently with, "Yes, but . . ."

"Well, now, let me put it to ya another fashion," Hooks said, the soul of patience. "Y'all have played baseball."

The tech rep hesitated a moment, then nodded.

"Well, figure y'all are out in the outfield, and there's a bit of a breeze blowin' at yore back," continued the LSO. "Now someone hits a high loopin' fly a little off to your left. Just from the way that there ball takes off, ya right away got a pretty fair idea about where it's gonna land, and so y'all can start running off after it. Ya know there's a wind now, y'all can feel it, and so ya speed up or angle off yore run accordingly. Right?"

Hooks' right hand moved through the air above the other man's head in a slow graceful trajectory. "But now, the ball has a little spin on it or the wind's a mite stronger than ya first figured, don't ya see, and there's something in the way that it's hangin' up that tells ya yore gonna have to put on a mite more gas to land that there ball right in yore mitt. Well, now, getting one of those jets aboard the carrier is the same sort of thing, don't ya know. Ya play it just that way. Ah don't know of any sort of formula that tells ya exactly what to do. Each time's a little different." Lewis looked very pleased with his explanation and stood smiling benignly at the other man, complacently scratching his haunch.

But the computer man was something less than satisfied. Despairing of getting anything mathematically analytical out of Hooks, he next buttonholed me. I guess my bright Wheaties-fed look seemed to suggest an intelligence more concrete than the Alabama cracker's.

"Yes, yes, I understand that," the tech rep persisted. "But all these things should have some sort of precise relationship that we can nail down. Something mathematically predictable."

"I don't know what to tell you," I said. "You can probably work out a formula for the basic angle of attack and power settings for each aircraft, but then you'll have to correct it for the variation in the amount of fuel the jet is carrying, the armament load and configuration, the weight of the pilot, and the thousand and one crazy ways the wind blows and the sea tosses, or the plane might get damaged. I wish you luck, because, until you do, we're still going to have to jockey our way aboard by feel and the seat of our pants like Hooks says."

The tech rep's job was troubleshooting the computers and automated systems of the aircraft and collecting data for the design of new setups. There was always something slightly condescending in his manner. He was an irritation, but too indefinite a presence for a reaction as strong as dislike. His only distinguishing characteristics were black, heavy-framed glasses and his clothes. The other civilians aboard wore sports clothes, giving the impression that they had dropped by on their way to a barbecue. Or they affected a sort of pseudo military outfit of uninsigniaed khakis. But the computer man always wore carefully pressed slacks, a pale blue shirt, and a bow tie—one of the ready-made affairs held by an elastic band. Listening to the nagging drone of his voice, I had the wild urge to suddenly yank way back on the bow tie, stretching the elastic to its limit, and then, *snap,* catapult that slide rule of a man out through the hatch, over the catwalk, and into the water beyond.

"Well, we would certainly appreciate some cooperation," the tech rep said self-righteously. "We're just trying to develop systems to make it a lot less hazardous for *you* people."

Hooks Lewis came up, laid a heavy paw on the guy's shoulder, and leaned forward conspiratorially. "I'll tell ya something confidential," he said in a low voice. "I don't think these pilots want it safer. If it's all safe and easy, they're gonna stop handing out all that extra hazardous duty pay. And secondly, it'll kill Charly here's sexy, daredevil image. He's like to have a terrible time to get laid. He won't be any different ya see than, well, you people." Hooks drew back and winked at me. The tech rep stalked out of the ready room.

I slid into an empty row of chairs to read over one of the accident reports that Lewis had brought with him. As he said, we had to either learn from the dead or join them.

Two rows in front of me, Frank Pastori and another one of the tech reps were conferring in quiet, confidential tones.

Gradually, without making an effort to eavesdrop, I became conscious of what the tech rep was saying. "I'll talk to the honchos who fire and hire when we get back to the states. But I'll level with you, Frank. You're sort of in-between. You're a couple of years too old to start out and train in the engineering program without any civilian experience, and you haven't got enough rank yet to be valuable as a sales rep at the Pentagon. Hell man, with your background and record, you've still got big things ahead. If you want my advice, stay with it until you've got your twenty in. Then at least you'll have your pension to fall back on."

Pastori shook his head. "I want out *now*," he said, his voice hushed and intense.

22

Why is it that death, like the ocean waves that batter sea rocks into sand, always comes in groups of threes?

Hooks Lewis stood on the landing signal officer's platform, shivering in the dark. He wore thermal underwear, flight coveralls, a foul-weather jacket and, on top of all that, his LSO jersey, but still his poor bones shook in the freezing wet blasts that swept over the flight deck, exposed and harsh as a winter steppe. His nose and eyes ran miserably, and he swiped at his face continually with the arm of his jersey, but he never took his eyes off the plane now swooping down in its final approach.

"That's it, babe. Right down the old groove."

Jack Tallman was returning from his second patrol that night. With the continuing deterioration of the weather, the Black Knights now bought all the night patrols. We lived in a sort of nether world, like bats fitfully dozing in the caves of the ship by day and emerging only at nightfall to swoop off on the long, grueling flights.

Tallman flew smoothly down the glide path in his final approach. At the right moment, he cut power, and the heavy Crusader jet slammed onto the deck and then bounced ahead. Tallman rammed on his power, and the plane took off, airborne again. His tail hook had not caught an arresting cable.

"It's a bolter," Hooks radioed. "Take it around again. But you were right in there. Good landing."

Hooks checked with primary flight control on Tallman's gas state. "He's got all day," he said when given the figure.

Tallman came around again on his final approach, and Hooks, anxious to get out of the bitter wind, began coaching him. Hooks had once been a shortstop on a backwoods college baseball team, and he was still the double-play keystone man. The pepper-upper. The chatterbox from the dugout. With great difficulty, the captain and the air boss had enforced a semblance of Navy radio discipline on him, but still the nervous chatter on the LSO platform went on incessantly. And when, in excitement or impatience, Hooks inadvertently keyed his mike button, the dugout chatter crackled out of loudspeakers on the bridge, in primary flight control, and in the pilot's headphones. "That's it, babe. Right in my lap. That's it. All the way, hey, hey."

Tallman, for the second time, hit right in the landing area, and once again the plane bolted forward and up into the air.

"What's the matter?" Tallman asked anxiously.

"I can't tell for sure," Lewis said. "It's your tail hook. It's not catching. It looks like its bouncing around. It must be loose. Take it around again. It'll catch."

"Am I hitting all right?"

"Hell, you're perfect."

But on the third try, the heavy reinforced-steel tail hook again bounced over the arresting wires without grabbing. It happened again on the fourth landing, and Tallman, his voice tight and a little breathless, reported that he did not have enough fuel left for another safe approach and landing. He elected to consume the little gas remaining to climb to ten thousand feet and eject. The aircraft would be lost.

Tallman's plane disappeared into the overcast. A radar fix was taken at the moment he radioed he was ejecting, and two guard destroyers were immediately dispatched to the area. They never found him.

The second death occurred just before dawn the next morning, right after I catapulted off into soot-black mist. Tom Hillyard, the stocky, taciturn lieutenant commander who had taken Alexander's place as squadron operations officer, made a normal landing aboard. He added power to taxi out of the wires, but his throttle evidently jammed. The plane rammed forward, out of control, plunged over the side, and sank.

Fatigue, the breakdown that sets in when metals or men are stressed beyond certain limits, was taking its toll.

The appearance of the Russian reconnaissance plane

worried Task Force 77 command. They could not allow the Russians or Chinese Reds to pinpoint the task force's position. Under cover of a thick thieves' overcast and intermittent squalls, the carrier and its escort vessels stole away to a new station, due east of Taiwan, maneuvering to keep the bulk of the island between it and the mainland of Red China.

The patrol was longer, more grueling. But now, because it took longer just to reach the Straits and get back to the ship, each flight had only enough fuel to make one pass over the Straits, rather than go down and back up again as we had previously. Our flight route was a rough equilateral triangle with the carrier at one point, the run down the Slot the far side, and as much time and fuel going as coming back.

Pastori took the first flight and stomped back into the ready room shaking his head. "It's cutting it awfully close on fuel with this armament load," he told MacCafferty.

"Well, what do you want me to do?" MacCafferty said, a little irritated. "Recommend to Flag that we move in closer? That will put us in MIG range."

Pastori didn't say anything.

"We could recommend that the Air Force take over the whole show when they finally get uncrated," MacCafferty said in the same unsparing tone of voice.

We had just gotten word that the Air Force was transporting a squadron of its shiny new Lockheed F-104 Starfighters to Taiwan. The Starfighter had just been delivered to the Air Force Air Defense Command earlier that year and,. in May, the plane had set the world speed record of 1,404 miles an hour, officially making it the world's fastest combat aircraft. It was not an attack bomber, nor was it an all-weather fighter with radar-controlled missiles. But the Air Force was planning to stage a big show in the Straits making 1,400-mile-an-hour blips on the Red's radarscopes.

The news appeared to anger MacCafferty. It incited him. The patrol schedule he set up became increasingly relentless. To make up for the reduction in time we spent over the Straits, MacCafferty increased the number of flights each pilot made.

On a landing, Walt Stovall's starboard gear collapsed. The tail hook caught, and the plane looped on its wing.

Stovall was not scratched, but the crash violently jammed his back and he was carried, in pain, down to sick bay. The flight schedule was tightened once again to take in the gap.

I picked my way through the treacherous jumble of tie-down wires on the dark flight deck out to the jet that was hooked and yoked to the catapult. I was due to relieve Pastori on watch in the ready plane.

It was so still and silent around the aircraft that I assumed Pastori had popped into one of the flight deck offices for a second, and I hauled myself up the side of the plane. But Pastori was in the cockpit, hunched over and intently staring straight ahead as if his thoughts were as black and turbulent as the sea that rose and fell just off the bow.

"What? . . . Oh, Charly . . . Is it time?" He looked startled, then embarrassed, as if I had caught him in some very personal act.

"Did I wake you?"

Pastori gave me a quick, nervous smile and wearily rubbed his face. "I only wish I *could* sleep," he said.

I jumped back down to the flight deck to let him climb out of the cockpit. We stood on the lee side of the airplane, under the wing, sheltered by the fuselage from the biting wind. Pastori looked up at the plane a moment, studying the streamlined white sculpture of the missiles hanging under the wing, then turned and peered at me. "What are you doing here, Charly?"

I was confused. "I came to relieve you."

"I don't mean that. I mean here, on this carrier, flying this plane."

I shrugged. "What are you doing here?"

Pastori shook his head. "I don't know. I just don't know. One war is enough for any man, and two is too many. I never wanted to be out here again. This is the last place I wanted to be."

"Where did you want to be?"

"When I was *your* age? In California or up in Washington, building fantastic buildings of native stone and redwood. I was going to be the Frank Lloyd Wright of the Pacific Northwest. I'm a graduate architect. Did you know that?"

I shook my head. "What happened?"

Pastori did not answer. His sad dark eyes gazed at the sea, but judging from their expression, he was not focused on anything within a thousand miles.

My own nerves were jangling like fire alarms. All the pilots were groggy from lack of sleep, and the flight surgeons were dispensing amphetamines like stewardesses handing out Chiclets. That afternoon, my fitful sleep had been a succession of nightmares in which I flew my strike mission with a nuclear bomb strapped to the plane's belly, dodging MIGs all the way, and then, just as I was about to release, I spotted this enormous missile headed directly at me, like a harpoon about to hit a fish. I woke up in a drenching sweat at the bottom of the bed. Faced with a catapult watch and several patrols that night, I popped down two amphetamine capsules the size of .22 caliber bullets. Now I was jumpier than hell. and I would rather stand out in the cold wetness of the flight deck talking to Pastori than be jammed down in the claustrophobia of the cockpit by myself.

"What happened with your architecture?" I prodded Pastori.

"The Korean War," he replied. "After World War II, I went back to college on the GI Bill. graduated. and was working as an apprentice draftsman for a fat fifty dollars a week when I was hauled back into the Navy. And when that war was over, I had a wife and two, then three kids. Take it from me, Charly, don't marry an Italian Catholic girl. They have tin ears for rhythm." But he said it in a gentle, mocking way, and I knew that Pastori's family had always been more of a pleasure to him than a burden.

A cold, impenetrable fog surrounded the ship, and ghostly wisps of it floated past the flight deck like reconnoitering phantoms. Pastori plunged his hands into his pockets and hunched forward, containing himself against the cold. "You don't remember it, you were probably too young, but after the Korean War a lot of good engineers and architects were walking the streets. There was a recession, and the Navy was a damn good place to stay," Pastori said hesitantly, almost apologetic. "I had ... well, a couple of decorations ... and with all my combat jet time and architectural training, the Navy wanted to send me back to college to get a master's degree in aeronautical engineering and design. I've been more or less specializing in development and testing ever since."

He looked back up at the plane and missile, brooding, then shook his head. "Buildings of redwood and stone my kids could point to," he said with a quickening intensity, "and instead I helped build this." He shook his hand, palm up and fingers curled in a gesture of angry contempt that was distinctly, expressively, Italian. A sudden rage flared up, bunching the muscles of his body. "What a fucking perversion of my life," he hissed, and the words came like the last sizzle of a fuse that had reached its charge. Pastori's right fist shot out and slammed into the missile with all his might, the bang of knuckle on metal exploding across the still flight deck.

I was stunned, half expecting to be instantly consumed in white heat. But the missile, as if impervious to his rage, did not blow. It remained stock-still, insolent in its fastenings under the wing. Pastori was doubled over, purged of his anger by the sharp pain of the blow. He stood there massaging his hand, at a loss for anything to say, then turned away and quickly retreated down the flight deck.

By the time Red Lucas came to relieve me on the catapult, my nerves were as frayed as battle pennants. I hunkered down on the ejection seat, hopped up on dexedrine, shivering and staring out at the black at the end of the catapult.

I wanted to vault out onto the deck and run. But where could I run to on that flat gray steel deck? I just crouched there in the dark with the circuitry of my mind setting off a storm of alarms and flashes as if it were corroding and shorting out in that foggy dampness. To make matters worse, my bowels were in revolt. It was a now familiar pattern of nerves, and that recognition in itself alarmed me.

Suddenly Lucas' basso profundo boomed up from below the wing. I scampered down to meet him.

"Anything up?" Lucas asked.

"No," I said, sucking my guts halfway to my throat to keep from crapping in my pants.

From the pocket of his flight jacket, Lucas pulled out a small paper package and unwrapped a hamburger. He took an enormous bite and stood chewing a moment, peering off into the wall of mist ahead. "Just what the hell is he trying to prove?" he growled in his deep rumbling voice.

I didn't say anything.

"You got the next launch?" Lucas asked.

"Yeah."

"Well, better go below and get yourself coffee and a hamburger or something, bucko. It's going to be one long, hairy night."

Lucas' face was screwed up in a troubled frown, and I wondered if he was as shaky as I was. But one did not ask about fear. It was like a no-hit ball game. Very bad form to talk about while it was in progress.

I started to walk away, and Lucas called after me. "Hey, Charly, your goggles."

"Oh, yeah, I forgot. Thanks," I muttered, fumbling about my neck for the red-tinted goggles hanging there. I slipped them on, and then beelined for the head.

Security is a quiet can. Seated there with my flight suit and bandoleer of .38 caliber tracers around my ankles, I had a moment of peace before the galloping heebie-jeebies hit again.

I wrestled back into my combat gear and moved out, not knowing exactly where I was going but still bouncing on the balls of my feet like a punchy fighter. In a sort of daze, I popped into the main wardroom to check out the evening movie. It was *Hellcats of the Navy* starring Ronald Reagan.

Reagan was peering through a submarine periscope, draped over the handlebars and wrestling it like a drunken sailor hanging on a barmaid.

The sub's executive officer strode over and reported, "We're right to the edge of the mine fields, Captain. What do you see?"

"Nothing out there but fog," Reagan said. He straightened up, turned to the engine order telegraph operator and barked, "All ahead two-thirds."

I moved on to the wardroom lounge next door. I ordered a hamburger from the steward on duty in the galley and then drew a cup of coffee. The coffee had been perking since dinner, and it was so black and thick the spoon almost stood up in it. I slumped down into a chair and squeezed the cup with both hands, trying to force the liquid heat up my arms and into my body.

"Excuse me. I'm rather curious. Why do you wear those red goggles?"

The chaplain who had officiated at Alexander and Cullen's funeral service sat down next to me. He smiled questioningly.

"I have a flight in a few minutes," I said.

"Oh," the chaplain said, nodding and smiling vaguely. He did not know what I was talking about.

"It has to do with the structure of the eye. The rods and cones in the retina," I explained. "White light, like in this room, temporarily blinds you for night flying. It desensitizes the parts of the eye you use for seeing in the dark, but the night-seeing rods are insensitive to red light. So you wear these glasses for an hour or so before your hop to allow your eyes to completely adjust to night vision. Otherwise, we'd have to hide in a dark box before a night flight." A good explanation, I thought, especially coming from a man who had a cement mixer for a mind. I was grateful for the opportunity to focus on something technical.

"Oh, I see," the chaplain said, nodding again. "Thank you. The things they come up with nowadays."

The man's face had a strangely evil, decadent look, almost Mephistophelean. It had a scarlet glow and his eyes gleamed as if he were peering into a raging fire. I looked about the wardroom. The walls, the plaques with the squadron coat-of-arms, the framed photographs of aircraft and ships on parade all reflected the flames of that same inferno.

A chair next to me slid out, and Pastori sat down. He looked at me anxiously and was about to say something when the chaplain interrupted.

"Which is your squadron exactly? I'm still trying to get all the planes and squadrons straight," the chaplain inquired, punctuating the question with a solicitous smile. "It's my first experience with the brown-shoe Navy."

"We're the Crusader squadron," Pastori answered suddenly, although the question had been directed at me. "Our job is all-weather attack. Nuclear attack."

"Oh, yes," the chaplain nodded appreciatively. "Those

202

are the planes with all the Marine guards around them. That's pretty involved stuff."

I nodded politely and sipped my coffee. Through the goggles, it looked like a cup of blood and even left the faint trace of rust in my mouth. My hands were noticeably trembling. I put the cup down and it made a brief rattling sound in the saucer, slopping coffee out over the side.

"I hope you don't mind my asking questions," the chaplain inquired. "I'm trying to get some background. You see, I'm going to be sort of the crew's radio correspondent." He laughed slightly to himself, as if we were supposed to be in on the joke. "Each evening, I'm going to give a report on the general announcing system. What the general situation is. What the various squadrons are doing. That sort of thing. I'm trying to think of what to call myself. Any suggestion? The chaplain on the *Essex* calls himself Essex Ernie." A faint chuckle. "His name is Ernest, you see."

"What happens if we really go to war, padre?" Pastori asked, his voice strained and intense. His eyes still had that distracted, strangely haunted look that I had seen on the flight deck, but now, through my flame-colored glasses, his expression was even more tortured.

"Oh, well, in that case, I guess I report things like the number of sorties flown, what targets were hit, and what type of ordnance was dropped, and especially rescues. I mean if any of our planes go down. I may even interview some of the pilots. That's generally what we did in the Korean War, and I understood it was very popular with the crews."

"Will you report the number of people we kill, mutilate, and burn to death? And announce how many of those were civilians? Or women and children? For a rough guideline, you can use the fact that in Korea it was estimated that we killed at least four civilians for every North Korean or Red Chinese soldier." Pastori's mouth twitched. He too was wearing red cellophane goggles, and there was a slight nervous fluttering of the muscles around his eyes and temple, where the goggles pressed into the flesh.

"Or why don't you report how those napalm missions are planned," Pastori ran on, his voice low but nonetheless tense and excited. "The intelligence officers give you a square marked on a map and tell you it's a suspected staging area. Then you go in and burn everything. And I mean everything. Huts, villages, rice paddies, even water buffalo. If you're interested in ordnance, padre . . . you might report what each type does to the people it hits—the bombs, the white phosphorus, the napalm. Just the ordinary stuff. Forget the nuclear weapons. They're too involved."

"I don't quite see the point of all this, Commander," the chaplain said, his voice stern with disapproval.

"The point is your reporting, Father," Pastori said flatly. "It seems to me as a chaplain you have an obligation to also inform men when they are in peril of losing their immortal souls."

Just then the duty steward, a Filipino in a starched linen jacket, appeared at the table and began busing the dirty ash trays, coffee cups, and sandwich plates the officers had left scattered about. As he cleaned the table, the chaplain intently probed Pastori's face, as if trying to read something in the two glinting, red-cellophane disks facing him.

"Are you a Catholic?" the chaplain asked.

"Not for a long time," Pastori said in a voice devoid of any expression.

"When was the last time you came to Mass or confession?"

Pastori was silent.

"Perhaps you too have a few moral obligations you're neglecting," the chaplain said with the hint of a smile.

"Can you offer me absolution for all my sins, padre?" Pastori said, with a hard cutting edge to his voice. "Is that your ultimate job aboard this ship? Many of us aboard have ultimate jobs. Charly's and mine is to drop a nuclear weapon somewhere in Red China, maybe tonight, maybe tomorrow, maybe never, but to be ready to do it. Is that your job, padre? When that time comes to offer us absolution without end. Forever and ever, amen."

"What sin do you think is beyond remission?"

Pastori did not speak for a long while, and, when he began talking again, his voice was low and strained and the chaplain had to lean forward to hear him. "In Korea, I was in a field hospital when they brought in a group of refugees. My plane, it had been shot up and I had to crash land. I was banged up but nothing serious. But the refugees, they were a scene from a nightmare. I remember a woman . . ." At this point Pastori's voice faltered, but then he continued again. "She was trying to breast-feed her baby, only the baby was long dead. It was filthy and bloody, and it was missing a leg. It had been blown off and she kept touching the wound like she was trying to close it with her fingers or make it whole again out of the thin air. And all the while she was crooning to it and trying to get it to feed at her breast."

He looked up at the chaplain. "To knowingly do that again, that would be beyond redemption."

"You can't blame yourself for that," the chaplain said softly. "You don't know . . ."

Pastori cut him off. "Padre, padre, padre," he said in a soft mocking voice, rocking his head. "In Utah they still have firing squads, and men, civilians, volunteer for it. For God knows what reasons. And do you know what they do? Into one of the rifles, no one knows which one, they put a blank cartridge. That way, each of the executioners has a loophole for his conscience. I don't even have that. The day before I saw that woman I wiped out an entire town. Just my wingman and myself."

Pastori turned to me, as if he remembered for the first time that I was still there, and now looked to me for confirmation. "You know who my wingman was, Charly?"

I knew—I had read the citation—but I didn't say anything.

"MacCafferty," Pastori stated. "We were returning from a routine patrol when we spotted this long truck convoy holed up in a village. They hadn't quite gotten their camouflage all up yet. And we hit them. We did a real professional job of it. We corked the front end of the convoy, and then racked over and burned the tail end. We had them trapped in the village between the shacks, and they couldn't disperse. Then we bored in and, Jesus, everything began blowing up. Some of the trucks were loaded with ammo, and there was so much exploding I can't even tell you if they were firing at us. But both of our planes were hit. We were going in so low, it might even have been exploding ammo that got us. MacCafferty was wounded, but he was still flying. I suggested we get the hell out of there, and he answered, 'Balls! You go!' and dove right back down. I followed him, and we kept going in until we had expended every shell and bomb we had, over and over, until we didn't even have fuel enough to return to the ship. Don't ask me why. I couldn't tell you to this day. It was some kind of madness or lust. The trucks were blowing, and we had the village in flames from one end to the other, and people were running out of the houses—some with their clothes on fire—and we kept boring in, raking everything with our guns, until there was nothing but flames."

Pastori stopped talking, his eyes intensely focused on that picture he had conjured up, and the fires of it flared on his face and were reflected in his goggles.

"How did you get back?" the chaplain asked anxiously.

"We were damaged and out of fuel, and I shepherded MacCafferty to one of those Air Force emergency dirt fields and we pancaked in. We wasted both planes. We'd overextended ourselves over target and hadn't tried to contact the rest of the flight, but the official report made us look like heroes. We were recommended for Navy Crosses, mainly because the skipper thought MacCafferty was going to lose his leg. The photo planes showed one hell of a lot of damage. There were more than a dozen troop and supply trucks destroyed, that was real enough, but the village—that truck stop—was described in the report as a major staging and supply area. It wasn't. It was just a village. And all the while I lay in that field hospital, the mangled and bloody. . . ." Pastori's voice broke at this point. Sitting next to him, I could see his cheek twitch and two wet smears pool under his goggles and then streak down his cheeks. He sprang to his feet and swiped at his face with the sleeve of his flight suit. Then, without another word, he shook himself to settle his bandoleer of bullets and shoulder holster in place, pivoted on his heel and fled for the door.

The night overcast smothered the world beneath a black wet quilt, suffocating the mountains of Taiwan, the sea beyond, and the task force. When the jet finally stabbed through, it was like surfacing from the sea itself. I let out a long deep breath. To my enormous relief, the sky above was clear of cirrus, and the stars and a slice of moon were visible, silver and very near. Over the radio, I could clearly hear the ship's controller calling Pastori, who was now inbound from the southwest.

I banked northwest, steering to pick up the China coast off Foochow. The ship's controller contacted me, but instead of routinely passing me on to Taipei control as I expected, he asked, "Are you in radio contact with Charger Four?"

"Negative."

There was a long puzzling silence on the other end. I continued on. The ship called me again, but this time there was a different voice.

"Charger Seven. This is the CIC officer. Are you in contact with Charger Four? Over."

"Negative. What's the trouble?"

"Would you try to contact Charger Four on radio for us," the ship requested.

I called twice, unsuccessfully, and then insisted, "What's the problem down there?"

"Charger Four hasn't checked in yet, and we can't contact him. We may be holding him on radar, but if it is him, he's way off base to the south and not showing IFF...."

Before the CIC officer had finished, I was banking to the south. "Vector me in on him," I demanded. Charger Four was Pastori.

"You'll have to abort your mission. I haven't the authority. . . ."

"Vector me in," I repeated.

The first voice immediately came up with the course and distance to the other plane. It was far south, and an oblique intercept at that.

"What time did Four launch?" I asked, and checked the clock.

The answer was bad news. Pastori did not have much time in the air left. I throttled up to full power and then cut on the afterburner. There was an explosion, and the plane surged smoothly ahead. The initial boom dissolved into a whispering hush, as the Mach needle swept to 1.0 and then moved relentlessly to 1.3 as the jet outraced the fury of its own sound. Just behind my seat raw fuel was being injected directly into the jet flames to produce a prolonged explosion that thunder could hide itself in.

The controller automatically read off the course and distance to Pastori's aircraft. I rechecked my fuel gauge and clock. In afterburner, the plane was consuming fuel six times as fast as it did cruising at subsonic speed, but it was my only hope now of catching Pastori. The controller gave me a new course and closing distance.

I checked my radar. There was not a hint of a contact. I was still out of range. "Is he flashing any IFF yet?" I asked.

"Negative."

Pastori must have had a complete electrical failure, possibly a circuit fire. He was a lost and blind man flying on the tip of a fading rocket and unable to see or hear his way home. You cannot be in a worse fix in a jet and still remain airborne.

The droning voice of the controller reported the bearing and distance again. Yet the void between Pastori and me was measured in time. Outside the cockpit only the stars were visible, and my passage in relation to them was indiscernible. Inside the aircraft, on the instruments, my course, speed, and altitude were constant, my relationship to gravity and the speed of sound were unwavering. Only the clock moved steadily and, as if geared to the clock like some specific portion of time allotted to Pastori and me, the fuel indicator dropped relentlessly. The clock might cycle around and around forever, but the fuel indicator, like life itself, had a definite end toward which the pointer was now falling.

Pastori and I sailed only in time. It flowed soundlessly about the jet like a sea, wearing life away, grinding it into heartbeats and breaths and hopes that were then swept away like bits of sand.

MacCafferty got the phone call in the ready room. He slammed out the door and ran down the passage to the Combat Information Center, pitching and heaving on his game leg like a drunk.

The watertight steel hatch to CIC was bolted, and he had to open it by cranking the heavy metal wheel at the center of the hatch. He flung it open, and for a moment his big body was lit by the eerie, electronic glow from within the room. He stood on the threshold, blinking, while his eyes adjusted to the dim red and green light.

The room was cavernous and low-ceilinged, crammed with banks of waist-high electronic consoles and paneled its entire length with large plexiglass charts on which numbers and hieroglyphics magically wrote and erased themselves. As MacCafferty's pupils widened, his eyes made out the dark shapes of men stationed in recesses behind the boards, working in a strange behind-the-mirror world where everything had to be written backward so that it made sense to the officers out front.

At the nearest radarscope, a skinny, very young-looking ensign sat on a stool doodling on the glass face of the scope with a grease pencil, occasionally glancing at the boards as if he were expecting a certain number to come up. The light from the radar gave his skin a ghoulish, unhealthy look, and made black splotches of a slight outbreak of acne about his mouth and chin.

MacCafferty quickly walked over to the controller and seized him by the shoulder, as if he were going to whirl him around.

The ensign was startled. "No, no that's not my flight," he blurted out in answer to MacCafferty's demand. He pointed down the ranks of radar consoles to several officers gathered about a scope. "Greenameyer has got the emergency."

MacCafferty immediately charged toward the group, almost knocking down an enlisted man who stood in his path in the narrow aisle between the banks of electronics.

"Charger Seven, this is Commander MacCafferty. Over." The harsh, hard-edged voice was unmistakable, even though muted by the radio. ". . . It's a lousy set up, Charly. The intercept is going to end up in a tail chase, unless Pastori starts circling in a lost plane orbit immediately. I don't know why he hasn't yet. I'm assuming the worst. That he has a complete electrical failure. I don't know what the hell he's doing so far south. Probably a combination of wind and bad navigation. His fuel's critical at this point. . . . What's your state? Over."

The question, coming from MacCafferty, had its irony. MacCafferty, who himself had taught me that only the pilot saw the gauge and could report anything that damn well suited him. The squadron commander must have been thinking the same thing, because he responded to my report, "Don't play hero games, Charly. I don't want two planes in the water. Cut back on your afterburner. It won't make that much difference at this point. No matter what happens, you're to be over the ship with fifteen hundred pounds. That's an order. I don't want two planes in the water. Over."

I acknowledged, but I kept on in afterburner a while longer, until I knew with a sick feeling in my gut that the chase was hopeless. I tried calling Pastori on the radio once more. Suddenly, as if in response to my call, a blip developed at the edge of the intercept radar.

I quickly adjusted the scope, and the contact came in stronger. I called again on that radio, half expecting the blip to turn toward me like a man being hailed. But there was no answer.

I reported the radar contact to the ship, and they confirmed it as Pastori's plane. Just then the blip began fading. I fiddled with the radar and then with a shock realized that the other plane must be losing altitude rapidly. I adjusted the scan lower, lower, until the yellow-green mark that was Pastori dissolved completely into the spreading stain of the radar's sea return.

"Frank!" I screamed into the radio. "Frank! Frank!"

In the Combat Information Center, the overhead radio

speakers had been turned all the way up so that MacCafferty, the CIC officer, and others present could follow the intercept unencumbered by earphones. I am told that my cry burst from the speaker filling the compartment with a fierce, protesting howl that slammed their ears and stunned them where they stood.

"What . . . what the hell's he yelling at?" the CIC officer asked excitedly, but he was immediately quieted by the expression on MacCafferty's face.

The squadron commander, his jaw clenched so tightly it seemed his teeth might shatter, was staring at the radarscope. His face, pressed next to the radarman's, was as dry and pale as a skull in the glow of the cathode ray. The controller's grease pencil hung confused and indecisive over a track that ended abruptly in darkness.

When the radar wand swept around the scope for the fourth time, revealing no contact, MacCafferty looked up. For a moment, he looked about at the thicket of radar consoles, the UHF and VHF radio receivers, intercepter controllers and carrier approach controllers, the closed-circuit television picture of the final landing approach, the repeaters displaying the aerial radar pictures picked up and broadcast by the giant Lockheed radar patrol planes, the graphs and the automatic navigational systems. Pastori was now beyond the capabilities of any of them.

Reluctantly, MacCafferty raised a hand mike to his mouth, "Rohr, this is Commander MacCafferty. We've lost radar contact with Pastori. You're to return to the ship immediately. Repeat. Return to the ship immediately. What state? Over."

I did not respond. MacCafferty repeated the call twice before I replied. "Roger, Charger Seven, returning home. State, fifteen hundred pounds. Over."

MacCafferty knew I was lying. He immediately began coaching me. "Throttle back as much as possible without flaming out. . . . Don't use your air brake in the penetration. Swap all your speed and altitude for distance. You'll need every bit of it. . . . If you get down to minimum before you're on the final approach, get the hell out of there. You've done it before."

I flew steadily, following directions automatically, as if there were no emotional energy left to generate fear. I glided down into the clouds, reacting unconsciously to the instruments and the controller's instructions, and then switched the radio channel to the approach controller who jockeyed me toward the landing glide slope.

My fuel reading was now below the minimum with which I could safely attempt a carrier landing, and according to MacCafferty's orders, I should have ejected. But the fuel indicator of the F-8 had an inherent error of as much as three hundred pounds, so there was a possibility I might still just have enough for one landing. If I was wrong, the plane would flame out and drop into the sea, sinking like a lead shot and exploding before I could get out. I did not weigh the odds. I simply refused to eject a second time into that black nightmare outside. I rejected the thought so automatically that it was no decision at all.

Then, quite unexpectedly, I was set up for a landing, and I had to keep coming straight on by the book with the throttle set at eighty-five percent, sharply aware that the thin thread on which my life was strung might break at any moment.

The controller, quoting standard procedure, informed me that if I didn't see the meatball within five seconds. I had to wave off and go around again. I did not even bother to "Roger."

It seemed considerably longer than five seconds when I finally broke through the scud, and my eyes adjusted and picked out the carrier's stern and the red beacon of the meatball. I was supposed to report my fuel state at that point, but since the needle was quivering on empty, there wasn't any point to it.

"Keep it coming," Hooks Lewis said quietly in my ear.

The deck lights came up toward me and I crashed down and stopped with a hard, painful shock.

I automatically goosed the throttle to taxi out of the arresting wires. The turbine revved up and then, just as the jet started to move, it flamed out. It was a photo finish.

I pulled off my helmet and oxygen mask and then slumped back against the seat and headrest, sitting absolutely still with my eyes shut, not thinking and not moving a muscle until the plane captain climbed up and helped me unstrap.

MacCafferty met me just as I was coming off the flight deck. We stared at each other without comment for several seconds, and then MacCafferty said, "They've dispatched tin cans to the area. They'll pick him up in a little while."

I didn't say anything. It could wait until later.

All of the squadron's pilots—those still left—had gathered in the ready room, and they greeted me quietly. "Tough luck," Chub Harris said, shaking his head solemnly. "Tough, tough luck."

Red Lucas was already airborne on patrol.

The head flight surgeon, the burly captain, was standing by, a bottle of medicinal brandy in hand. Disaster's bartender. He gave me a small sad smile, nodding sympathetically, all the while his eyes examining my face carefully as if searching for some telltale symptom, like the rheumy eyes that foreshadow yellow fever. "Something for the nerves?" he inquired with the same bedside smile.

"Anything."

The doctor poured a stiff drink into one of the coffee mugs. The hot flash of brandy triggered something. Suddenly tears were streaming down my face. All I could think or say was, "Oh, shit!" I looked from MacCafferty to the others, confused and embarrassed, and then left the ready room before anyone could say anything.

I was on my second cigarette when MacCafferty came into the stateroom without knocking and sat down on the edge of the bunk.

From the breast pocket of his flight jacket, he took out the mangy, disintegrating butt of a cigar and lit it with his steel Zippo lighter, squinting and one-eyeing me through the billowing smoke and blowtorch flame. "You all right?" he said finally.

I held out my right hand straight in front of me with the elbow locked. There was a slight tremor at my fingertips, but other than that, my hand was steady. "I'm all right," I said. "It's Pastori. I don't think they're going to find him."

I described to MacCafferty in detail my two encounters with Pastori that night. All the while I was talking, MacCafferty frowned at me, puzzled and faintly hostile.

"I don't understand what it is that you're saying, Charly," he said finally. "Was he irrational?"

I shook my head.

"Well, what are you suggesting?" MacCafferty said im-

213

patiently. MacCafferty was fighting the idea. He was chewing on it like a tough piece of beef that he could not quite digest but which he could not spit out either.

"I'm not suggesting anything. He's out there in the water, probably dead, and that's the bottom line."

"You've had a similar emergency. You've been in the water," MacCafferty said.

"I'm just a kid on his first tour. Guys like you and Pastori, you don't get into that kind of trouble. He's been through two wars, and he's been a test pilot. He's got ten different ways to cope with an emergency that I haven't even thought of. If he's got his head on straight."

"What the hell are you talking about?"

"I don't know what the hell I'm talking about," I shouted. "You knew him better than I did. You tell *me* what happens to a man like him when he sits brooding, adding up his life, and has doubts about what it all comes out to. What does that do to you when you're out there and you run into trouble? It must be more paralyzing than fear."

MacCafferty stared at me, his eyes cold as stone.

"You tell me why he didn't wear his Navy Cross," I added.

MacCafferty sprang up. For an instant I thought the squadron commander was going to belt me. But instead he hobbled across the room and back again—pacing—ignoring me. At one point he paused to study a photograph of Lucas, his wife, and two boys on the bureau. Then MacCafferty whirled and went to the door, turning back to me at the threshold.

"Pastori was . . ." he started, then stopped. For reasons of his own, the instinct and secret knowledge of years of experiences I was only scratching, MacCafferty knew what I knew. The search-and-rescue destroyers racing over the horizon would not find a ripple in the sea to indicate where the man Pastori was.

MacCafferty's anger and arrogance were gone now, and he looked bitter and somehow betrayed. "I don't want you to say anything about this. It's a straight accident. It will serve no purpose to say anything to anybody about what you think. His wife and family will have enough grief to cope with."

I nodded my agreement. "Yes, sir."

214

He still stood in the doorway. "You're on the schedule for the oh-six-hundred launch," he said finally. It was a question.

"Yes, sir. I'll be there."

24

Neither I nor anyone else in the Black Knight squadron flew the next day. A weather front suddenly moved in, shredding and ripping the gray shroud that enveloped Taiwan, the Straits, and the Chinese coast. By afternoon, the sky was clear with only scattered scraps of cumulus that were blown before the wind like bits of paper and rags.

The wind tore across the flight deck in a numbing gale and whipped up suds of whitecaps and spindrift. Almost the entire air group was launched that day. The other squadrons' planes, suddenly freed after being caged so long in the hangar deck, now sprang eagerly from the carrier. To port, just clear of our flight pattern, the aircraft carrier *Midway* raced on a parallel course into the wind, its catapults also booming off aircraft in a steady barrage.

The sea glittered with ships. In the Pacific, east of Taiwan, an armada had gathered. The carrier *Lexington,* launching its aircraft, drove in a line abreast of us and the *Midway,* and all about the three great carriers were a score of destroyers and destroyer escorts deployed in an antisubmarine screen.

The Black Knights were immediately relieved of the patrol. Like the exhausted survivors of a tough, lonely battle we sat back and watched the fresh replacement troops take over, viewing them with contempt and a sense of wonder at their enthusiasm.

NEWS OF THE DAY

(TAIPEI)—FOUR CHINESE NATIONALIST SABER JETS SUNK THREE COMMUNIST TORPEDO BOATS AND DOWNED FIVE MIGS IN A SWIRLING AIR-SEA BATTLE OVER THE STRAITS OF TAIWAN YES-

TERDAY. ACCORDING TO NATIONALIST MILITARY
SOURCES HERE, THE BATTLE BEGAN WHEN A
SUPPLY CONVOY TO QUEMOY WAS ATTACKED BY
FOUR RED TORPEDO BOATS. A PATROL OF NA-
TIONALIST SABER JETS SANK THREE OF THE
COMMUNIST CRAFT WHEN THEY IN TURN WERE
JUMPED BY A ESTIMATED THIRTY-TWO MIGS
FROM THE MAINLAND. IN THE DOGFIGHT THAT
FOLLOWED, THE SABER PILOTS CLAIM THEY
KNOCKED DOWN AT LEAST FIVE MIGS AND
ROUTED THE REST WITHOUT LOSING A SINGLE
NATIONALIST AIRCRAFT.

"Bullshit!" Red Lucas snorted. "Facts are facts, and
the hard facts are that Chiang's squadrons are outnum-
bered three to one by the Reds. Those Russian MIG-17's
fly faster and twelve thousand feet higher than those old
Korean War-surplus North American Sabers that we gave
to the ChiNats. There ain't no way, bucko, that they've
killed seventeen MIGs in three weeks without losing a
single aircraft. I mean that's flat-out propaganda, and I,
for one, resent being fed it." Lucas was the voice of experience.

In Taipei, the U.S. Air Force checked the film from the
Sabers' gun-cameras, then flew it to Tokyo to the Pacific
Air Forces Commander. The combat reports were then
transmitted to ComCarDiv to ComAirGroup to Com-
VA-219.

"Apparently the Communist pilots have been kept from
training by a jet fuel shortage in Red China," Steinberg,
the intelligence officer, explained. "They're no match for
the Nationalist pilots. Some of the ChiNats have up to
fourteen hundred hours in their Sabers. That's more experience than most of you have."

"That's not what you told us when we scrambled a
month ago," Lucas rumbled.

Steinberg shrugged. "A month ago we didn't know."

The great deadly squadrons of MIGs massing behind
the Bamboo Curtain since Korea had not mastered basic
fighter tactics. In combat, they split up and separated, and
the American-trained ChiNats, constantly covering each
other in tight, disciplined pairs and quartets of fighters,
simply pounced on the stragglers and lone planes and

picked them off, one at a time. The Red pilots panicked, zagged when they should have zigged, and one even crash-dived into the sea trying to escape. They forgot to drop their wing tanks or cut in afterburners to get combat speed. On one gun-camera film a MIG pilot, in confusion, dropped his flaps and hung in the air fat and slow as a target sleeve, while a pair of Sabers ripped him to pieces.

No American aircraft had been involved in the dogfights to date. Yet the dragon we knights had charged forth to slay had now turned out to be a paper dragon conjured up by our own fears and incomplete intelligence. It breathed smoke, made horrible faces and banging, clanging noises, like the dragon the kids haul down Grant Avenue in San Francisco in the Chinese New Year Parade, but it was still a paper dragon.

Then what had killed Luke Alexander, Marty Cullen, Jack Tallman, Frank Pastori . . .?

25

That evening, immediately preceding the dinner prayer over the general announcing system, the chaplain read off the box score of the number of sorties each squadron had flown that day. The squadrons aboard now competed with each other to launch the most flights. In the wardroom, the pilots talked excitedly about the air show over the Straits.

The Air Force was streaking down the Slot in their gleaming new F-104 Starfighters at Mach 2.2 to impress the Red radar. Bulky C-119 Flying Boxcars made round-the-clock airdrops of supplies to Quemoy with the U.S. Marine squadrons now on Taiwan flying fighter escort in Douglas F4D Skyrays at night and swept-wing, scoop-nose FJ Fury jets during the day.

Yet, all the excited chatter at dinner suddenly subdued when the Black Knights sat down at the table. Pilots in other squadrons, guys I had known since flight school, became remote, fidgeted uncomfortably with their silverware. The others in the squadron felt it also, and tacitly we all began gathering in the ready room to go to the wardroom together. At that, our table was always quieter, almost funereal, as if any joviality were improper.

One evening at dinner, one of the pilots from the A3D heavy bomber detachment quietly voiced the rumor that the Black Knights were going to be disbanded as a squadron, because of our heavy losses. I dismissed it as scuttlebutt, but it suddenly made me realize that the other pilots, now launching in flashing parades over a sun-sparkled sea, regarded the Black Knights as a jinxed outfit. We were men enamored of death. I studied the faces of my squadron-mates about the table, then after dinner fled to my stateroom and stared long into the mirror. The eyes that now examined me so anxiously from the other side of the looking glass were deeply etched with fatigue and the face had a gray pallor.

Once, over a beer at the North Island Officers' Club in San Diego, a lieutenant in the Coast Guard who had just returned from a geodetic survey cruise to the Solomon Islands told me that he could spot the natives there that still secretly practiced cannibalism. Their brown skin had a grayish hue and there were black circles under their eyes. Staring now into my own shadowed, blood-flecked eyes, I knew the story was true. But it was not the eating of human flesh that caused the change in appearance. It was the dark recognition by each man of the cannibal within him.

Each combat report from the Straits now had its own stabbing twist of irony. At ten o'clock on the morning of September 24 a spearhead of six Saber Jets took off from the field at Taipei. They were the first Nationalist combat planes to be equipped with air-to-air Sidewinder missiles.

In the fall of 1958, the United States had fifty-four different guided missiles in its armory. Of all these, the Sidewinder was the simplest and the cheapest. Its infrared heat-seeker was less complicated than a living room radio, and it was generations of technology behind the radar-guided Goshawk missiles with which the Black Knights had stalked the Straits. But all of the missiles had been developed since the Korean War, and none had ever been fired in combat.

Just north of Quemoy, the ChiNat Sabers spotted the contrails of a flight of over twenty MIGs flying at 39,000 feet and maneuvered onto the MIGs' tails. While still three miles away, the ChiNat flight leader and his wingman each quickly fired a Sidewinder. Moments later, two MIGs disintegrated in midair. The ChiNat Sabers fired a total of six missiles and shot down four MIGs, before they closed within range of their .50 caliber guns and the dogfight began. To the Nationalist Chinese that day went the historical distinction of making the first actual kills in combat with a guided missile.

The news depressed me, but another mystery now preoccupied me. Days would go by without MacCafferty appearing in the ready room or even showing up for meals. His personal appearance—a military obsession with close trims, knife-edge creases, and glittering brass surfaces that he had kept up even during the patrol—suddenly deteriorated, and on his rare emergences from his stateroom, his khakis were sweat-limp and sleep-rumpled, his hair shaggy and uncombed.

One day I needed his signature on a missile inventory and went to his stateroom. I knocked on the door and thinking I had heard him say, "Come in," I stepped into the compartment. MacCafferty, dressed only in his underwear and a grubby terrycloth bathrobe, sat hunched over the edge of his bunk massaging his leg. The leg thrust out from under the robe, exposing the twisted and gnarled bloodless white flesh. Shiny white scar tissue sheathed the shattered bone and now atrophied muscle of the mutilated calf. MacCafferty brutally squeezed his lower leg, as if, with pain and violence, he could force life into that withered shank. He started when he saw me, and with a quick, embarrassed movement hid his leg beneath the robe.

MacCafferty glanced perfunctorily at the report and took it to the desk to sign. On the desk were several crumpled Baby Ruth candy wrappers and a half-eaten hamburger, now crudded with congealed grease and blood. An ash tray overflowed with the chain of cigarette butts whose stale smoke now thickened and fouled the air of the compartment.

A dark stubble bristled from MacCafferty's cheeks and jaw, and in the dim yellow light of the desklamp the flesh of his face looked jaundiced and slack, as if undermined from within by fatigue and about to momentarily cave in. Without a word he handed me the signed report, and the eyes that met mine were, I imagined, haunted and grief-stricken.

On the way back to the ready room I wondered if I had seriously misjudged the man. The whole patrol already was becoming distant and unreal to me, a reign of terror that I had dreamed and through which I had not really lived.

But the explanation for MacCafferty's behavior was not grief. The next night, just before dinner, I ran into Stan Haverman in the wardroom head, and while we were poised over adjacent urinals, the deck officer accounted for the squadron commander's sudden seclusion.

Several days after the weather broke, MacCafferty had appeared on the carrier's bridge. A launch was in progress, and a half-dozen officers crowded the bridge. Haverman—at the time the officer of the deck with a pair of heavy black binoculars hanging about his neck as the millstone of office—the ship's navigator, and several ensigns frantically hustled about, checking and rechecking the wind, the carrier's course and speed, the escort destroyers' positions, dispatching messages and keeping track of the aircraft being launched. Occasionally, Haverman sang out something to the captain, who grunted an acknowledgment without turning his attention away from the activity on the deck below.

The captain sat slouched in a raised swivel chair in the port wing of the bridge, commanding a view of the entire flight deck. A small closed-circuit TV set displayed a picture of the aircraft in the final landing pattern, an area blocked from his sight by the ship's superstructure. The captain—a bearish man, thick-set and grizzly—swiveled and shifted his weight to peer at different things below with heavy heaving movements. MacCafferty stood directly behind him, rocking nervously back and forth, toe to heel, trying to catch his attention.

It appeared as if the captain was deliberately trying to ignore the presence of the squadron commander and, at the first lull in activity, MacCafferty moved around to directly confront the senior officer.

"Your squadron's had it tough," he responded to MacCafferty's question. "You really came through in the clutch. Take a little rest. Let some of the others get in their share of the flight time. Okay?"

"We've been off a week now, sir. We're more than rested. We want in this show," MacCafferty insisted.

The captain nodded. "Well, let's see what happens in the next couple days. I get the feeling that the pressure's easing off. In another week or two, who knows but we may be back in Yokosuka boozing rather than fighting World War III. Let's just see what happens, huh?" He swung his chair away from MacCafferty, dismissing him abruptly.

MacCafferty stood fast. "Captain, just what the hell is going on? I've been getting a runaround from CAG too." He bit off his words, straining to contain his anger.

The captain swung back around, glanced quickly at the other officers on the bridge and, evidently taking activity for deafness, replied to MacCafferty in a low but rough and ominous voice, "You push too hard, Tom. Take a rest. You've lost a lot of planes. I don't want to risk losing any more. We've got enough to explain."

"Explain?" MacCafferty was outraged. "What is there that we have to explain? We lost those planes because we were out there on the line when no one else dared fly. When no one else *could* fly. The Reds knew we were there and that we had the missiles to blast them if they moved on the islands. No one else could see their hands in front of their faces, but we were out there to stop them. What's there to explain about that?"

"Okay. Okay," the captain stage-whispered. "Maybe it's just as you say. Maybe you single-handedly stopped World War III from happening. I don't know. How do you figure it? How do you score it? I don't know."

The captain held out both hands, appealing to MacCafferty. "I'm not sure what the hell counts anymore. We're not really at war. Fact is, we're supposed to be trying to stay out of one, but Jesus Christ, half your squadron has been wiped out. You just push too hard, Tom. I gave you your head. I figured that you knew what you were doing. You were the squadron commander. You knew the aircraft and you knew your pilots. You really grabbed the dirty end of the stick, I grant you that. But how is it going to look on paper to someone sitting on his ass at a desk at ComAirPac? Do they really know how it was out here two, three weeks ago? Christ, I'm not even sure anymore. They'll see we lost pilots like Alexander, Hillyard, Pastori—all out of one squadron. You shouldn't lose men like Pastori in an operation like this. Everyone is going to wonder about that."

The captain paused and looked at MacCafferty. The squadron commander was so furious he was speechless. The captain gestured vaguely to take in something beyond them, just over the horizon. "Look, Tom, you can see it for yourself. It's a milk run now, the Straits. I wouldn't be surprised if the Air Force were already taking Congressmen and their wives along for the ride and dropping them off in Hong Kong to shop on the way back."

"No one else was out there," MacCafferty whispered

223

from a throat constricted with rage. His eyes glittered and his legs appeared to be trembling with anger. "No one else. We were there to stop them when there was no one else." Before the captain could answer, MacCafferty whirled and lurched from the bridge in that stiff-legged, pitching march of his.

26

On October 6, after shelling the island of Quemoy for forty-four straight days, the guns of Red China fell silent. The Communists declared a cease-fire, as they phrased it, "out of humanitarian considerations."

The next day, the captain summoned MacCafferty to the bridge. The captain greeted the squadron commander with a shy, hesitant smile and immediately said, "These just came in, Tom. I thought you would be very interested in them." He handed over two dispatches.

Without a word, MacCafferty read the messages quickly. Then he reread the second one, lingering over it with his brow knitted, as if trying to see something between the neatly blocked lines of type. When he finally looked up, his mouth was twisted into a brutal smile, ugly in its pride. "Thank you, sir, for showing them to me."

"You may have the copies, if you like."

"Thank you, sir. Will that be all?"

The captain held MacCafferty with his eyes a moment, then shook his head. "You know, Tom, there probably won't even be a campaign ribbon."

MacCafferty hurried immediately to the ready room, and had the entire squadron assembled. When we were all gathered, he announced in a loud voice, "This ship has just received two messages. The first is from ComSeventhFleet to all commands. It reads, quote, 'I am proud of the fleet's excellence in operations, hard work, and fighting spirit during a critical time of international tensions. Its response was in the highest traditions of the Navy. To all hands, a well done.' The second message, also from ComSeventhFleet, is specifically addressed to this command and the air group." MacCafferty glanced up, his bright hawk eyes sweeping about the room, and then read, " 'Your performance and devotion to duty during a

most critical period was of great significance. The courage
and sacrifices of your officers and men operating under
extremely hazardous conditions significantly impressed all
with our combat effectiveness and determination to defend
our commitments in this strategic area. I am honored to
have you all in my command.' "

A couple of the enlisted men, huddled together in their
dungarees at the rear of the ready room, cheered, but the
pilots remained silent. At that moment the captain came
up on the ship's general announcing system and read both
messages himself.

Between those lines of Navy command dispatches was
MacCafferty's vindication.

That evening MacCafferty, newly barbered, his cheeks
pinked from close shaving, and wearing fresh khakis—
heavily starched and ironed to sharp creases like sheets of
cardboard—arrived several minutes early for dinner in the
wardroom and took a place at the head table reserved for
the carrier's department heads and squadron commanders.

The chatter at dinner that night was manic. Rumors
ricocheted around the tables like Ping-Pong balls. The
ChiComs had already reduced their build-up. No, it was
just a ploy. They would resume shooting in a few days.
The carrier would be on the line for another two months
at least, no matter what happened. No, we were being relieved in a week to return to Japan. No, Hong Kong. We
were immediately detached for a good-will visit to Sidney
Australia. President Eisenhower himself was flying out for
an inspection. No, Vice President Nixon. Chiang Kai
shek.

But whatever happened now, it was apparent that just
over the horizon the crisis was somehow ending, like a
high fever that comes in the night and is gone in the
morning.

The aerial parade down the Straits continued, but on a
reduced schedule. The Black Knights resumed flying the
next day, and I had an occasional patrol, sunlit and
uneventful, riding in an echelon of four planes down the
middle of the Straits.

Stubby TF transports, buzzing angrily and looking like
giant horseflies with their blunt noses and high wings

shuttled between the carrier and Taiwan or Okinawa, coming and going with high military brass and the first mail in weeks. I received a letter from my mother, extremely concerned because she had read in the newspaper that my ship had suddenly pulled out of Japan, destination unknown, and she had not heard from me in months.

There was no letter from Nancy, but in the same mail delivery there was a bill from the Diners' Club for a dinner Cullen and I had splurged on at a steakhouse in Hawaii. It was like opening a time capsule. The back newspapers and magazines, which had not reached the ship since we scrambled from Japan, now poured in. I descended on the wardroom lounge, gathered up a stack and retreated to a corner to work my way through them. Mine was the historical American quest for principle—just what the hell are we doing here?

I grabbed up a back copy of *Time* magazine and sat back. On the first page, I read:

FOREIGN RELATIONS

Policy Under Pressure

For Secretary of State Dulles, architect of the strong Far East policy that has kept Red China locked up inside its borders since 1955, it was a week of unrelenting and bitter pressures. On Monday, he conferred with President Eisenhower on Quemoy, found the President occupied and deeply disturbed by U.S. and European press criticism. On Tuesday, only minutes before his press conference, Dulles sent down for a handful of State Department mail to be picked at random, read many letters from the U.S. public that said something like "Don't let's have a war just on account of Quemoy and Matsu," but many, many more that simply pleaded "Let's not get into a war." The basic U.S. policy on Quemoy—hold the islands against Communist aggression in the Pacific, but negotiate if the Communists agree to a cease-fire—was not obviously understood by everyone. . . .

I flipped to the next page where *Time* ran a box summarizing editorial opinions from around the country.

JUDGMENT AND PROPHECIES

New York Times: With commendable if somewhat belated flexibility the Eisenhower Administration is now undertaking a "clarification" amounting to a realignment of our China policy to bring it more in line with both the military realities and with overwhelming public opinion at home and abroad. The pity is that this more flexible policy was not adopted long before the Chinese Communist attack.

Seattle Times: Talk of Munich has not obscured the fact that most of the free world's people do not consider the tiny offshore islands to be the rightful or logical place to draw the line against Communist expansion.

Dallas Morning News: The U.S. and liberty cannot afford to offer an island sacrifice to the Red Moloch.

Columnist Walter Lippmann: We should prepare for the passing of Chiang's regime. And we should go before the world in favor of a Taiwan settlement, asking no special privileges, strategic or economic, for ourselves.

Detroit Free Press: If the islands are not defensible or not worth defending, why not just say so, pull out, and forget the demands that Red China first agree to cease fire.

Lewiston (Idaho) Tribune: Secretary of State John Foster Dulles has taken the U.S. to the brink this time against the advice and wishes of America's allies, presumably the U.S. Senate and probably the American public. If the U.S. backs down from this position, the whole free world position in the Far East may indeed be at stake.

Chief of Naval Operations Arleigh Burke to the *New York Herald Tribune:* My fear is that too many people in the U.S. are not willing—probably because they do not understand the problem—are not willing to stand up for principles. You let one doubtful area go, then the next area becomes a little more doubtful and you become a little weaker—a little weaker in your own spirit.

I threw down the magazine, unable to read another line. In a way, I envied the Walter Lippmanns, the editorial writers, the Chiefs of Staff, each of whom saw things with such absolute clarity through their individual polarized glasses that screened out all conflicting bands of light. For me the truth of the situation threw off a blinding, painful glare. I could not look at it directly any more than I could stare into the blazing sun outside.

I wandered next door to the coffee mess. The chief steward, a bald-headed old black man, was fluttering about nervously, straightening cups and saucers and emptying ash trays, telling everybody that Chiang Kai-shek himself and ComSeventhFleet were coming aboard for an inspection in a week. The ship was going to stage an air show and firepower demonstration in their honor.

27

Allan Phelps' unruly hair and eyebrows seemed to be made from the same bristling orange fiber as his baggy tweeds. The rumpled suit, the full, unclipped curling hair and the tie askew under the soft collar gave the English man an undisciplined, almost seedy air that reminded me of several of the younger professors at Southern Cal. Phelps was the Far Eastern correspondent for a London newspaper. He was also, as I quickly discovered, engaging, full of odd quirks of humor, sardonic to the point of outrage, and totally contemptuous of military ceremony.

"Nelson, you screaming faggot," Phelps yelled down from the afterbridge on which he and I stood observing. "Get in there and fight for some decent shots this time or I'll have you keelhauled, or whatever the hell they do in the Yank Navy."

Fortunately, the blaring of the carrier's band and the roar of the helicopter that had just landed drowned out his voice. He turned to me. "When we were on Formosa I lined up a tour with some of your top brass in the Military Advisory and Assistance Group there, but that rollicking, frolicking fag was off somewhere chasing young Chinese boys. London really bit my arse off for not having any photos to accompany my deathless analysis of the U.S. military posture in the Far East."

The object of Phelps' abuse was a heavy-set photographer in a bush jacket, who at the moment was struggling in a pack of a dozen or more other photographers on the flight deck. He hopped up and down, frantically trying to shoot with a Rolliflex held at arm's length over his head.

The seething, jack-in-the-boxing cameramen and the rhythmic movements of the band were the only signs of life among the frozen, squared-off formations on the flight deck. The band played while standing at attention, lined up next to a Marine honor guard arranged in radiant blue lines across the deck. The black leather straps of the Marines' caps, normally cinched above the bill, were secured snugly under their chins to prevent them from blowing off, although there was not enough wind at the moment to launch a Kleenex. The ship's senior officers and the Seventh Fleet staff, all in gleaming white dress uniforms decked out with swords and medals, were paraded alongside the carrier's island.

The sea was calm and unruffled, an opal blue under a sky bleached by the sun. As the helicopter landed, enlisted men in immaculate white uniforms immediately formed two ranks at the helicopter's door. In the glaring sunlight, they looked like a corridor of salt pillars. Between them stepped Chiang Kai-shek, smiling and blinking, a lean figure in a khaki uniform. The Generalissimo acknowledged the salutes and shook hands with ComSeventhFleet, a stocky man half a head shorter than Chiang. Together they strode forward, followed by a half-dozen U.S. Navy and Chinese staff officers all trying at once to act friendly and cordial but at the same time keeping exactly in step with everyone else, resulting in a jerky unnatural gait like a march of marionettes.

The group paused directly below Phelps and me to inspect the honor guard. I was awe-struck by the presence of Chiang, a gaunt old man with yellowed skin like shining parchment stretched tautly over a shaven skull. Chiang's mouth seemed permanently drawn into a tight little smile or grimace.

"Look at him," Phelps exclaimed quietly. "He looks more like an ambulatory mummy every day. Who would believe that a few weeks ago he was raising holy hell with your boys because they wouldn't let the Nationalist planes loose to bomb the mainland. He still believes he is going to invade and liberate Red China. He's a dangerous, fanatical old man who's been in power past his time, and, God help you, you're stuck with him."

As Chiang, the admiral, and the Marine captain commanding the honor guard moved slowly down the ranks, the photographers broke from their huddle and scattered across the deck. Oblivious to the formalities, they sprinted between the formations, crouched and lay down on the

231

deck, jockeying for their individual camera angles and positions like skirmishing guerrilla fighters.

Chiang and ComSeventhFleet paused several times during the procession and smilingly posed for the photographers. No official notice was taken of the break from ranks. A ragtail, unruly mob of reporters now swirled through the uniformed formations, shattering the neat, regimented military frame of reference.

The press had descended on the ship in a flurry of motley sports clothes and cameras like busloads of tourists. Along with a dozen other junior officers, I was assigned to escort them about the ship. My personal charges were two Japanese reporters, with whom I had great difficulty communicating, and Phelps, whose alert gray eyes seemed to catch everything and, for some secret reason, find amusement in it. He spoke with a mild English accent—tempered by years abroad—but he had a quirk of suddenly launching into cockney or a very British Colonel Blimp manner like a disk jockey doing imitations.

The ceremonies ended on the flight deck below, and Chiang, ComSeventhFleet, and their retinue of war lords disappeared into the fortress of the island. Phelps turned to me, cleared his throat, mumbled to himself Blimpishly, "Ahem, yes, of course. Well then, Leftenant Rohr, what's next on the schedule?"

I checked my watch. "In about ten minutes or so, there is a press conference in Ready Room One. I'll show you where it is."

"Aren't you going?"

"No, it'll be a little crowded for space, so we're just supposed to drop you off and leave. I'll meet you all back in the wardroom for lunch. After that, you may as well come back here. It's the best spot to watch the air show from."

"What exactly is going to happen?"

"There's going to be a giant fly-by of aircraft from all the other carriers in the area and the Marines on Taiwan. A cast of thousands."

"Thousand aircraft," repeated one of the Japanese in a soft hiss, starting to write.

"No, no, old man," Phelps interrupted, putting a hand on his shoulder. "Just American hyperbole." The Japanese reporter looked confused.

"Then our air group will launch," I continued. "You won't be allowed on the flight deck at all then. It's very dangerous." I looked sternly at the Japanese to make sure they understood.

They smiled and nodded vigorously.

"The various squadrons aboard will demonstrate their specialties. The Spads will lay down a napalm pattern and the A-4 Skyhawks will go through their loop-the-loop acrobatics for nuclear delivery, and then there'll be high-altitude precision bombing and strafing runs. . . ."

"Right! Fireworks. What's a proper Chinese celebration without fireworks?" Phelps exclaimed.

Just then the photographer Nelson came up. He was a thickly built, hulking man with a completely shaven head and a fierce, drooping black mustache. But the Tartarish appearance was offset by his large, soft, watery eyes.

"Well, did you get anything, besides sexually aroused by all those flat-bellied young Marines?" Phelps asked him.

Nelson looked at him with hurt, reproachful eyes, and without a word hunkered down in the shade of a bulk-head to fuss with his cameras. He unloaded, then loaded, two Rolliflexes, carefully sorting the exposed rolls of film into specific, baggy patch pockets of his bush jacket.

Phelps turned back to me. "I imagine you can expertly brief us on all the intricacies of the aerial maneuvers while it's happening," he said pleasantly.

"I'm afraid I'm going to have to leave you after lunch. I'm flying."

"Oh," Phelps responded with interest. "What is it you're doing?"

"We're the grand finale. My squadron is going to put on a missile shoot. Shoot down a couple of jet target drones. They're flying them down here specially from Oki-nawa."

"Well, that's going to be exciting for us," Phelps commented. "Probably old hat to you."

"No, I've never actually fired one of these missiles. Some of the senior pilots in the squadron have worked with them on test runs, but that's all. They're too expensive to practice with. The electronics in them cost more than a Rolls Royce."

"Is this a nuclear device?" one of the Japanese reporters inquired.

I hesitated, then shook my head apologetically. "All I'm allowed to say is that the aircraft and weapons systems have a nuclear capability," I recited.

"Not today, I hope," Phelps mumbled, his tangled, woolly eyebrows arching.

"Today we'll use the air-to-air missiles with a conventional warhead."

"Comes in all sorts of sizes and colors, I suppose. Well, are you very excited about bagging your first plane, so to speak?"

"I don't know if I am yet. We're going to draw straws after lunch to see who makes the actual runs."

"Well then, best of luck," Phelps said heartily. He pushed out his hand to expose a bony wrist and brought it back to study his wristwatch in a peculiarly brusque, exaggerated movement. "If we're to get seats up front, we might get started heading in the direction of that press conference now," he suggested.

Two obsolete Grumman Panther jet fighters, which were being flown from Okinawa, were to be the radio-controlled target drones for the missle shoot.

MacCafferty was to make the first missile shot. With all the lieutenant commanders in the squadron dead, MacCafferty decided that the honor of the second shot, and the choice of two back-up shooters, would be made by drawing straws. Jack Webster plunged his hand into the helmet filled with paper slips and drew out the piece of paper marked "2d alternate," Red Lucas drew "1st alternate," and the wad that I unfolded was penciled "2d shooter."

Harris let out a loud howl at the injustice of the junior man in the squadron getting the shot, but there was no really serious complaint. We had all too recently survived the trial of the patrol for rank and seniority to again claim its privileges.

For several days MacCafferty had been edgy about the demonstration. He snarled at the squadron officers or petty officers who approached him with routine business, and snapped at the tech reps about minor adjustments. That sort of nervousness was out of character for him

234

But missiles were not bullets or bombs which unerringly bull's-eyed where he aimed them. Missiles often had devious electronic whims of their own. There were a dozen tales about missiles going awry, locking on planes that inadvertently strayed into the target area, or turning on the aircraft that fired them, and now the stories came back to haunt the squadron commander.

At the air group meetings planning the air show, MacCafferty insisted that the other squadrons land before the Black Knights' missile run. The civilian engineer for the electronics firm that produced the missile guidance system insisted that the parade assembly area was well out of any conceivable danger zone. MacCafferty then questioned the wisdom of having the kills so close to the ship. The tech rep responded, "Unless your pilots confuse a quarter-mile-long warship for one of the drone aircraft, Commander, I don't think there's any real danger." That ended MacCafferty's voiced objections, but not his nightmares.

The air show started with a titanic parade of aircraft. The squadrons from the carriers *Midway, Lexington,* and *Ticonderoga* and the Marine squadrons on Taiwan swept in low over the ship in silver echelons, their engines and jet blasts consuming the sky in thunder.

As soon as the great fleet of jet fighters and bombers passed overhead, then our catapults began firing aircraft off the flight deck at intervals of only seconds. As each squadron was luanched, they rendezvoused, then peeled off and hurtled down the carrier's starboard side. The dart-shaped A-4 Skyhawks dove at the sea, one closely following another, spitting a red stream of rockets at a target sled.

Next, the scoop-nosed FJ Fury jet fighter-bombers skimmed in so low they seemed only a few feet above the water. Just as they approached the target sled, they suddenly zoomed straight into the air, rose in perpendicular flight from the sea, then released their dummy bombs and looped over on their backs. The aero-batics were designed to protect the planes from the nuclear blast and radiation of the real bombs the Fury pilots were trained to drop.

The Douglas Spads, thick, truculent workhorses, lumbered in with the shattering roar that only a propeller-driven warplane can generate, and set the very seat itself on fire with canisters of napalm.

The Black Knights rendezvoused in a loose formation far astern of the carrier. We circled at high altitude, waiting impatiently for the other squadrons to complete their demonstrations of firepower. The sky was cloudless with unlimited visibility, and in the distance at the end of the ship's wake, the napalm drop was a vibrant red-orange splash of paint on the turquoise sea.

Over the radio, the ship's controller finally contacted the drone-control plane for a preliminary radio check. He then called MacCafferty. The squadron commander answered up snappily. The radio channel for the pilots and controllers was being piped over the ship's general announcing speakers so the spectators could follow the intercept. The point of kill had been plotted to be off the starboard side, hopefully in sight of the press gallery. The VIPs would be following it on radar.

It was to be a straight, head-on intercept, nothing tricky, but the controller was taking his own sweet time about setting up. The checkout with the drone-control plane was interminable, and then the controller ran MacCafferty and me in turn through two separate IFF checks.

I looked at Lucas, who was loosely riding on my starboard wing, and shook my head in disgust. Lucas hand-signaled me to switch to the squadron tactical frequency.

"Guess they don't want us to shoot down the wrong plane," Lucas said.

"We may shoot down one of the butterflies in my stomach by mistake. They're getting big enough," I answered.

MacCafferty's voice broke in. "Maintain your radio discipline. Get back on the assigned freq immediately," he snapped.

Just then, the controller, apparently satisfied he was sending the right plane to destruction, ordered MacCafferty to an intercept heading.

Like jousters at opposite ends of an enormous tournament ground, both planes wheeled and headed directly at one another. MacCafferty's excitement now focused on the mechanical procedures of the intercept. The radar had been sharply tuned, and it was exceptionally clear of snow and interference. Each time the controller called off the closing distance to the target drone, he scaled down the search pattern more finely.

At the edge of the scan, a ghost of a blip materialized. "Contact! Zero-zero-eight degrees. Twenty-eight miles. Over."

The controller merely rogered, not confirming that the contact was his target. "Charger One, your bogey, zero-zero-eight, twenty-five miles," he reported routinely.

The blip came straight at MacCafferty. He worked the target selector cross hairs onto it, all the while reporting the direction and closing range and, between reports, swearing under his breath, "Lock on, you bugger, lock on!" But he couldn't fire without confirmation from the ship. The controller had yet to even officially acknowledge that the contact was his bogey. The controller's voice was like some chiding echo, each time correcting MacCafferty's contact reports the mile or two closed.

"Contact. Zero-zero-six, eighteen miles."

"Roger. Charger One, your bogey, zero-zero-five, sixteen miles."

"Contact. Zero-zero-five, fourteen miles."

"Roger. Your bogey, zero-zero-five, thirteen miles."

At eleven miles out, the radar locked on the contact and began to track automatically. But MacCafferty still had no confirmation that it was the target drone. He snapped out another report.

"Roger," the controller answered, and then, finally, as if reluctant to make the commitment, "Charger One, that is your bogey. That is your bogey."

"Judy! Judy!" MacCafferty shot back, indicating a lock-on.

There was an infuriating stretch of silence, and then the order came. "Fire at will! Fire at will!"

He jammed down the button.

For a moment, nothing seemed to happen, and then very gently, as if caught in the eddy of some chance current, the slender lance of the missile floated out from under the wing. It accelerated quickly and shot ahead of the plane, streaming white smoke. "Bird away!" he reported excitedly.

MacCafferty could not keep the streaking missile in sight. He banked right and shoved the throttle balls to the wall to chase after it. Any moment he expected to see the explosion.

The trajectory of the smoke trail puzzled him. It was dropping much lower than expected, in a downward arc as if gliding for the wave tops. Supposedly, the radarman or the drone-control pilot could also confirm the kill.

Then, a little to the left and below, just where it should not have been, MacCafferty spotted the drone. The obsolete Grumman Panther jet was tooling along right on course, unscratched and unmolested.

The drone-control pilot and the ship's controller began talking at once. "I still have a strong radar contact on course," the controller reported.

"Well, I'm still getting normal signal responses up here," the drone-control pilot said. "But it's out of sight at the moment."

"Charger One, do you have an eyeball on the drone? Over."

MacCafferty stared dumbfounded at the jet fighter, now passing abreast of him.

"Negative," he responded. It seemed somehow shameful to admit he could actually see the target his guided missile had just missed.

The others decided that they definitely still had something, and turned the reprieved aircraft around.

MacCafferty banked back to rejoin the squadron flight. "I had a definite lock on target. The radar was operating, but the missile seemed to fall away fast, too fast, as if it had an underpowered rocket or malfunction," MacCafferty answered the question on the radio.

"The drone's in sight, under control, and unscratched," the drone-control pilot reported with a note of glee in his voice.

MacCafferty tersely informed the ship that I would take the second run as scheduled in case the problem was in his equipment. After another seemingly endless series of checks and identifications, the target plane and the interceptor were again squared off.

My run was an exact duplicate of MacCafferty's.

With the second missile failure, the shoot was ordered terminated. The radio-controlled drones did not have enough fuel to return to Okinawa, nor could they be landed aboard the carrier. The control planes were ordered to shoot them down with their cannons. MacCafferty and I were denied the privilege of even cleaning up the operation.

The commander of the air group met MacCafferty on the flight deck and accompanied him back to the ready room. ComSeventhFleet had ordered an investigation of the missile failures, and the captain wanted a preliminary report by that evening. As he was about to step out the door, CAG turned back to MacCafferty and said solemnly, "I understand the Generalissimo expressed his extreme disappointment."

For the first time since I had known him, MacCafferty seemed at a loss for what to do next. He just sat at the duty desk staring absently at his hands, pressed palms down with fingers spread out on the desktop in front of him, as if he were holding on for support. The civilian tech rep for Marion Electronics, the contractors for the missile, and Chief Simmons, the squadron's chief electronics technician, tried to ask him questions. MacCafferty's responses were short and angry.

I went over the firing with them, step by step, and then we went down to the hangar bay to check out my plane. I climbed into the cockpit and energized the equipment, but without a radar contact or actually firing the missile, we could not reproduce what had gone wrong.

The avionics crew dismantled part of the radar and wiring, and hauled the equipment and one of the missiles to their shop, where they reassembled and hooked up the entire system across the floor and on top of work benches. I stared at the naked nervous system of wires, printed circuits, transistors, condensers, tubes, and innumerable little black boxes jamming every inch of the radar and missile containers, and I did not believe for one moment they would ever ferret out what had gone wrong in that electronic tangle.

MacCafferty limped in and watched silently while the technicians pored over the circuit diagrams in their manuals and attempted to retrace them in the confusion of hardware spread over the compartment. All the while they made brief, cryptic remarks in what sounded like Esperanto. MacCafferty sprawled in a chair against the wall and just stared straight ahead, the thick, raised blood vessels on his broad forehead pulsing and looking like saber scars in the unshaded lighting. He frequently reached down and massaged his game leg.

An electric buzzing and cricket chatter of sharp metallic clicks brought my attention back to the hardware.

Simmons looked up at the tech rep. "Well, I guess it's not that."

"Well, what the hell is it then?" MacCafferty raged.

The tech rep, startled, peered at him over the rims of his eyeglasses. He blinked, started to say something, but then thought better of it and, embarrassed, adjusted his glasses and bent forward to intently study the mechanism before him again.

MacCafferty stood up and began restlessly pacing back and forth across one short wall of the compartment, and then sat down again.

The dialogue between the technicians as they took jump readings with their voltmeters and traced out the circuits with pencil tips had all been incomprehensible to me, and I was surprised when they began bolting the missile plates back on.

MacCafferty, completely absorbed in his own thoughts, started when he noticed the technicians were finishing up. He jumped up. "Well, what is it? What did you find out?"

The civilian tech rep looked up with maddening slowness and turned to MacCafferty with an embarrassed little smile. "Well, it turns out that it wasn't very serious after all."

"What was it?"

"It seems that the vertical correction signal isn't properly hooked up to the control mechanism for the missile vanes. It's actually a little thing, but it probably would never be discovered in operations until you fired off a few missiles. We can make all the adjustments right on board."

"*All* the adjustments?" MacCafferty blurted. "You mean none of the missiles would have worked?" He looked stunned.

The tech rep shrugged. "Well, they all operate off the same guidance system. . . ."

MacCafferty's fist hit him squarely in the face. The engineer reeled back against a work bench and caught it for support, his knees buckling under him. The blow had

240

snapped the frame of his glasses right in half at the bridge, and each separate lens dangled from an ear, falling drunkenly across his face.

I jumped in front of him, but MacCafferty did not make another move toward the man. He stood with his fists up, ready to strike out, but just looked in bewilderment from his victim to me to Chief Simmons and then spun and lurched out of the compartment.

28

The carrier sailed into Hong Kong on a sea sparkling like a field of gems. We cruised a few hundred yards off a spectacular seacoast of hills and cliffs, alternately lush and rocky, that plunged directly into the surf, or broke into brief fjords. On that bright, sun-washed morning, I would not have been too surprised to suddenly confront a school of mermaids on the rocks beckoning to me. But the ship had made its approach with the crew at General Quarters, its five-inch deck guns manned and ready, because the passage to Hong Kong passed within the range of Red Chinese offshore batteries.

The patio of the Correspondents Club, high in the hills above the city of Hong Kong, looked down on the harbor. I leaned over the balustrade, sipping a gin and tonic, and all about on the steeply climbing green slopes were the magnificently landscaped homes of the wealthy Chinese and British colonials. They rose up in white sugar lumps and heaps of pink, magenta, and pale orchid as if advertising the fact that along with rockets, printing, and water torture, the Chinese had also invented paint. Across the bay, just beyond the sprawl of the city of Kowloon, were the brown hills of China itself, looking at a distance like mounds of ants.

Kowloon, part of the British Crown Colony, was on the mainland. That afternoon I had taken a tourist bus to the outskirts where only a wire fence and a stretch of barren no-man's-land separated it from Communist China. For the hell of it, I threw a rock over the fence.

Now below me in Hong Kong harbor, a Matson liner, vanilla as an ice cream sundae and carnival-decorated, bobbed near shore amid the comings and goings of rust-plated tramps, schooners under sail, tottering ocean-going junks, high-bridged river steamers that looked like orange crates under power, racy Chris Crafts, and racing sloops. At the breakwaters near shore a coolie frantically poled his frail sampan, trying not to be swamped by the wakes of the larger ships churning by.

Small water taxis that looked as if they were held afloat by the old tires that hung from their sides as fenders scooted busily in and out of the harbor traffic. Double-decker ferryboats ceaselessly shuttled between the island of Hong Kong and Kowloon on the mainland. Two of the ferries now operated exclusively as liberty boats for the carrier anchored in midharbor.

The carrier rode at anchor, the smashing hurricane bow heading into the tidal current, straining at the anchor chain. The great armor-plated mass and its towering radar scanners dominated the harbor and dwarfed everything about it. The carrier's flight deck was empty now, the planes all tied down below, out of sight on the hangar deck and secured under guard. We were to be moored in Hong Kong for a week. Then we sailed off again on a routine training exercise.

Closer to shore, the escort destroyers had nested next to a large amphibious assault ship that the U.S. Navy had moored in Hong Kong harbor as a permanent station ship.

"Well, hello there, Leftenant Rohr."

I spun around to confront the smiling florid face and outstretched hand of Phelps.

"I ran into your chum Tail Hooks Lewis in the bar, and he mentioned you were out here by yourself *brooding,* as he put it."

The carrier's wardroom had been extended the hospitality of the Correspondents Club and immediately began using it as its officers' club. Hooks, Lucas, and the others were at the bar inside playing Liar's Dice and ritually drinking up before going out on the town.

"What are you doing here?" I was surprised to see Phelps.

"I live in Hong Kong. I was meeting some airline's public relations chap up here for a drink. Public relations types always seem to like places called the Correspondents Club or the Press Club. Lord knows why. Dreary places really. I rarely come here myself, but I'm delighted to run into you again. I didn't get a chance to thank you for taking me in hand aboard your ship, showing me the grand tour and all that."

Phelps' pleasure was genuine and open. In the reddening afternoon sun, his unruly eyebrows and hair were more like bristling copper wire than ever, and his shaggy tweeds looked entirely at home against the red brick of the club.

"Well, nice to see you again. Sorry that I didn't get a chance to say good-bye on board the ship before you took off," I apologized.

Phelps dismissed it with a wave of his hand. "I imagine that you were pretty well occupied, especially after that snafu with the missiles."

I nodded.

"You lost half your squadron out there on patrol?" Phelps asked incredulously.

"Damn near."

"That's a hell of a thing," Phelps swore. "It's some sort of hellish nightmare like going through the bloody flak at Cologne, only to find your bombs are all duds."

Something in Phelps' intensity caught me. "Did you fly in the war?" I asked.

Phelps nodded.

"Fighter?"

"Oh, no, nothing so vainglorious. The few to whom we all owe so much are almost all dead now, you know. No, I came in later when the back of the Luftwaffe had been broken, and we were taking our bloody revenge on the German cities."

"Still, it was something," I said.

"It was systemized, schedulized horror. Endless hours of bloody boredom punctuated by a few moments of stark terror."

"Still, it was something," I repeated.

"You're a damn fool if you believe that," Phelps said quietly, almost offhandedly.

"Maybe I am," I snapped, suddenly angered. "But I'll tell you something you didn't get in your high-powered press briefings by CincPac and the Generalissimo. We were out there on that carrier ready to launch World War III. Not that I didn't lose a lot of sleep thinking about it. But I was primed and ready to go. It was the only way I could justify my being there. The men who got killed. The selection process that I had gone through. And then nothing happened. Nothing."

"Good Lord, you sound as if you'd almost rather have flown into Red China and launched your nuclear missile."

I stared at Phelps, started to say something, but could not find the words and just shook my head in frustration. 'How long can we do this? Go to the brink and then just . . just . . . back off."

Phelps just shook his head with a sort of sad acknowledgment. "Not indefinitely," he answered in a dry and caustic voice. He frowned, as if composing his thoughts, and the tangled copper wool of his heavy eyebrows hooded his eyes. "For what it's worth, I have great faith in mankind's instinct for self-preservation. At the moment, everything seems to be building toward a big blowup. But I believe that geopolitics, like the geology of the earth itself, has certain natural relief valves when the pressure builds up to world-shattering degrees. My guess is that the United States and the Communists are going to get into a dirty isolated little war somewhere, not unlike Korea. Bloody and weary and endless as hell itself, fought with relatively conventional weapons within definite boundaries like some grotesque game, to keep it from spreading. No smashing victories. No stunning defeats. Just the gradual bleeding of young men and national wealth over the years."

"That's a hell of a thing to look forward to."

"It is better than the alternative of a nuclear holocaust," Phelps said in a tone as brittle as glass crystal.

Below me, a whaleboat circled about the carrier. It was the security patrol—a boat officer and several enlisted men, all armed to the teeth with carbines, pistols, and concussion grenades. They were on the lookout for Red Chinese frogmen. Scubaing spies and saboteurs. If bubbles were spotted, the orders were to depth bomb the area with grenades. The next night, I had the duty. Another patrol.

I looked down at my empty glass. "Let's get a drink," I said to Phelps.

"That's the first thing you've said that makes sense since I've been here."

The crowd gathered around the bar had grown considerably. I plunged in and drank up with a vengeance, making jokes and eager conversation to heave back the depression hovering like a black cloud at the edge of my consciousness. I was loud, flushed, sweating, and slightly drunk. At some time in the evening Phelps politely took his leave and Hooks' face, red and joyous as a circus balloon, bobbed toward me through the crowd. "We're going to town," he hollered.

I followed him through the jam and almost rammed into MacCafferty. He slouched against the bar, favoring his good leg, regaling several other squadron commanders. MacCafferty was the only one in his dress uniform.

"It was like flying through a coal mine. It was so dark, I couldn't even see my own wingtips," MacCafferty boomed, and even in that din his voice rumbled half the length of the bar. "So I radioed the controller on the destroyer for a radar fix. 'I think you're in trouble,' he said. 'The only radar contact I have on my scope is in a landing pattern over the Red base at Swatow.' "

The other officers laughed. The patrol was now another sea story in MacCafferty's stand-up repertoire. He glanced toward me, and the eyes that met mine were amused but cold and implacable as ever.

What happens to men like MacCafferty? Do they just fizzle out like a drink gone flat, or turn sour and bitter? Or do they continue to seethe like a volcano, spewing occasional black puffs of anger, until one day they explode? MacCafferty would undoubtedly rise to air group commander, then captain of a carrier, but all the while a selection board of admirals in the Pentagon would have to make a subtler and subtler decision. Just how far could they trust Tom MacCafferty?

I plunged outside after Hooks. A half-dozen of the barroom commandos were trying to squeeze at once into the cab, a compact British make. In the darkness and press of bodies, I couldn't tell who was what. Everyone was talking and shouting at the same time. I discovered I was sitting on Chub Harris' lap.

"Charly, hey Charly, y'all in?" Lewis wailed from up front.

"Yeah, in the back here. Is Cullen in? Cullen!" I called out, then remembered and felt embarrassed.

Hooks was next to the Chinese driver, who was pa

tiently working to extract a destination from him. "Oh, hell, man, you know, gals. Suzie Wongs. Wham-bam. Hey Red, what *thee* hell is the name of that honky-tonk?"

"Moon Gardens," Lucas yelled back.

"Hell yes, that's it. Moon Gardens, driver. *Mushi, mushi.* Hey, how'd y'all know that, Red?"

"I've got friends in low places."

"Ain't you something, though."

The humid miasmic heat of jammed liquored-up bodies in the cab was stifling. I lunged for a window, rolled it down violently, and yanked open my tie and shirt collar. Behind me, Harris reached a hand around and offered me a bottle of beer he had toted along. I took a swallow and handed it back, feeling slightly nauseous. Harris thirstily drank up. In the brief illumination of a passing light, his fat wattles quivered and his moist face glowed yellowy-looking, pudgy, and waxen.

I peered at him. "How the fuck is a clown like you still alive?"

"Boy, get that smell," Harris said.

"Wait till we get to Subic Bay in the Philippines. That's where we're headed next," someone in the front seat said.

"Where'd you hear that?" I asked, leaning forward.

"It just came in on an ops schedule last night."

"What's it like there?"

"Like Tijuana years ago, only with no bullfights and more Navy. Whorehouses in a hot stinking jungle."

The cab jolted to a stop under a large gaudy neon light.

I don't remember much about the Moon Gardens. I was on the dance floor and a girl was shoving her crotch provocatively into mine, but she didn't really seem to be paying attention to me or even the music. The whole purpose of our being there seemed to be the crotch bumping.

The girl insisted on my buying her several drinks there—it was evidently a house rule—and then we left the club and hailed a cab outside. We drove only a few blocks, off the bright neon-buzzing commercial street into an unlit alleyway. There was the soft cluck of chickens about me in the darkness and a fetid coopy smell. The girl took me by the hand and led me through a door directly into a cramped room where there were several children huddled together asleep on the floor, breathing thickly. Under a bare yellow bulb, an ancient woman with prune-wrinkled flesh and white hair sat sewing. She glanced up and then immediately returned to her mending as the girl pulled me up a flight of rickety wooden steps.

Her "apartment" was above. It was actually a large room with a jerry-rigged partition of curtains separating her bed and a space with a sink and table. The floors were bare, and the quarters smelled strongly of cheap, sweet perfume. An old center-sagging double bed and a nightstand spilling over with boxes and jars of makeup, pomade, colognes, and soap slivers was jammed into the girl's crib. A douche bag hung in one corner, and pictures were pasted on the wall—pages torn out of magazines— of Frank Sinatra, President Eisenhower, and several Chinese movie stars I didn't know.

The girl sat down on the bed; I gave her the money and we undressed immediately.

"Big muscles," she said, squeezing my shoulder. "You Marine jungle bunny?"

"No, I'm not a Marine jungle bunny," I said, irritably.

The whore had a slender provocatively round body, but I felt absolutely no desire. Her fingers caressed and gently pulled at me. "You like that?" she asked.

"Yes . . . sure."

But when she felt no response, she said, puzzled, "You don't like me?"

" 'Course I do, baby. Probably just had a little too much to drink or something. That's all. It'll be all right."

I turned on my side and pressed against the girl, holding her tight. But her pulling and tugging did not seem to have any effect. I was limp and impotent, blocked off from the blood that now throbbed in my head.

"How come you that way?" the girl asked, troubled. "You don't like me?"

"No, no, baby, it's not you," I said, running my fingers along her thigh, trying hard to respond. "You're terrific. I've had too much to drink or something. I just don't feel in top shape."

"You sick?" She was worried.

"No, I don't feel sick. Look, I'm not going to throw up or anything. I just don't feel great . . . but you're all right. It's not your fault."

"You want me to do something else?" She made a suggestion with her lips and tongue. "You like that?"

"Yeah. Great."

The girl turned about and went down on me. I leaned back and shut my eyes. When I looked up, I saw, over the backs of her thighs, Frank Sinatra on the wall watching me with great amusement, a Tyrolean hat cocked rakishly over one eye, winking and grinning encouragingly. President Eisenhower stared down with stern disapproval, and the Chinese actors, as if deliberately ignoring the sexual struggles below, gazed off into the distance.

The girl stopped and turned around again. "No good," she declared. Her hair was in her face, and she pushed it away with both hands and wiped her wet mouth with the back of her hand. "You feel very sick?" she asked, frowning.

I leaned back and closed my eyes. The bed felt lumpy and sagging and the sheets faintly greasy. "No, never mind. You can keep the money. It's not your fault," I said.

I lay still a moment and then got up and put on my shorts and went over and washed my hands very carefully in the galvanized-iron sink, drying off with a limp moldy-smelling towel I found there.

Downstairs the ancient woman, still mending beneath the light of the bare yellow bulb, did not look up as I went out.

As I came aboard the carrier, Stan Haverman greeted me. He was the officer of the deck. "Good liberty?"

"Yeah. Great. It must have been," I answered. "I feel awful."

Haverman grinned expectantly, as if he wanted to hear more—he had the duty and had not been ashore in Hong Kong yet—but I hurried past the quarterdeck toward the staterooms without further comment.

I don't know why, but on impulse I stopped in Pastori's stateroom. It was empty now. The chaplain and mess treasurer had packed off all Pastori's clothing and books. Evidently no one, not even the stewards, had been in the room since, and the air in the compartment was stale and musty as a tomb. There was no sound except the hush of the ship's generators whining six decks below me like a distant wind. I sat down on the bunk in the dark, trying to communicate in that thick silence with Pastori's unhappy ghost.

Nothing stirred, and after a while, I flicked on the bedlight. Taped to the bottom of the upper bunk above Pastori's bed, where those who officially gathered up his personal possessions had never looked, was a photograph of his family. His wife, a plump pretty woman, stood with her arms outstretched to hug their daughter and the two boys, both already dark gangly reflections of their father. It damn near broke my heart.

I snapped off the light and went on to my own compartment. There, in the mail on my desk that had been delivered to the ship that day, was a letter from Nancy in San Diego.

Dear Charly,

I just ran into Ernie Scholl at the North Island O Club. He told me about resigning his wings. Then, almost as an afterthought (he was a little drunk), he told me about Marty Cullen and Frank Pastori. I was stunned. I immediately asked about you, and he said he had seen your name in some accident report but he was pretty sure that you were all right. I just got up and left the club. If I could have, I would have phoned you immediately. As it was, I just walked out of the club and left my date standing there. He's a very nice guy and very good-looking (be a little jealous, please), and I've only seen him a couple of times. I don't know what he thinks, and I've discovered that I don't really care very much. It's one of the discoveries I've made this evening sitting here thinking, smoking, and crying a little. The main one is that I still love you. I wanted to get that on the record before anything else in hell happens. I love you. There! I may regret saying it in the morning, but I won't take it back. I keep crying. For the first time since I was a child, I want to pray for someone. You. But I find I can't. I'm not on very comfortable terms with God these days. But that's not what I'm crying about, although it might be reason enough. I keep thinking about that dear, sweet Mrs. Pastori and their children. And funny, sweet, gangling, high-spirited, gung-ho Marty. Lost! I can't even bring myself to say, "Dead." It's a terrible nightmare.

I want to call Mrs. Pastori, but I don't know what to say. I don't even know how to re-introduce myself. I'm Charly Rohr's ex-wife, and we met, etc., etc.

You really put me through hell, Charly, and when you left, I hated your guts for a while. I was going to hurt you as badly as I could in the divorce. Now it all seems so childish and self-centered. Maybe not that exactly, but just not very important at the moment. I love you and you are alive. That's important. How we've cheated or mistreated each other, I don't even want to think about, not even if I see you again.

Please write to me. No ties or promises, just write. And come to see me as soon as you get back to San Diego.

I'm still afraid of you. You've become a bastard, you know. But also I'm afraid for you. I wanted to give you something before you left, a poem, but then we got into that fight, or fights, and I never did. It's "An Irish Airman Foresees His Death" by William Butler Yeats, and when I came across it, it reminded me so much of you that it terrified me—

> I know that I shall meet my fate
> Somewhere among the clouds above;
> Those that I fight I do not hate,
> Those that I guard I do not love;
> My country is Kiltartan Cross,
> My countrymen Kiltartan's poor,
> No likely end could bring them loss
> Or leave them happier than before.
> Nor law, nor duty bade me fight,
> Nor public men, nor cheering crowds,
> A lonely impulse of delight
> Drove to this tumult in the clouds;
> I balanced all, brought all to mind,

The years to come seemed waste of breath,
A waste of breath the years behind
In balance with this life, this death.
            —the end—

I don't understand what Yeats means by "a lonely impulse of delight." Some day you might try explaining it to me, although I accept the fact that I may never understand it. It seems to me something very cruel and destructive. Charly, the newspapers here aren't worth a shit. What the hell is going on out there?

Darling, be careful. And please write to me.

My love,
Nancy

I reread the letter twice.

It was hot and humid in the compartment, and I stripped down naked and lay back in my bunk, wide-awake and cold sober. Actually, I was beyond being sober—off into the deepest possible thought. Like the Irish airman, "I balanced all, brought all to mind." And I wanted out.

Not out like Pastori and a thousand like him, who had gotten out once and then hauled back to Korea. Not four more months in WestPac, a year more on active duty, and then years in the reserves, dangling, until I was jerked back for the next Big Power confrontation or undeclared war over Berlin, Lebanon, or Indo-China. I wanted clean out.

I got up from the bunk and started moving about the room, plunging into drawers and lockers, sorting everything into different piles. I looked at the largest stack a moment and then, still naked as a babe, grabbed an armload and carried it down the passageway and laid it down right outside MacCafferty's stateroom.

I made several trips, and all of it together made a tight, neat stack exactly as wide and high as I am. Then I banged on MacCafferty's door like a goddamn five-alarm fire warning.

"What . . . what the hell you think you're doing?" His eyes were still rheumy and confused with sleep, but his mouth fell open at the sight of me standing there bare-ass with what must have been a stupid grin on my face.

I pointed to that man-sized stack of all my uniforms, with the Navy wings right on top, pinned to the dress blues, and said, "I'm turning in my uniform. I'm not playing anymore."

"What the hell you think you're doing?" MacCafferty said again. And I repeated it all over again.

"Just what the hell do you think you're doing, Mister?" MacCafferty asked a third time.

I pondered a moment and then said, "I'm going for a swim," because standing there bare-ass and ready for anything, it was the fastest way out.

I marched right up to the quarterdeck. The morning sun was just rising, and the OOD stood watching it, almost formally at attention, with the official officer of the deck telescope tucked under his arm.

I strode over, came to attention smartly and saluted him, pivoted aft, saluted the ship's flag, and then executed a beautiful swan dive.

From fifty feet up, the landing smarted a bit. Just as I surfaced, the patrol boat putt-putted by. I yelled and splashed water at them so that they'd know it was just good old fun-loving Charly Rohr, the All-American boy, and not start shooting and dropping concussion grenades all over the place. Then I rolled over on my back and floated, and just let the current carry me for a while.

are you missing out on some great Pyramid books?

You can have any title in print at Pyramid delivered right to your door! To receive your Pyramid Paperback Catalog, fill in the label below (use a ball point pen please) and mail to Pyramid . . .

PYRAMID PUBLICATIONS
Dept. M.O., 757 Third Avenue, New York, N.Y. 10017

NAME_____

ADDRESS_____

CITY_____STATE_____

1_____ZIP_____